Last Call

A Murder On The Rocks Mystery

LAST CALL

A Murder On The Rocks Mystery

by Cathi Stoler

To my family: Paul, Lauren, Mike, Madison,
Delores, Dan, Sue, and my nieces and nephews. I love you all.

Praise for Books by Cathi Stoler

Cathi Stoler's *Bar None* is a New York crime novel with a modern twist - dark, deadly and loaded with memorable characters. Sidle up to the bar and order a few rounds of this smooth, potent drink. You won't regret it."–Alex Segura, author of the Anthony Award-nominated Pete Fernandez Mystery series

Jude Dillane is my favorite new heroine! You'll definitely want to belly up to her bar, the Corner Lounge, for a tall cool one, a little heat, and a New York mystery that will keep you guessing until the very end. –Jess Lourey, author of the Salem's Cipher thrillers and the Mira James Mysteries

Stoler's *Bar None* is a perfectly toxic cocktail of corruption, embezzlement, and murder.–Reed Farrel Coleman, *New York Times* Bestselling author

A captivating tour of downtown New York's food scene, *Bar None* is a modern twist on a classic whodunit that will keep you guessing until the very end. –D.A. Bartley, author of *Blessed Be The Wicked*.

Preface

New Year's Eve

1999

Times Square was packed. Nearly half a million revelers were squeezed in as tight as the cork in a champagne bottle, ringed by barricades in an area forty blocks square. Many had been there since that morning, waiting in the cold for the glittering Waterford Crystal ball to drop.

Security was tight. It was the dawn of a new millennium which brought fears of a Y2K disaster bringing down computers and creating havoc amongst anything electronic.

Over five thousand police officers were on hand to make sure nothing went horribly wrong—although the crowd was well-behaved, many of them wearing oversize glasses and waving banners as they cheered and yelled into the cameras.

No one was having a better time than the four young tourists from Denmark who had arrived in the city the day before. Worming their way through the crowd, the two men and two women pushed in as close as they could to have a close-up view of the ball drop and watch the entertainment, a popular band playing their latest hit.

One member of the group, Lukas Janssen, decided to step away from his friends for a few moments to buy a souvenir for his younger sister. "I think she would like one of those T-shirts," he told his girlfriend, Isa Mulder, and pointed to a man a few yards away selling shirts with a millennium logo on the front. At six feet four inches, Lukas stood well above the crowd around him and had no trouble plotting a path to the vendor.

"Hurry back, Lukas," Isa told him, giving him a quick hug. "The new year will be here in just a few minutes and I'll want to give you a special kiss." She smiled as he walked away and turned back to her friends, Elias and Sara, who were waving small Danish flags at a TV camera that scanned the merrymakers.

At ten seconds to midnight, the ball began its descent and Lukas was still not back. Isa thought he may have gotten turned around in the mass of people, and gave her attention over to the cheers and chaos that erupted at the stroke of twelve, sure he would join them shortly.

The crowd dispersed soon after, but Lukas was nowhere to be found. His three friends looked up above the sea of people leaving the area, searching for the tall blond man in a red ski jacket. Isa's eyes widened with worry. "I don't see him. Where did he go?" Tears began to spill from her eyes as she fought her way through the remaining crowd, calling his name.

"Maybe he stopped for a beer," Elias ventured.

"Not without us," Isa told him. "He'd never leave us here wondering where he is."

She shook her head. "Something has happened to him. I know it."

Three days later, Lukas Janssen's body was discovered in Tompkins Square Park on the east side of Manhattan. No one knew how or why he wound up there. The young man had been stabbed through the heart and died instantly—the first victim of the person who would become known as the New Year's Killer.

A guy walks into a bar...

Chapter One

New Year's Eve

2018

The ball was about to drop, and everyone's eyes were fixed on the TV over the bar. I guess it had been a good idea to follow my landlord Sully's advice and lug the flat screen down from my apartment for the night. The Corner Lounge wasn't the kind of bar where five TVs were tuned to whatever sports games were being played, but being New Year's Eve, I relented from my prohibition of television in the restaurant, and it seemed to be paying off. I just didn't want to hear any "I told you so's." from Mr. Smart Mouth.

"Three…two…one…Happy New Year!" The glittering Swarovski crystal ball ended its descent, and the crowd in Times Square went wild, roaring their good wishes into the faces of the numerous TV cameras that swept the area.

It was a bit more subdued at The Lounge, if only because the number of people present was just slightly fewer than the crowd at the country's hottest New Year's Eve venue—although the noise level seemed just as loud as everyone shouted "Happy New Year!" before kissing the person closest to them and lifting their glasses in a toast.

Dean, my head bartender, and I had been busy popping open champagne bottles and filling flutes for the customers who numbered three deep at the bar. I grabbed three glasses and moved down to where my boyfriend, Eric, and Sully were seated. Handing one to each of them, I leaned over and gave Eric a big kiss on his lips, then planted one on Sully's cheek. "Happy New Year, boys!" I clinked my glass against each of theirs. "Let's hope it's a good one."

Eric gave me another long, lingering kiss and nuzzling my ear, whispered, "It will be, Jude. I promise." Then one of his pals from work called out to him and he went off for bro hugs and good wishes with his buddies who'd joined him for the evening.

Sully nodded, knowing there was more to my words than their simple meaning. The last year had been pretty tough on all of us, and it was definitely time to move on to something better.

"A good year? I'll drink to that." Sully downed his champagne in a few gulps then held out the flute for a refill.

"Philistine." I shook my head and poured him more of the bubbly. "Sip this one."

"Hey," Art Bevins, one of my regular customers, called to me, "don't forget us." He pointed to his spot in front of the bar.

"I'd never do that." I smiled and handed over a glass to Art and one to the young man with him.

"Jude, meet my brother, Michael. Michael, Jude. She owns the place." Art made a loose gesture with his hand that encompassed the dining room and bar. "Mikey just got in and we came down to celebrate. I didn't even give him time to unpack. He's staying with me over the holiday break." Art was smiling so wide I could practically see his tonsils.

I shook my head at Art and held out my hand to his brother. "Nice to meet you, Michael." He was tall, blond, and handsome in a hipster kind of way, scruffy stubble on his face, plaid shirt with a black T-shirt under it, jeans and sneakers—a uniform—just like the black jeans and black turtleneck that I wore to work every day. Art had told me all about his younger brother, who was a senior at the University of Maryland, majoring in medical research.

"I think Art's mentioned you once or twice."

He laughed, assuming his brother spoke about him way too much. "You, too. I've heard all about you from this guy."

Art hooked an arm around his brother's shoulders. Or tried to. He was a several inches shorter and a few drinks ahead, and his aim was a little off, his arm landing somewhere around Michael's shoulder blades. Art's dark eyes shone with pride and you could see how much he loved his brother. "Mikey here is the real brains in the family. A science wiz. Going to find a cure for everything that ails you."

"Starting with over-imbibing, no doubt," piped in Tony Napoli, another regular customer and one of the "10th Street Irregulars," as I called them. He was with Oscar Lupe and Jim Deems, two more from the group, who'd come in just after midnight and finally managed to elbow their way to the bar.

I leaned over and gave each of the three men a peck on the cheek. "Champagne?" I didn't have to ask twice.

All three nodded like bobbleheads. I placed their drinks in front of them and moved down the bar to see to my other customers as Art introduced Michael around.

A little while later, Michael shrugged into his jacket and leaned over the bar. "Nice to meet you, Jude. I'm heading out to another party downtown." He looked over his shoulder at Art and pointed up to the ceiling. "Make sure my brother gets home safe," he added before he went back toward the group.

After a while, when I glanced up at the Irregulars, Sully, Art, Oscar, and Tony were laughing at something one of them had said and Mikey was gone.

I didn't have time to dwell on it. Busy didn't describe the scene at The Lounge. Hey, not that I was complaining. I was in business to make money. So was my partner, Pete, the chef and soul of the kitchen, who popped out from his station at his huge 8-burner Garland stove to swoop me up for a New Year's kiss and grab a bottle of champagne for the kitchen staff.

Well, so far—an hour in—things looked good for the year to come. I hoped it would last. But somewhere, deep inside, a little voice said, *Good luck with that, Jude.*

I ignored it. How I wished I hadn't.

Chapter Two

The new year was barely five hours old and already it felt like an eternity. I gave last call over an hour ago and hustled out Sully and his crew amidst protests of "Aw c'mon, Jude. Just one more for the road."

Fortunately, their road was either upstairs or around the corner and I sent them on their way. Pete had hung up his apron and closed the kitchen hours ago. Eric was upstairs sleeping in my warm and cozy bed where I longed to be snuggled up next to him. I'd sent him home when I found him nodded off at one of the dining room tables, snoring lightly, head resting on his folded arms. All that was missing was the milk and cookies.

Now, I was alone and appreciating the post-celebration quiet. I didn't like big celebrations or big crowds. Hadn't since I was a teenager. So of course, I went into the restaurant business where the bigger the party and the larger the crowd, the better.

I gave my beautiful bar one more swipe with a clean bar cloth and steeled myself to take a good look at The Lounge. It's soft, pearl-gray walls with hand-rubbed streaks of silver were overpowered by the mess that surrounded them. Gold and silver decorations were dripping over floor lamps and sconces, and noise makers and hats were in piles on tables. My sleek black chairs were set helter-skelter all over the floor. Happy New Year! Well, my porters would be in soon to clean up and we'd be ready to open in time for New Year's Day brunch. Thankfully, Dean was working the early shift and I'd get to sleep in.

I put the evening's take in a bank bag and headed for the safe in our basement office. Once I was done, I went back upstairs, bolted the front door, flicked off all the lights and walked past the kitchen to the back door. I was surprised to see it was slightly ajar—not good when you're in a deserted bar on your own late at night. There'd been so many people in and out, I couldn't keep track. At one point I'd looked over at Eltee, our bouncer, by the front door. He gave me a big smile and a thumbs up. All that was missing was the velvet rope and a few stretch limos filled with celebrities.

My imagination was getting the best of me. It was probably just one of the customers sneaking outside for a smoke who came back in and didn't close the door all the way. I grabbed a bag of trash the kitchen porter had forgotten sitting next to the door and set the alarm.

When I stepped outside to lock up, I thought I saw movement by the dumpster. It was at the end of the alley next to a fence that abutted the backyards of the buildings on 10th Street. The area was poorly lit. There were deep, dark shadows surrounding it that made it difficult to see. Was someone there?

Thinking about the open back door had my nerves working overtime. I stopped myself from calling out and stood as still as I could. I let my eyes adjust to the dim light then took another look. All was quiet. I must have imagined it. No one was there waiting to jump out at me. Just darkness and shadows I'd noticed before. I walked toward the dumpster and hesitated for just a moment before I lifted the lid. When I did, I let out the breath I didn't realize I'd been holding. There was nothing in it that didn't belong. I tossed in the bag of trash and made my way to the building's entrance at the other end of the alley on Avenue B.

Up in my apartment, Eric was sound asleep, a sweet smile on his lips. *I hope he's dreaming about me, something nice,* I thought as I slipped in beside him, falling asleep the moment my head touched the pillow.

Chapter Three

I awoke to Eric kissing me lightly on my forehead. I smiled up into his soft brown eyes. He was looking at me with a silly grin that spread from ear to ear.

"What?" I asked, smiling back as I lifted my face for a real kiss, then satisfied, snuggled deep under my comforter.

"I didn't mean to wake you, Jude. I'm leaving for home now. Go back to sleep."

"What time is it?" I mumbled, starting to sit up, worried I'd missed my shift at the bar.

"Just ten," Eric replied, gently guiding me back down and placing the covers over me. "I promised mom and dad I'd be at their house by eleven for New Year's lunch with *Abuela* Carmen."

"Umm," I mumbled and turned over. "S'okay." A second later I was asleep again. When I finally awoke at two o'clock, I felt rested. I usually didn't get this much sleep, but considering it was almost six in the morning when I went to bed, I deserved it.

I'd forgotten that Eric was spending the day with his parents, sisters, and his grandmother who was visiting from Puerto Rico. It was going to be a hard day for all of them. These were the first holidays the family was observing since George, Eric's identical twin brother, was killed.

I knew how horrible it was to lose a family member. I'd lost of all of mine a long time ago and their absence still haunted me. But for Eric's parents it must be twice as unbearable—looking at an exact replica of the son who'd died. I knew Eric was doing everything he could to ease their pain, but I also knew it would never go away, not entirely. Nor would his.

Okay, Jude, great way to start the day. I shook off my melancholy mood before it got any worse and headed for the kitchen to make a pot of coffee. While it was brewing, I picked up last night's sticky clothes that I'd thrown on the floor and tossed them in the hamper.

It's a new day, a new year, and time for a new black turtleneck and jeans.

I got to The Lounge a little after four. Brunch was almost over, and Dean was behind the bar chatting to two pretty young women. Smiling his movie star smile—according to him working the bar was just a rehearsal for his eventual stardom—he was probably charming the pants off these ladies. Well, not literally—at least not right now. At six foot two with a great build, blond hair cut into a fade, and blue eyes that sparkled like the Mediterranean awash in the sun, he was what Sully jealously called a babe magnet.

When one of the women went to the ladies' room, I noticed the other one ask for his phone. Giving her a sexy stare, he handed it over. Tossing a sultry look of her own right back, she punched in a number. Hers no doubt. Whether he'd use it or not, I'd probably never know.

The Lounge had a thriving singles vibe going on. The bar was full for our Monday through Friday Social Hour from five until eight p.m. But the real fun started later when the heavy hitters arrived, especially on Thursday nights.

What can I say? New York singles liked to start the weekend early and The Lounge was getting a reputation as the place to do it. I always made sure Dean was working with me on Thursday nights. He knew how to handle that crowd with its Tinder hook-ups, Snapchat, and constant texting, pouring on the charm with the drinks and never missing a beat. I, on the other hand, took over the service bar and chatted with the older folks like Sully and his pals, who kept me company until the noise level got to be too much for their more sensitive senior ears.

Working behind the bar instead of being on display in front of it was much more suited to my temperament. I was happy I had Eric as a boyfriend. I waved at Dean, pointed at my watch and held up ten fingers. Then I went off to find my partner and chef extraordinaire, Pete.

"Hey, you," I said as I entered the kitchen. "How many covers did we do today?"

"About sixty, I think," he replied looking at the call slips stuck on a pin for orders he'd filled.

"Pretty good for New Year's Day, hangovers and all," I said. "I'll check the book when I go back out to see how many reservations we have for tonight." Pete nodded and I continued in a more serious tone. "Wanted to let you know someone left the back door open last night. I got a little spooked when I was leaving."

"Jeez, Jude, I'm sorry. You know the kitchen crew and I all left together through the front as soon as we were done. We went over to the Silver Bullet for a New Year's drink to chill out after the crazy night we had. I'll make sure to have someone check it before we leave from now on."

I remembered waving to Pete and his team as they flew out last night. The kitchen had been really busy. "Not your fault," I replied.

Pete was silent for a minute. "There's something else, Jude." He was frowning as he spoke.

My stomach clenched as I waited for him to continue. What now?

"You know that new knife I just ordered, the really expensive one from Japan?" he asked. "It's missing."

I did know the one. And it was expensive. More expensive than any other knife we'd purchased. I remembered what he'd told me when convincing me of the benefit of spending a pile of money to buy it.

"It'll last forever, Jude," he'd said. "It's seven inches of specialty steel and iron," he continued his pitch, "and the blade is a sharp as they come."

"Is it missing like you misplaced it? Or like it was stolen?"

"I've looked everywhere and it's not here." He looked me in the eye. "Considering what you just told me about the back door being open, I think it's probably been stolen."

I gulped. That meant that someone had been in the restaurant while I was there by myself. I stumbled back into the counter behind me and Pete put out a hand to steady me.

"Are you okay?" he asked, realizing what must have been going through my mind. "Jeez, you could have been—"

I cut him off. I didn't want to go there. "I'm fine, all in one piece. But we need to do something about that door to make sure none of the customers open it to go outside." Maybe I had seen someone by the dumpster, after all. A few minutes earlier and I might have run into him while he was ransacking the kitchen. A chill crept down my spine.

"Was anything else missing?" I asked, bringing myself back to the present.

Pete shook his head. "No, just the knife as far as I can tell. It's strange, don't you think?" He gestured toward his work surface that held his collection of knives and other expensive utensils. "I'll look again but I really think it's gone."

The restaurant had an alarm system but we didn't set it during work hours. I always locked the front door when I was there late, and bolted it before I left. Up until now, I had no reason to think the back door would be open.

"Let's get Sully's alarm guy in to put a separate one on the back door. And we'll put up a sign that it's an emergency exit only." He hesitated. "This way, if anyone's here late, no one will be able to get in. Okay?"

By anyone he meant me. "Okay." I checked my watch. "I'd better get back to the bar and relieve Dean. I told him he could have the night off. I think he has big plans for the evening," I added, smiling.

Pete made the curvy shape of a woman with his hands. "Big plans, huh? No doubt," he said and laughed.

Chapter Four

Sully was sitting at his regular seat at the bar, a Jameson on a coaster in front of him, when I returned. Dean looked more than happy to see me, and I noticed the young woman from a little while ago at a table in the dining room, texting away. He gave me a sly look as he said goodbye and walked over to her. I wondered how she'd gotten rid of her friend, but hey, that wasn't any of my business.

"So," I said to Sully as I planted myself in front of him, "how are you today? Feeling the effects of all that partying in those old bones?" I could never resist when I had the opportunity to get in a little dig about the difference in our ages—my thirty-four to his fifty-nine.

Sully tilted his head and looked at me. "You know that song? What is it? Something like, 'Let's party like it's 1999'? Well, it isn't. And I can't even though I tried."

"Don't suppose you want another one of those, then?" I cast my eyes down to the nearly-empty glass on the coaster.

"Didn't say that, did I?" He lifted one eyebrow and held up his glass for a refill.

"All of the Irregulars get home okay?" I asked as I poured the deep-golden Irish whiskey.

"Yup. At least I think so. Saw them all off except for Jim. I guess he left early."

Probably three thirty instead of four, I thought, smiling to myself.

Sully picked up the Irish and swirled it around. "Has Art been in today?"

"I just came on, so I don't know. Why?"

"I saw him the hallway a little while ago. He was really upset, looking for his brother." Sully shook his head. "Seems the kid never made it home last night. Well, this morning."

"He probably stayed over with one of his friends." I chuckled. "Sounded like they were going to party for a while."

"That's what I told Art. But he said Mikey told him he'd be home for sure. Maybe really late and not to wait up. He's been trying to reach him, but the calls go straight to voicemail." Sully took a gulp of his drink. "He was acting strange. Hyper and angry more than worried."

"Maybe he's feeling a little overprotective, younger brother and all?" I ventured. "I'm sure he'll—" I was interrupted when Carlos, the bus boy, came flying into the bar, his arms waving in the air.

"Ms. Jude! Mr. Sully! He ran over to us and I could see his eyes were practically bulging out of his head.

"Carlos. What hap—"

"*Dios mio! Ven rapido.* Hurry. Hurry." He made a waving motion to get us going. "Outside in the dumpster...*un cuerpo*...a, a body. *Muerto!*" The words tumbled out in Spanish and English, Carlos tripping over them as he tried to tell us what he'd seen.

A dead body? It finally registered and Sully and I scrambled out of the restaurant through the back door and down the alley. The trash Carlos had been transporting was strewn all around the dumpster and its lid was up against the fence behind it, creating a dark shadow over the opening. Carlos stopped a few yards away from the gaping chasm and crossed himself, muttering prayers to heaven.

Sully and I crossed the remaining space together. When we reached the dumpster, he went into marine mode, all senses on high alert. He moved in front of me and put his arm out to block me from seeing what was inside. His body jolted back when he looked down into the space. Taking a deep breath, I moved from behind him and peered into the cold metal box. I had a terrible premonition about what I was going to see and dreaded it, hoping I would be wrong. I wasn't.

It was Michael Bevins. He was on his back, one arm bent under it. His legs were splayed open, partially concealed in a mix of trash bags and cardboard boxes that made a macabre scene feel even more surreal.

Cold, lifeless eyes gazed up at me from a gray face. Blue-tinged lips were opened in surprise as though he were asking how this had happened. He was wearing the same clothes he'd had on last night, jeans, a T-shirt, and the checkered lumberjack shirt he'd worn over it. Only now, it was stained with a wide rusty swath down its front and around the knife that was protruding from his heart.

Moving as far away as possible from the body, I fumbled out my cell phone and punched in 9-1-1. The new year had started all right, and it was going downhill fast.

Chapter Five

A few minutes later, the police arrived, and Sully and I were still trying to process what we'd seen, shivering in the cold January temperature. Turning me away from the dumpster, he tried to tell me it was going to be okay. I'd been through this before and no matter what he said, somehow, I didn't believe him.

Shocked as I'd been, I recognized the body immediately. Art's younger brother was dead in my dumpster. I also recognized the knife sticking out from his heart.

"That's the knife that was stolen from the kitchen," I'd whispered to Sully just as the police were approaching us. He had no idea what I was talking about since I hadn't had time to explain the theft.

He shook his head slightly, letting me know to keep quiet. Then he greeted the police, Patrolman Rodriguez and Patrolman Vastic, who had responded to my call. They secured the scene and asked us a few questions.

"Did you know the victim?" Rodriguez asked.

"We met last night." I motioned toward the restaurant. "His name is Michael Bevins. He's the brother or one of our customers." *Or was,* I thought.

Rodriguez jotted it down. Then continued. "Who discovered the body?"

"Our busboy, Carlos." I pointed to the man just inside the back door. "He was bringing out the trash.

Rodriguez nodded toward Vastic, who walked over to Carlos. "And what time was that?"

"About ten minutes ago." I was shivering all over in the frigid air and my teeth were chattering as I spoke. I had my arms wrapped around my middle and Sully was shuffling from foot to foot, both of us trying to ward off the icy cold. The patrolman noticed we were freezing without our coats, then told us we could wait in The Lounge until the detectives arrived.

As soon as we were inside, Sully demanded in his marine command voice, "What the hell was that about the knife?" I quickly explained about the open back door and Pete's knife being stolen. I'd recognized its curved handle.

"I've got to tell Pete." Panic tinged my words. "He should know before the police question him."

Sully nodded. "But do it somewhere private." He gestured toward stairs to the office. "I'll keep watch up here."

I stuck my head into the kitchen and told Pete I needed to speak to him.

"Can this wait?" he asked, busy at the stove, totally unaware of what was going on in the alleyway.

I shook my head and he followed me down to the office, asking on the way, "What's Sully doing by the back door?"

I quickly explained everything that happened since I left him earlier and stepped behind the bar. Pete listened in silence, taking it in. Then he exploded. "My knife? Used to kill someone? Oh my God." He looked like he was going to be sick and I didn't blame him.

"We don't have a lot of time to figure this out," I said, taking his hands in mine. "We have to tell the police it's our knife and that it was stolen. The truth," I added.

"My knife, you mean, with my fingerprints all over it. They'll think I did it."

"Stop this," I chastised him. "The body wasn't there when I left this morning about five. You were home by then, and later, weren't you?"

I knew he could hear the apprehension in my voice. *Please let him have an alibi,* I begged silently.

He nodded. He knew I was worried that he'd gone bar hopping on his own with no one to vouch for his whereabouts. "And, before you have a heart attack, Marlee was with me. She met me and the crew at the Silver Bullet. After a few drinks we went home, and she stayed until I left for work today."

I sighed in relief. "Okay, good. Now, let's go upstairs and let the cops know about the knife."

When we got back upstairs, Sully was snarling. The alley was now a full-fledged crime scene. Just wide enough at the street for a truck to enter, it opened up into a wide T shape at the top where the dumpster was located. Now, it was filled with a police cruiser, CSU techs, an ambulance, and jarring, flashing lights. Looking around as a Crown Vic entered, adding to clutter of vehicles, Sully jutted his chin in the direction of the dumpster. "Look who just showed up."

"Shit," I muttered under my breath, looking at Detectives Ortiz and Delmonico from the 9th Precinct who exited the car and made straight for the dumpster.

Unfortunately, I'd met them last year when I discovered the body of Ed Molina in Sully's apartment. Things did not go well with them then and I wasn't holding out much hope it would be any different this time. Delmonico had a chip on his shoulder as wide as the Verrazano Bridge, and wore it like a badge of honor. I instantly bristled when he was anywhere near me. He was a living example of the stereotypical dumb cop as far as I was concerned.

It didn't take long for them to notice us coming out of The Lounge; this time we all had our coats on. "Well, Ms. Dillane, we meet again. Isn't this a coincidence?" he asked, turning to his partner, Ortiz, then back to me. "Care to tell us what happened here?" He gestured with his arm to include the alley and dumpster.

Sully fielded the question, ignoring Delmonico and speaking directly to Ortiz. The detective had also been a Marine and the two men had established a tenuous connection the last time they met.

As efficiently as if he were explaining a combat mission to new recruits, Sully gave them a blow-by-blow description of our actions since Carlos came screaming into the restaurant.

"And what about you two?" Delmonico asked. I explained about the back door being open and that I might have seen someone near the dumpster but later realized I must have been mistaken. There was no body in it at five a.m.

Then, Pete related our thoughts that the knife used in the murder had been stolen from the kitchen, since I recognized it when Sully and I looked at the body.

"Whose knife?" Delmonico focused on me, looking up from the notebook he'd been writing in as he spoke.

"Ours," I replied, throwing him a withering look that silently added, 'you asshole.'

"Which of those two brilliant patrolmen let you go back into the restaurant together?"

I just shrugged. I wasn't giving up either of them. Even if they knew better than to let witnesses, or would-be suspects, hang out together.

Delmonico shook his head in disgust. He pointed at the three of us. "Get back inside and stay put until we can get to you." He called over one of the patrolmen. "Take them inside and make sure to keep them separate."

Ignoring Delmonico, Sully turned to Detective Ortiz. "Michael's brother, Art Bevins, lives upstairs. I'd like to go with you when you tell him about his brother. We're friends and I think it will help if I'm there." His voice was flat and unemotional as he spoke, although his blue eyes told a different story. Sad, dull and full of pain.

He glanced at Delmonico. "I'll be glad to give you a statement and answer any other questions you have once we're done." His voice had gone steely, as if daring the detective to contradict him.

Art's apartment faced the 10th Street side of the building and he probably hadn't seen or heard all the commotion in the back. I knew Sully wouldn't want him to come downstairs to this.

"You want to wait and we'll do it together?" I asked.

"No. This happened under my command and it's my responsibility." He squared his shoulders and looked toward the street. Technically, that wasn't true, but one look at his face and I knew I couldn't argue with him, neither would either of the detectives.

Once a marine, always a marine, I thought. Thomas "Sully" Sullivan would never shirk his responsibility.

"Maybe you can keep him upstairs until they take the bo…uh, take Michael out of the dumpster." I noticed that the CSU people were setting up to move

Michael's body to a stretcher. "It might be easier for him if he doesn't see his brother this way." I dipped my head in their direction.

We both knew nothing would make it easier for Art. He'd been frantic when he thought his brother might be missing, looking everywhere. His death would take that to a whole other level.

"Ok, Sullivan, let's go." Ortiz took Sully's arm and they moved toward the building's entrance. Pete and I walked back to the restaurant, escorted by Patrolman Vastic, who looked more than relieved to be out of Detective Delmonico's path.

Chapter Six

Inside the restaurant, Pete went back to his kitchen and I slipped behind the bar. Fortunately for me, our new bartender, Kara, who'd been trailing Dean and was still in the restaurant when Sully and I ran outside, had quickly jumped in. The bar wasn't very crowded, and she seemed to be handling it well. Looked like she was going to be a keeper.

I'd shown Patrolman Vastic to a table in the back of the dining room and had one of the wait staff bring him some coffee. He could still keep an eye on me and peek into the kitchen to check on Pete if he felt the need. But at least he was semi out of sight of our customers.

Some of them had heard the commotion in the alley and were speculating as to what had happened. The yellow crime scent tape had kept them from satisfying their curiosity. I just shrugged my shoulders and poured their drinks. I wasn't going to be the one to tell them about Michael's death. I looked down to the empty corner seat—Sully's usual place—and willed him to appear. I knew it was wishful thinking; he'd be hours with Art and then the police.

Two of the 10th Street Irregulars, Oscar and Jim, plopped themselves down at the end of the bar. Jim lived in Sully's other building and the police had already questioned him.

"Jeez, Jude." Jim, who was always a little jumpy, shook his balding head, sneaking a nervous glance at Vastic. "W-w-what the hell happened back there? His question came out with a slight stutter he couldn't always control. The cops wouldn't tell me anything. Just wanted to know if I heard or saw anyone this morning. They told me they might have more questions."

I watched him shudder at the thought of speaking to the police again.

"Don't worry about it," Oscar piped in then focused on me. "It's bad, isn't it?" He tilted his head toward Vastic who was texting. I hoped Detective Delmonico didn't catch him or he'd be in even more trouble.

Oscar, who liked to gossip, was gearing up for a long chat and I couldn't oblige. "Listen guys, I really can't say anything. So, what'll it be today?" I poured their drinks and moved to the other end of the bar. I liked these guys, but I wasn't about to tell them information they should learn from the police.

Just then, Delmonico walked into the bar. He crooked a finger and summoned me to the table where Vastic was waiting. I kept my temper under control and walked over, pasting a smile on my face. "Coffee, Detective, while we chat?"

He glared at me and shook his head no, then told Vastic to go back outside.

"So, Ms. Dillane, let's go over your story again, shall we?" He couldn't fit any more sarcasm into his words if he tried. He really didn't like me, but that was his problem, not mine.

I repeated my story, up to and including when I'd recognized Michael and the knife used to murder him. Then I crossed my arms and waited.

He closed his notebook and nodded at me. "Don't think about leaving town, Ms. Dillane. We'll want you to give us a written statement."

I bit my tongue to keep from laughing. Did he think I was planning to run off to Rio for winter break?

"Of course," I managed to say, then got up to leave.

"Please send your partner over," he said in a more neutral tone. Maybe he realized how ridiculous he sounded, but I doubted it.

When Pete was done speaking with Delmonico and the crime scene techs had finished up, it was pretty late. Only one couple remained in the dining room and the bar was practically empty. I gave last call and got ready to close for the night. I still hadn't seen Sully. If he was with Art, I didn't want to disturb them. I'd catch up with him in the morning.

The diners had left, and Pete was in the kitchen working on tomorrow's menu. I poked my head in and told him I was ready to go home. He closed down the kitchen and checked the back door, then walked me to the front, waiting until I set the alarm and locked up. He escorted me around the corner to the building's entrance. "Want me to come upstairs with you?" he asked.

"No, I'll be fine." I shook my head and pecked him on the cheek before I went inside. "Get home safe," I added. I wished Eric had been here with me, but he was spending tonight at his family's home and going to work from there tomorrow. I'd call him as soon as I was upstairs and fill him in on this horrible day.

I was so tired when I got off the elevator, I didn't notice the note tucked between the doorknob and the jamb until I was about to put my key in the lock. My mouth went dry and my hand started shaking as I slowly reached for it. When he was stalking me, my ex-boyfriend, Roger used to leave me notes like this. But he was in jail in California. It couldn't be him. I unfolded the paper and my breath caught in my throat.

FORGET WHAT YOU SAW

KEEP OUT OF MY BUSINESS

OR I'LL DESTROY YOURS

The message scorched my hand as if was on fire. I flung it to the floor and rushed inside the apartment, locking the door behind me and blocking it with my body.

"I didn't see anything." I kept saying it over and over again to my silent apartment. "*Nothing.*"

I don't know how long I remained there shaking but, finally, my breathing slowed and I was able to stand. I opened the door an inch, slid my hand out, and retrieved the note. Then I double-locked the door and stood there for a long time. Finally, I walked to the living room window and peeked out, expecting to see the murderer staring up at me.

How, with all the police swarming over the building, had he managed to get in and leave me his note? Had the killer forced his way into the building? God, had I just missed him? Or was he still somewhere inside, lying in wait in the stairwell, ready to attack? These were just some of the possibilities that sped through my mind as I huddled on my sofa and stared into my darkened living room. It was too late to stop the others, like a knife through my heart, from burrowing deep into my brain.

23

Chapter Seven

I woke up on the couch feeling stiff and sore. My eyes darted around the room until finally allowing my mind to understand I was alone. I slowly uncurled and tried to get a grip on the situation. I'd fallen asleep before I had a chance to call Eric. Maybe it was for the best. Telling him about Michael's murder would be hard enough. Having to explain that the killer had left me a warning would be terrible. Eric would want to find him and tear him limb from limb. Not that I'd mind.

I walked to the window and looked out on a bright and sunny view that had seemed so threatening and grim last night. Just as I began to turn away, a huge black SUV pulled up in front of the building. A far cry from the polices' Crown Vic, it sported government plates and I wondered what it was doing here. A moment later, a tall woman—long, black hair whipping in the wind—exited from the driver's side. She looked up at the building as I watched her. She had a leather folder tucked under her arm.

A couple of minutes later, my doorbell rang. "Who is it?" I called out as I approached the door and looked through the peephole.

"FBI," came the reply as my eye focused on credentials held up close enough so I could read them.

FBI? What the hell were they doing here? "Just a minute," I replied. I knew I must have looked awful, spikey hair standing up more than usual, dressed in clothes that looked as though I'd slept in them, which I had. I quickly ran my hands down my T-shirt and smoothed my jeans as best as I could. There was nothing much I could do with my hair. Then, I opened the door.

The woman from the SUV stood in front and introduced herself. "Ms.

Dillane," she said with just the slightest southern accent, "I'm Special Agent in Charge Garlinger from the FBI's Behavioral Analysis Unit." She put out her hand, which I shook. "I'd like to speak with you about yesterday's homicide behind your restaurant." Her voice had softened at this. "May I come in?"

I moved aside and invited her in. Her eyes slid past me taking in my apartment. Aside from the balled-up throw on the couch where I'd spent the night, it was neat and tidy with the light from the window adding an optimistic warmth to a cold winter day.

The real mess was in my bedroom where my vintage wardrobe was scattered all over as usual.

I took her coat and scarf—both from designers I coveted—and gestured to the armchair facing the couch. "Please, sit." She did then I sat on the couch and looked at her. Either the FBI had really upped their pay scale, or she was independently wealthy. The rest of her clothing lived up to her outerwear; her suit, a single button Armani, if I had to guess, fit her perfectly and her red-soled Louboutin ankle boots had the soft sheen of the supplest leather. Her face was long and angular, with ice-blue eyes that reflected intelligence and were now directed at my own.

She'd caught me checking out her outfit. Shit. She was here because of a murder and I was thinking about fashion. I could feel my face going pink and tried to cover up my embarrassment. "Is your partner going to be joining us?" I asked. Didn't agents always work in pairs? Or was that only on television? I guess I wasn't entirely up to speed on my FBI procedures.

"I'll be partnering on this case with Detectives Ortiz and Delmonico from the 9th Precinct. I believe you met them yesterday." Her voice was calm and measured, and despite her pleasant smile, she wasn't giving anything away.

I nodded and gulped. "Yes, I'm acquainted with the detectives," I rose, hoping to change the subject and not to have to explain our previous connection. "Some coffee, Agent Garlinger?"

"Yes, thanks. That would be great." She sat back and settled in like she might be there for a while, placing her leather folder on her lap.

I got the coffee started in my small kitchen and went back into the living room. "So, why is the FBI involved in this? Wouldn't the NYPD handle a murder here, in the city, on their own?" I asked, the sounds of the coffeemaker gurgling behind me. I could see she was assessing how much to tell me. "It's not that I don't want to help. It's just that I don't understand why you're here."

"There've been some similar murders we're looking into." She paused. "The work of someone we've been tracking for a very long time."

"You, as in the FBI?" My brain put the pieces together slowly as though I were working on a complicated jigsaw puzzle, and it finally all fit. "Tracking? As in searching for a serial killer?" I asked, my stomach clenching at the thought.

Agent Garlinger nodded her head. "Yes," was all she replied as the coffeemaker let out a beep that made me jump.

"Then, there's something I need to show you." I rose from the couch and headed for the kitchen.

The coffee had long gone cold by the time I finished telling Agent Garlinger everything that occurred on New Year's Eve and the following day and turned over the note that had been left on my door. I'd put it in a plastic baggie in case there were fingerprints on it, other than my own, that is.

"You have no idea where this could have come from?" she asked for the second time, holding the baggie by a corner and looking at the squat block lettering. "The writing doesn't look familiar to you?"

"No." It almost looked like a child could have written it, except for its deadly message.

"Okay, we'll get back to this in a bit." She slipped the note into a pocket of her folder and continued with her questions.

She'd been focusing on my words intently and jotting down notes as I spoke. She stopped me a few times to go over several details of what I'd seen and heard.

"Just a few more questions, to fill in the blanks, if you don't mind."

"Okay." I nodded.

"Did you notice anyone in the bar who looked suspicious or didn't fit in?

I shook my head. "We had a special New Year's Eve menu and a lot of people from the neighborhood were there. Some of my regular customers came later for the ball drop and other people just wandered in." I tried to picture the scene, but all I could see was a lot of bobbing heads. "It was so busy and noisy, I barely had time to look up from pouring drinks."

"How about anyone approaching Michael?" Her pen was poised over her notes.

"No, no one that I saw. As I mentioned, he was with his brother and his brother's friends. He told me he was going to a party and asked me to make sure Art got home safe." I could feel my eyes filling with tears and willed them away. *He's the one who never made it home*, I thought. "It was after midnight when he left. I think he was meeting some friends."

She looked up and her blue eyes seemed to go darker. "Did you see if he left alone, or with someone?"

"I'm sorry," I replied. "I didn't see him leave. At some point, I just noticed he wasn't with his brother's group."

"They would be?" Her pen poised in front of her as she waited for my answer.

"I call them the 10ᵗʰ Street Irregulars, local guys from the neighborhood who come in at least a few times a week. There's Sully—Thomas Sullivan, my landlord, who lives on the tenth floor, plus Art Bevins, Michael's brother, who's a screenwriter and lives on six. Tony Napoli's apartment is on Eighth Street and Avenue A. He works for a tech company. There's Jim Deems. He has a garage right around the corner and lives in Sully's building across the way. Then there's Oscar Lupe, from Eleventh Street and Avenue A, His building is right next to Jim's garage. Oscar's a cable repairman. And, also," I paused. "I think they were all together when I noticed Michael was gone." I lifted my hands in front of me. "Honestly, it was just so crazy..." My voice trailed off.

"But it wasn't too long after midnight, correct?"

"I think so. I really wasn't paying attention to the time." I pushed myself to remember, but nothing much was coming. "The bar and dining room were still busy, so it couldn't have been that late. Most of the partygoers left between two and three a.m. When I gave last call just before four, most of the Irregulars were still there and a few other diehards." I paused. "Pete and the kitchen crew left about one a.m. and I'm pretty sure Michael was gone by then, since he'd mentioned a party. "Why is it important?"

"Well, for one thing, we don't think he made it downtown. We found his phone in his shirt pocket and there were a lot of missed calls between one and one thirty."

"Was it turned off?" I asked.

She nodded.

That seemed wrong. In my experience twenty-year-olds never turned off their phones, practically never even had them out of their hands. "So where did he go?"

"We don't know," she answered. "We think when Michael left The Lounge, he was lured back here, or somewhere close by." She sighed. "How that was accomplished, I couldn't say. He was a big guy, It wouldn't have been easy to kill him somewhere too far from here, then move the body to your dumpster. It seems more probable that the kill site is nearby. We're still searching for it."

Her words chilled me to the bone. "Lured?" I asked. "Michael didn't know anyone from around here except his brother and his brother's friends." I was puzzled. "How would some stranger get him to go anywhere with him?"

I could see from her expression she was considering her reply. "It could have been anyone. A stranger, someone who pretended to know him, or a person who'd been watching him, caught him unawares and attacked." She lifted a shoulder as if to say she didn't know. "Someone saw an opportunity to kill and took it."

"What are you saying? You think it's someone he met at the restaurant who did this?" Had there been a murderer in our midst on New Year's Eve, one who now had me in his sights, as well?

"Agent Garlinger?" I asked. "What's really going on here?" She understood I meant more than Michael's murder.

"Ms. Dillane," she began.

"It's Jude, please."

She cleared her throat and started again. "Jude, we have reason to believe this began nineteen years ago, with the disappearance and murder of a Danish tourist, Lukas Janssen, on New Year's Eve in 1999." She paused, choosing her words carefully. "He was with his friends for the ball drop in Times Square when he suddenly vanished. Three days later his body turned up in Tompkins Square Park." She paused, giving me time to let that sink in.

"You didn't catch his killer, did you?" I asked, already knowing the answer.

She shook her head. "No, we didn't. He's still at large—"

"And you think it's the same person who killed Michael Bevins?" I interrupted.

"Yes, and two other men, as well. All of them, including Lukas and Michael, were tall—over six feet—well-built men in their twenties. Not the type to be easily overcome. After they were murdered, they were left somewhere in this neighborhood." She looked directly into my eyes. "The killer's been quiet for a while, but now with Michael's murder, we believe he's resurfaced and has started killing again."

My body started vibrating and I felt a cold flash of anger at her words. "So, I'm right. You do think it's someone from around here…from the Lower East Side." It came out more as a statement than a question.

"It's a strong possibility since all four bodies were left in this neighborhood. So, anything you can add, any detail you remember, or something that struck you as odd or suspicious can help." She put down her pen and looked right at me. "Especially if he thinks you saw him and could identify him."

I nodded, feeling sick that this cold-blooded murderer had killed, and was still killing, right where I lived. "Of course," I replied, racking my tired brain for something more. All that came through were the words from the note I'd been left: KEEP OUT OF MY BUSINESS OR I'LL DESTROY YOURS!

The thought that I might have seen him had prompted this sick love letter. Happy New Year to me.

Chapter Eight

Agent Garlinger's words were playing over and over again in my head like a song lyric I couldn't shake as we moved from my apartment to the restaurant downstairs. We wouldn't be opening for business for hours, but the kitchen was already bustling, Pete and his team doing the prep work for the evening's dinner service.

I introduced her to Pete, who I knew she'd want to speak with, and then we walked out into the alley, which she wanted to examine. The crime scene tape was still in place, swaying with the slight breeze that was flowing through. It separated the back of the alleyway where the dumpster was located from the narrower section near our back door.

Garlinger pulled out her iPhone and started snapping pictures, capturing the dumpster as well as the buildings behind it and on either side. I imagined this was how she operated. Looking at and assessing the evidence. When she was done, we went back into The Lounge where I steered her to a table, then poured us more coffee from the pot that was always brewing in the kitchen.

"I'd like to speak with the person who found the body." She looked at a page in her folder. "Carlos Milagros. Is he available?"

"No. He won't be in until later, just before we open," I replied, "if he comes in at all today. He was very shaken up by this and the police called the EMTs. They were worried he was going into shock. They checked him out and gave him a sedative. When the detectives were through questioning him, I had one of the waiters take him home." I remembered how terrified he'd been and wasn't sure if he'd be able to tell her much of anything. "He lives farther downtown near the seaport," I added.

She made another note. "I'll speak with him later. How about Thomas Sullivan?" she asked. "He was with you when you went outside to check the dumpster. Correct?"

I nodded. "As I mentioned, Sully, Mr. Sullivan, is my landlord. He's also a good friend. He had just stopped in when Carlos found Michael's...body." My own gave an involuntary twitch at this. "He volunteers at the Big City Food Coop, but he might be home today." I knew he was concerned about Art's mental state but kept that to myself. "I can call him if you like."

She probably knew all about Sully, me, Big City, and the murder that rocked its foundation last year. The one Sully and I had become very involved in that almost got him killed.

Agent Garlinger nodded and I got up to use the phone by the bar. I didn't know how Sully would react to more questions, and I didn't want her to hear if he had a fit.

"Speak," he answered with his usual greeting.

"It's me," I replied. I turned my back to the agent as I continued, whispering into the phone. "There's an Agent Elaine Garlinger from the FBI's Behavioral Analysis Unit with me in the restaurant. She's looking into Michael's death and would like to have a word with you."

My statement was met with silence. "Sully," I hissed. "Did you hear me?" This wasn't a good time for him to be difficult.

"Tell her I'll be down in a few minutes." His voice sounded strange, like he was far away. "I...I was just on my way to check up on Art. He'd like to get Michael's body released as soon as possible and arrange the funeral." He paused and I could tell from his breathing, he was pacing. "The FBI? What the hell does she want?"

What the hell do you think? I wanted to say, but by then he was gone.

I relayed Sully's message and Garlinger nodded her understanding. "Can I ask you something?" I said. "These other murders? When did they happen and how exactly are they related to Michael's?" If we had a serial killer living in the middle of Alphabet City, I wanted to know about it.

"I can only tell you the basics. You understand that, right?"

"I deserve to know, don't you think?" I tapped my finger on the folder where she'd stashed the killer's note to me. I knew she couldn't give me all the specifics, especially facts that the FBI were holding back, or details only the killer would know.

Her eyes narrowed and her voice became even more serious. "It's a pretty gruesome tale. You sure you want me to continue?"

"Yes, I do," I replied with more conviction than I felt, praying I could hold it together and not toss my cookies all over her Louboutin's.

She started with the discovery of the first killing on New Year's Day in 2000, Lukas Janssen, then moved on to the other two cases. "In 2007, a man named Peter Finley, a banker with North Star Bank, left his friends at a bar near Times Square around one a.m. and was going to grab a cab to his home in the financial district. His body was found two days later under a bench on the walkway in John V. Lindsay Park along the FDR Drive. Cause of death was a knife through the heart."

God, I knew that park, had been there a hundred times. All I could do was nod at her words, the image of Pete's Japanese knife plunged into Michael's chest and all that rusty, crusted blood came floating up in front of me.

If she noticed my reaction, Garlinger didn't let on. Well, I'd said I wanted to hear about the murders, hadn't I?

"In 2014," she continued, Jake Hammity, a construction worker, went missing after a party at a friend's apartment on 12th Street. A knife piercing his heart was what killed him, too."

"Where was his body found," I found myself asking, "and when?"

"He was discovered a week later on the back deck of the former New York City Free Municipal Baths on Eleventh Street."

"I know that building." I'd heard it was for sale again. I thought the gracious old building with its limestone façade and soaring arches was beautiful and stopped to admire it anytime I happened to pass by.

Garlinger took a sip of coffee before continuing. "So, you know it was closed for a while. Now, it's an event space and photography studio on the bottom floor with an apartment on top. There'd been a big New Year's Eve party there and a crew was coming in to clean up afterwards. They're the ones who found him."

"Was he also—"

"Killed with a knife through his heart," she finished.

Without realizing it, I was clutching my arms across my chest as if to protect myself from what I was hearing, this gruesome tale of murders that had happened all around what I thought of as my friendly and safe neighborhood. How wrong I'd been to think I'd be secure from harm when no one was.

"Why do you think he brings the bodies, here, to this neighborhood? Doesn't he realize that might help the police find him?" I was puzzled.

Garlinger sat back and looked up at the ceiling. "There's more than one type of serial murderer and more than one way they behave." She brought her attention back to me. "Film and television often portray them as evil geniuses who make meticulous plans then make mistakes on purpose because they want to get caught.

"But that's pretty much a myth. And I certainly don't think that description fits our killer. He's more spontaneous and opportunistic. Goes hunting on New Year's Eve. He may count on his target's senses being dulled—"

"From partying?" I asked.

Nodding, she continued, "He finds a victim, kills him then dumps the body where it will be discovered and leaves the murder weapon at the scene."

"Why here?" I asked again.

"I believe it's his comfort zone. A place he knows. Maybe he wants everyone to see his work, and if he's here in the midst of it all and can secretly watch people doing just that, it gives him more pleasure and satisfaction."

For once I was speechless. Pleasure and satisfaction? Who could be this way?

Still in thrall to Agent Garlinger's words, I looked up and noticed Sully was standing behind her. How long had he been there? Had he heard what she just told me? Looking at him, I couldn't tell. His expression was calm. His grey hair was brushed back, and he looked like he'd shaved. He was wearing a blue broadcloth shirt that matched his eyes and tailored black wool pants. He was pretty duded up to speak with an FBI agent, I thought.

As I rose to introduce them, Sully moved into her line of sight.

"Thomas!" She couldn't hide the affection in her voice or the warmth that came into her eyes.

"Lanie." He smiled as he looked down at her. "It's been a long time."

What had just...How did he...? While these thoughts were going through my mind, I realized neither of them noticed I was still there. Okay, then. That was my cue to leave. On my way out, I poked my head into the kitchen and asked Pete to send out some sandwiches to Sully and Agent Garlinger. I had a feeling they'd be there for a while.

Chapter Nine

Sully and Agent Garlinger? Maybe I'd misread the situation, but I didn't think so. They knew each other. That explained his silence when I mentioned her name on the phone. He definitely knew it was his Elaine "Laine" Garlinger. And there was no way she couldn't have known it was her Thomas "Sully" Sullivan.

If I'd been shocked by the story she told me, I was nearly as blown-away by their greeting. A dozen questions flew through my mind. I couldn't wait to speak to Sully and find out their connection. A third degree was definitely on the agenda.

But right now, I had something more important to deal with: calling Eric and filling him in on what had happened since he left for the Bronx just yesterday.

Eric answered up on the first ring. "Honey bun, I've been trying to call you. Why aren't you picking up? I was getting worried." All this came out in one long breath.

"Oh, Eric," was all I managed to get out before bursting into tears.

"Jude! What is it?" He sounded frantic and I didn't want that. He knew I hardly ever cried.

Through my tears, I told him what had happened, and he said he'd be at the apartment in an hour. Then I went to sit on the couch and wait for him. I wasn't a stranger to death. This wasn't the first body I'd found, or unfortunately, even the second. They seemed to be piling up around me and I didn't understand why.

I blamed my bad luck on my Catholic mother for naming me Jude, after the patron saint of helpless causes. I think she and my dad had been trying for a while before they had me, and she was grateful. Wouldn't Judith have been just as nice? She was beautiful and smart. Okay, she did cut off someone's head, but still.

My pity party was in full swing when I heard Eric's key in the lock. I ran to him and threw myself into his arms. He led me to the couch and pulled me onto his lap and I snuggled into him. He was long and lean and our bodies fit together perfectly. He held me until I stopped crying, whispering that it would all be okay. What an optimist.

He tipped my face up toward his and I looked into his soft brown eyes. "C'mon, Jude, go get dressed and I'll take you out for lunch." Guess he'd noticed I wasn't looking my best in my disheveled T-shirt and jeans.

Twenty minutes later I was showered and decked out in my sixties Emma Peele, *Avengers*-style black cat suit. "Me-ow!" Eric's eyes lit up. "You look nice." He bent down and gave me a luscious kiss. "Hungry?" he asked.

"For you? Always." I kissed him back and batted my lashes, which I'd darkened with black mascara. "But that will have to wait until after lunch."

We went to the Dive Diner on 9th Street and Avenue A and sat at a small table in the back. I hadn't had much more than coffee since yesterday and I was starving as well as wired. I ordered a big cheese and bacon omelet with fries, a bagel, a piece of chocolate cake, and coffee. Eric just shook his head, wondering how I could eat so much food and never gain an ounce. I'd told him long ago it all went to height. He, on the other hand, was having a nice healthy salad.

We discussed Michael's murder and the possibility of a homegrown killer that Agent Garlinger had raised.

"She might be wrong," he suggested. "The killer could have spotted Michael and decided to target him." He waved his fork in the air for emphasis. "It sounds like he was the exact type he went after."

"But what if she isn't? What if it's someone from The Lounge? One of my customers?" I glanced down at my plate, the food suddenly not very appealing. "I couldn't stand that."

"Jude, there's nothing you can do. Let the police and the FBI do their job."

His phone rang, and he finished his thought as he reached for it. "Maybe this time they'll get him."

I watched him while he spoke and thought how lucky I was to have him. He was right, I should leave it alone.

"Listen." Eric clicked off his call and interrupted my thoughts. "I'm going to stay at your place for a few days. I don't want you to be by yourself."

"That's crazy. You don't need to. You have too much work right now." Eric was an accountant and tax season was in full swing, plus they were pitching a big, new account.

"You don't have to babysit me."

"Don't forget the note he left you."

"He was probably just trying to scare me. That's all." I hoped I sounded braver than I felt.

"Be that as it may, you're stuck with me full time, for now."

"Well then, pay our check because we're going shopping. There's a long, burgundy velvet coat with gold braid trim at that new vintage store, Mata Hari, up the block and it has my name on it."

Eric rolled his eyes at the ceiling as he got up to pay the cashier. And again, I thought how lucky I was to have found him, Saint Jude notwithstanding.

The coat was a standout. A rich, lush velvet with gold braiding all the way up its deep cuffs and around the collar. It was a perfect fit, as well. Snug through the bodice and waist and flared enough on the bottom to swirl around my hips. Plus, it was just the right length for someone as tall as me.

As I handed over my credit card, I gazed out the store's large front window and had the weirdest feeling that I was being watched. I looked up and down the street, but there was no one around. I shook it off and thanked the sales clerk for his help. Eric and I left and walked home arm-in-arm. Still, it was all I could do not to look over my shoulder every few steps.

Chapter Ten

In my apartment, I slipped out of my new coat and gently hung it in my already over-crowded closet. If Eric ever moved in permanently, we'd have to figure out where to put his clothes. As I walked back into the living room, I fished out my cell from my bag.

"Don't do it," Eric said.

"What?" I asked, acting as though I didn't have a clue about what he meant.

"Call Sully."

"Why not?"

"I know you, Jude. You're dying to know about Sully and Agent Garlinger's relationship." Eric emphasized the last word. "Let him tell you when he's ready to talk about it."

"But…"

"No buts." He took the phone from my hand and placed it on the coffee table. I stared at it for a minute, willing it to ring with a call from the man himself. No luck with that.

While Eric opened his laptop and connected to his office network, I decided to do some research of my own. "I'll be in the bedroom in case my phone rings," I called out pointedly as I left the room, but Eric was already too deep into the spreadsheets opening across his computer to even hear me.

You'd be amazed at how much information about the FBI you could find online just by Googling them. Guess they really were trying to be more transparent these days. I started by searching the New York office and its

Behavioral Analysis Unit. That led me to its profilers, Agent Garlinger's section, although they didn't mention her by name. It covered a lot of ground and I decided to get back to it later.

Next, I typed in "serial killer" and hit the mother lode. The most interesting site featured an article about the motivations of serial killers and also explained the misconceptions associated with identifying them. Kind of like what Agent Garlinger had told me, but much more in-depth.

By the time I got through all of that, my mind was buzzing with ideas on how to identify the killer. I looked at my watch and realized I'd have to hustle to be on time to open the bar. Maybe I could try out what I learned on some of my potential suspects, a.k.a. customers.

I said goodbye to Eric but didn't mention my idea. He wouldn't find it amusing.

We'd been lucky so far that police were keeping the murder quiet for now and no reporters were sniffing around. Somehow, I believed Agent Garlinger had a lot to do with that. It was an active case and a high-profile crime. It had the potential to go viral and if she wasn't careful, off-track. She'd want time to continue her investigation before the media scarfed it up and turned it into a big story they'd harp on for days. I knew it would only be a matter of time before that happened.

There'd been a small article in the paper about a body being found on New Year's Day on the Lower East Side. It hadn't mentioned Michael's name or the name of my restaurant. Once they found out how Michael had been murdered, the media would be here with their notepads and their cellphones, scrounging around for every gory detail. If, or actually *when*, they tied his death to a serial killer, they'd be like vultures circling and waiting to get their little piece of flesh.

This was all going through my mind as I set up the bar and got ready to open, cutting the fruit and restocking the bottles. It was Thursday and that meant party time, never mind that everyone had been out partying just three nights before for New Year's.

Dean would be in soon for Social Hour and, if we weren't too busy, I could spend an hour downstairs in my office, catching up on my always-mounting pile of paperwork.

Sully usually came in about now to have a Jameson and keep me company. But today he was a no-show. I figured he was avoiding me, giving himself time to figure out how much he wanted to tell me about Agent Garlinger.

I let out a long, loud sigh as I wiped down the bar's gleaming wooden surface and jumped as I heard a voice whispering in my ear.

"What's the matter, Jude girl, something troubling you?"

"Jeez, Eltee, you scared me." I shook my head at our big bear of a bouncer, who'd moved so quietly, I hadn't heard him approach me.

"You should be paying a little more attention." He looked me in the eye. "Don't you think?"

Had he been talking to Eric? "You're right." I held up my hands in surrender. "But now that you're here, I feel much safer." Even though I was being sarcastic, he knew I meant it. Eltee had saved my bacon more than once, and last year's trouble flitted through my mind as I spoke. We definitely couldn't do without him.

He shook his head and smiled.

"Pete made pasta carbonara for family dinner, so if you're hungry, you'd better get some before it's all gone." Eltee was always hungry. He loved to eat and he especially loved Pete's cooking.

He lifted my chin gently until my eyes met his. "Be careful, Jude," he said then went off to have some dinner.

A few minutes later my first customers began to fill up the stools at the bar. Among them, Tony Napoli, neighbor and one of the 10th Street Irregulars. Now was my chance to test out my theory that the killer could have been one of my customers.

I said hello and placed a coaster down in front of him. "Your usual?" I asked. He nodded and I poured him a Johnny Walker Black Label neat, with a side of soda.

Tony always hunched over the bar and placed one hand on each side of his drinks as though I might take them back.

"Anything new going on?" he asked as he cut his eyes toward the alley side of the restaurant.

"No." I shook my head. "Why? You've heard something, haven't you?" I wanted to put him on the defensive to see where it would lead.

"Me? Nothin'." His Brooklyn accent slipped out and his face showed surprise. "I just thought the cops might have told you more about how the investigation was going."

I chuckled. "You know how tight-lipped they can be."

"But wasn't there some FBI woman in here asking a lot of questions?"

Like you are, I thought. "Excuse me a second," I tipped my head to the left and moved down the bar to take care of some other customers. Tony didn't seem to miss much and I could feel his eyes on me now.

How had he known about the FBI, I wondered? I hadn't mentioned it to anyone. Maybe Sully discussed it with him, but I doubted it. Was Tony surveilling The Lounge to check up on how the police were progressing? I remembered the feeling I had of being watched this afternoon and shuddered.

When I got back to Tony, I nodded toward his glass. "Get you another one?"

"Sure." He slid his glass toward me.

"Want me to start a tab on your card?" I asked. He never used a credit card and always paid cash.

Tony gave me the strangest look, slightly puzzled and a little annoyed. I was sure he was sure I knew that. "No. I've got cash." He pulled out a fold of money from his pants pocket and peeled off a few twenties.

I rang up his drinks and placed his change on the bar in front of him. "You've lived in this neighborhood a while, haven't you?" I made my question sound casual.

"A little over ten years. First on Eleventh and C, now over on Eighth and A." His voice was wary, and he looked down into his scotch. "Why do you ask?" His eyes came up and met mine. All the warmth had left them.

I answered his question with another of my own. "So, the neighborhood had already changed when you moved in? Gotten rid of the drug dealers and the pimps?"

"It was well on its way but not as gentrified as it is now."

I leaned in close before I spoke again. "So, you must have been here for that other murder, right? The one from five years ago? Where they found the body in back of the old Public Baths on Twelfth Street?" I tossed out these questions one after the other in my most confidential tone. "I heard the guy was killed by a knife through his heart." I was practically whispering now as I waited for that to sink in and watched for a reaction. Tony just sat there stone-faced and I continued. "Who do you think could have done such a terrible thing?"

Avoiding my question. he cut his eyes to the front door, where several people were entering. He gave them a quick glance then looked back at me. A habit? I wondered, or self-preservation?

"Listen, I gotta go." He threw back the rest of his scotch, picked up his change, and pulled out a five for a tip. "See you next time, Jude."

I just nodded as he left, watching as he slipped out the front door. I wondered if I had just managed to poke the beast in his lair. And would he poke back?

About nine thirty, I decided to take a break and go upstairs and have dinner with Eric. I called back to the kitchen and asked them to send up a steak for Eric and an order of mac 'n cheese for me, my favorite comfort food.

The bar wasn't as crowded as I'd expected. People must have still been feeling the effects of their New Year's celebrations, and Dean could manage on his own for an hour or so.

"I'm leaving you in charge, so behave," I told him, eyeing the raven-haired young woman sitting across from him who was flirting for all she was worth. "Is that the same woman from yesterday?" I asked, all sweetness and innocence.

"Ouch!" he replied and shooed me away.

Eric had spread out his paperwork all over the coffee table and was so deep into the profit and loss of one of his clients, he hardly noticed I'd entered the apartment. I went over and sat on the couch facing him until he looked up and smiled at me. That smile. Warm, open, and generous, it instantly lit up his face. And mine. I bent over and kissed him.

"Dinner will be here in a few minutes." I gestured to his papers. "Leave this for a bit." I rose from the couch. "I'll go set the table and open the wine."

He was about to protest, when I held up my hand. "Work can wait for half an hour. Besides, it's late and since you're staying over, maybe you should give it a rest until tomorrow."

The food was delicious, as always. One of the benefits of owning a restaurant was that you always ate well, especially with a chef like Pete.

Dinner was quiet with both of us focused on our own thoughts. I considered sharing my plan to be the cat among the pigeons—in this case, the folks at the bar—to see if I could flush out the killer. Eric definitely would not approve and would try to get me to stop. That wouldn't work. My intuition told me I was on to something. What Agent Garlinger relayed about serial murderers, and what I had learned on my own this afternoon, solidified my thinking. It was someone from this neighborhood—a person who targeted Michael Bevins, most likely in The Corner Lounge, the only stop he'd made since he arrived.

I filed my thoughts away, loaded up our dirty dishes, and got ready to return to the bar. "Don't work too much longer," I told Eric, who "um-hummed" as he immediately sat back down in front of his computer.

Downstairs, The Lounge was quiet. Only a few tables in the dining room were occupied. The same for the cocktail lounge, and just a few stools at the bar were filled.

"Everything okay?" I asked Dean.

"Slow," he replied, shrugging his broad shoulders. "Oh yeah, I almost forgot Sully stopped by. Wants you to meet him for breakfast at ten at his place tomorrow. He said he's taking the day off from work."

"Okay." I looked at my watch. I decided to make it an early night. "Why don't you take off? I'll close up on my own."

"You sure about that?" I could tell he was thinking about New Year's Eve. Of course, the police had questioned him, and he knew I'd been here on my own when the killer was roaming around.

"Positive. Pete will keep me company until I close." He needed to write up the food order for the weekend and we could work on it together.

"And, Dean, be careful going home, okay?"

"Always," he replied, his blue eyes flashing me a peculiar look.

Looking at him, it had suddenly hit me. Dean was tall, blond, and handsome, the exact type that turned on our serial killer. I gulped and tried to swallow my fear. I could only hope I hadn't put him in his sights. If I had, I'd never forgive myself.

Chapter Eleven

I knocked on Sully's door exactly at ten the next morning armed with a bag of croissants from the bakery across the street.

"Enter," Sully barked out. "In the kitchen."

I shook my head and followed his command. I found him standing over the coffee maker, measuring out the scoops. "Right on time." I waved the bag of goodies in front of him, placed them on the counter, and went around to the cupboard to find a plate.

I knew Sully's apartment nearly as well as I knew my own. His 'penthouse pad' as he called it, was on the tenth and top floor of the building. Mine was on seven, plebe territory.

Old habits die hard, as they say, and Sully was living proof of this. Not one thing was out of place. Ever. His marine 'neat and orderly' training carried over to his civilian life and his apartment. I could walk through it blindfolded, maneuver my way around the dark-brown camelback sofa, teak-wood end table, and sixty-five-inch flat screen TV, on my way to the gleaming granite and Spanish-tile kitchen, and not trip over anything. I thought of my messy apartment a few floors below where I could barely find anything I was looking for.

"So," I settled myself on a stool across from Sully as he finished with the coffee, "are you going to tell me about you and Agent Garlinger?"

"Not much to tell." He shrugged. "She's an old friend."

"Don't give me that." I shook the croissant I was holding back and forth in front of his face like a Catholic school nun wielding her ruler. "That's bull. Talk," I demanded. I remembered the look on his face when he'd greeted her.

Sully bit back a smile. He'd been baiting me, and it worked.

I just shook my head at him and waited.

His tone changed and a shadow crossed his bright blue eyes. "She's the youngest sister of a first sergeant, Riley Garlinger, who was in my battalion during my tour in Iraq." Sully sat across from me and toyed with his coffee cup. "He was a good soldier, one of the bravest.

"By February 27, 1991, Saddam Hussein knew he was losing the war. He had just issued a retreat order to his troops in Kuwait, but the ones at the Kuwait International Airport never got the order." Sully shook his head. "U.S. Troops from eighteen divisions went in fighting under horrible opposition and it took the whole day for us to secure the airport." Sully stopped and took a deep breath. "It was bedlam. As the Iraqis retreated, they destroyed everything they could get their hands on, including hundreds of oil wells that they set on fire. One of the guys in Garlinger's platoon was badly injured and Riley went back through the fires to get him. Just as he was pulling him back behind our lines, a sniper bullet hit him in the chest and he went down. The medics did everything they could to save him, but it was too late. The bullet had nicked his aorta and he bled out."

I could hear the emotion in his voice as he spoke. It was raw and painful. I could see by the look in his blurry eyes how hard this had been for him to tell me.

"I'm so sorry." I put my hand over his, which had been resting on the counter. "Is that how you came to know Elaine Garlinger?" I asked.

He nodded. "When I got back to the states a few years later, I paid my respects to Riley's family. I wanted them to know how brave he had been, what a hero he was in his last moments of life." He shook his head. "Elaine was the youngest of his siblings, the only girl among three big, burly brothers." He smiled. "She was in college, planning to study for a law degree and then move into law enforcement."

"Obviously, she did."

"I kept in touch with the family, and her, for a while, but it's been a long time."

I thought of the capable woman I'd met who was now Special Agent In Charge of the FBI Behavioral Analysis Unit profilers. I did some quick math in my head. Sully would have been about thirty-two then and Garlinger twenty or twenty-one, if she was in her late forties as I suspected. I knew there was more to the story than Sully was telling me, but I didn't want to push it. I'd get him to spill at some point. Instead, I changed the subject.

"I've been wondering about something," I started. "How long has Tony Napoli been living in the building?"

"Tony?" Sully sat back and gave me a strange look. "Why do you want to know?" His voice had turned gruff, his softer stroll down memory lane all but forgotten.

"Just curious." I hoped I sounded casual and not confrontational.

"Yeah, right. What gives, Jude?" Sully wasn't buying it.

"I just think…his behavior is a little…peculiar. Know what I mean?"

"No, I don't." Sully crossed his arms over his chest in a combative pose. "What the hell are you getting at?" he demanded.

I got up and started pacing. "He seems awfully interested in the murder. Was asking me a lot of questions."

"Well, maybe he was just a little nervous about finding a body in his own backyard," Sully replied sarcastically.

"I guess." I shrugged. "But there's other stuff, too. He never uses a credit card, always pays with cash. I think that's odd. Don't you?" I was warming to my theme. "Does he even have a credit card? Maybe his credit is really bad. Or maybe he doesn't want to leave a trail. You know, something the police could follow to recreate a record of his history, where's he's liv…"

Something made me pause, and when I looked up Sully's eyes were cold and distant. "Stop!" He held up his hands. "What makes you think this is any of your business?" he asked. "And, why all this interest in Tony? What are you up to, Jude?"

I hesitated, trying to figure out how to frame my answer so Sully wouldn't go ballistic. "I'm worried that one of my customers could be the serial killer. Some of what Agent Garlinger told me makes me think the killer lives in this neighborhood." I didn't mention the note I received. Whoever the killer was, he knew where I lived. Only someone who already knew me would know this information.

One look at Sully's face and I knew I should have kept my thoughts to myself and my mouth shut tight.

"Are you crazy?" he shouted. "Tony? One of The Irregulars? You can't be—"

"I'm not saying it's him. I'm just thinking about the possibilities. Michael hadn't been anywhere else on New Year's Eve. He and Art came down to The Lounge right after Michael arrived. He didn't have time to meet anyone except the people at the bar."

"Well, stop thinking. Right now. You hear me! None of these people are killers. You got that?"

"Yes sir. Whatever you say, sir," I barked back as I turned on my heel and stomped out of the apartment, slamming the door so hard the coffee cups on the counter rattled.

Chapter Twelve

B ack in my apartment, I wasn't feeling any better. My head hurt and there was a knot in my stomach. I plopped down on the couch and just sat there muttering.

Of course, Eric noticed. I wanted him to notice. He got up from the kitchen table where he'd just punched off his cell phone and came and sat down next to me. "What's the matter? What happened?" His face was filled with concern, his eyes squinted and sad, looking at me. Adorable.

I shook my head. "I'm an idiot. I had a stupid fight with Sully."

"What about?"

"Oh, just some stuff." I lowered my head and hid my eyes from his. I didn't want to tell him my theory yet. I knew he'd be extremely upset if he thought I was looking for the killer.

"Well, you'd better get over it quick."

My head snapped up. "Why? What's going on?"

"Pete just called. He wanted to warn you that there's a camera crew and a reporter filming in the alleyway." He paused and took my hand. "I told him you were with Sully and he was going to call upstairs."

"What!" I snatched my hand away. "Why didn't you tell me this?"

"Jude. I just did."

"Well, not soon enough." I got up and ran to the door, slamming it too, as I headed for the elevator. *This is all we need,* I thought, *The Corner Lounge on TV as the site of a brutal murder. Better yet, a murder that was the work of a serial killer.*

I punched the call button on the elevator a half dozen times in frustration and had almost decided to take the stairs when it arrived. When the door slid open, Sully was standing there. We stared at each other for a minute, not saying a word. I got in, turned around to face the front, and kept my eyes straight ahead. As the elevator started its descent, I felt Sully take my hand in his. I let him keep it there. If we had to face the music, it would be better if we did it together.

I avoided the alley and went into The Lounge through the front door, quickly locking it behind me. Sully, eyes blazing like the fire from an artillery tank, stormed around the corner to the alley.

My least favorite reporter in the world was standing at its entrance, eyes on the camera lens, speaking into his microphone. Jared Jones was a sensationalist. The more lurid the story, the better. If not, he'd make it so. His station, WVEX, was the slagheap of pseudo news and innuendo. It had found an audience that thrived on discovering the worst in people and played to these viewers shamelessly.

I peeked out from one of the side windows as he was winding down his presentation.

"A vile murder of a vital young man found not thirty feet behind me in a dumpster belonging to The Corner Lounge, a favorite neighborhood bar and restaurant. Sources say he was stabbed through the heart and bled out in this, his final, filthy resting place filled with garbage and detritus from New Year's Eve."

The cameraman moved his camera and zoomed past Jones, pointing to the ground beneath the dumpster—which I knew was dark with dirt and stains, not blood. Then he swung back to him. Jones's face beamed with his most sincere expression, and I watched as he uttered his famous tagline and pointed a finger at the camera.

"This is Jared Jones from WVEX, and you know I won't rest until I uncover the truth, the whole truth, and nothing but."

He'd barely finished speaking when a hand reached over past his mic, grabbed him by the front of his designer suit, and practically yanked him off his feet. It was Sully in action. His other hand was clasped over the camera lens.

"What the hell is…" Jared Jones was in shock, trying to push away this crazy person who'd grabbed him.

Sully was having none of it. "You see this space?" He yanked Jones harder, bunched his jacket in his fist as he twisted him so he was facing toward the alley. "It's private property and you're trespassing." He gave Jones's lapels a final twist then tossed him away like he was bag of feathers. Jones fell to the ground, landed on his butt, and started scrambling away from this madman. "Now get the hell out of here. And don't come back."

He turned to the cameraman who had wisely stopped filming and was backing away toward the station's truck.

Ooh-rah, Sully! His marines would be proud. He'd put the fear of God in me and I was just watching. If I were Jones, I would have been out of there in a heartbeat.

Thankfully, the restaurant hadn't opened for business yet, and no one was around to witness this altercation. Although, I had a sneaky feeling Agent Garlinger would have more than appreciated it.

"How did he find out?" I asked Sully as I let him in the back door. "What sources?"

We moved to the bar and sat down. Sully looked over at the station's mobile truck and the cameraman packing away his equipment. Jared Jones was sitting in the front waiting for him to finish up. Every few seconds he looked over at our big glass window and sunk a little lower in his seat. The creep knew Sully was inside, probably afraid he'd come back out and kick the crap out of him.

Once this story ran, other reporters would be showing up. It was only a matter of time before they put Michael's murder together with the other New Year's murders and came up with a serial killer.

"I thought Agent Garlinger was keeping the murder on the down low."

"It was bound to get out, Jude. People noticed the police were here. Rumors get started." I wasn't surprised. Where crime was concerned, New York was as leaky as a sieve holding water. Nothing could contain the gossip.

Sully just shook his head. "I know. She's not going to be happy about this."

I bit my tongue and held back my, *Oh, you know what makes her happy?* "I think I should give her a heads-up about JJ's report. Maybe she can speak to the head of the station and squash this for now. What do you think?"

Sully didn't seem to be listening. He was focusing on a spot above my head and was in a zone far away. "Sully?"

"Yeah. good idea. Call her. And about before…you know…I…" He shrugged.

This was about as much of an apology as I would get from Mr. Never Wrong. I sucked it up. "No, I was out of line," I told him. What I didn't say was that I wasn't giving up on my investigation. I just wouldn't tell him any more about it.

Friday was my day to do bar and restaurant chores and it was already getting away from me. What with breakfast, my altercation with Sully, and our little skirmish with the media, nothing had gotten done.

"I think I'll check on Art," Sully said as he got up to leave. "See if any of those media creeps contacted him."

"Okay." I nodded. "I'll see you later then."

I poked my head in the kitchen where Pete and Alain had their heads together at the prep table. "I'll be in the office working on the schedule and ordering. Did you send me your food order for the weekend?" I asked Pete.

"Yup. It's done." We'd decided it was a good idea for Pete to write down what he wanted all in one place, so we wouldn't forget an item as we'd done once or twice in the past. You might not think being out of fresh parsley was the end of the world until you had to send a busboy out to three grocery stores to scramble to find some.

"I emailed it last night." Pete looked up and smiled. "Make sure to come up in about an hour. I have a few tapas dishes I'm trying that I want you to taste," he added as he was whisking something creamy-looking in a small metal bowl.

Never mind that I'd just eaten breakfast, my stomach started rumbling at the thought of Pete's food. It really was a good thing that I never gained weight, or I'd be five hundred pounds and counting.

Downstairs, I sat at my computer and brought up Pete's list. The first item stopped me cold. It was a new knife to replace the one the killer had stolen. I just stared at the type on the screen and felt chills creep down my back.

Stop it! I told myself. I needed to concentrate on my work, the business of running a thriving, successful restaurant and bar. I sent the knife order to the Bowery restaurant supply company we used. Then I scanned the rest of the list and placed my order with several of our Hunts Point Market purveyors, who'd deliver the meat, fish, vegetables, cheese, and specialty items for our menu.

Of course, the murder outside The Lounge made my mind wander back to the murders I'd become involved with last year and my undercover stint at Big City Food Coop, which was housed within the market. My chills were back, reminding me how close Sully and I had come to being killed ourselves.

I shrugged them off again and reminded myself to concentrate on business. I brought up the site for Citywide Wines & Spirits, our wholesaler, and sent in a list of what we needed for the week, including the organic wines we'd added to the menu that our customers were raving about.

When I was done with ordering, I made the schedule for the week, giving myself the day off on Saturday as I did almost every week. It was the one perk I allowed myself as the 'boss.' I slotted in Kara to trail Dean and Molly for a few shifts and hoped she'd be ready to take over one or two afternoon shifts on her own pretty soon.

I put the to-be-paid bills in a pile for Eric to deal with—one other perk of having an accountant for a boyfriend—and was done with the business side of the restaurant for today.

I was just about to call Agent Garlinger when the internal phone line rang. It was Pete letting me know it was time for today's tasting.

Chapter Thirteen

Pete was waiting for me at a table near the kitchen, plates, silverware, and wine glasses laid out on a crisp white tablecloth. Our tastings were serious business. Pete tweaked the menu often, not only to keep up with the latest trends and seasonal fare, but also to create some of his own.

Since I loved to eat and my palate wasn't exactly what you'd call discriminating, there was hardly anything I ever rejected. Pete, on the other hand, was able to evaluate his own food impartially and often eighty-sixed a dish I'd loved.

"Red or white?" I asked as I slipped behind the bar to choose a bottle of wine to complement our lunch.

"Let's have a white today," he replied, and I pulled out one of the organic wines I had just reordered. I opened a bottle of Private Reserve chardonnay from California and brought it along to the table. I poured the wine while Pete reviewed what we were about to eat.

He had three dishes set on the tablecloth and uncovered each one as he named what it contained.

"This is a chicken liver mousse with candied bacon topped by a quail egg. Next, we have grilled cheese triangles made with Saint Andre cheese and truffle oil. And finally, deep-fried figs battered in almond flour and stuffed with *crème fraîche.*"

My mouth was watering before I even took one bite. Pete had outdone himself. Everything looked and tasted delicious, and I was all for adding each dish to our growing appetizer menu. He wasn't sure about the chicken liver mousse and would ask Alain and the rest of the kitchen staff to rate it before he made a decision.

As we sipped and ate, we spoke about the effect the murder might have on our business and our clientele. Pete's food had taken The Lounge beyond a neighborhood place to a starred restaurant with a following, and diners from all parts of the city were reserving tables.

"It could go a couple of ways, Jude." Pete lifted one shoulder. "People could stay away because of the fear of crime on the Lower East Side." He said the last with air quotes around his words. "Or, we might get a lot of looky-loos who just get a thrill out of a serial killer murder and stop in for that reason." He paused. "I'm not sure that's the kind of exposure we want."

I told him about Jared Jones and how Sully had handled the situation. He shook his head and laughed. "Sully's still got it, hasn't he?"

I'd known Pete for a long time—well before we were partners—and trusted his judgment. "Pete, I've been thinking about who could have killed Michael Bevins, and…I'm afraid it could be one of our customers."

He rocked his chair back onto two legs, his tall frame tilted on an angle, and looked down at me through narrowed eyes. "How did you come to this conclusion?"

I could see the worry settle in his face, his mouth an unhappy straight line.

I related the theory Agent Garlinger had told me about the serial killer using our neighborhood for his dumping ground. Then I added my own thoughts about who could have stalked and killed Michael.

"I think it's someone who met him here on New Year's Eve. Someone who's lived here for a long time," I added softly. I didn't mention my suspicions about the 10th Street Irregulars or that Sully had gotten extremely pissed off about that idea.

Pete pushed his chair forward on all four legs and leaned in across the table, his palms pushing down on it and his eyes as intense as laser beams. When he spoke, his words were harsh. "Jude, don't do this. Murder is a matter for the FBI and the police. Not you. Let. Them. Do. Their. Jobs." There was steel in his voice and his message was clear.

I understood what he was leaving unsaid: Remember last year? The last time you meddled? You were lucky to survive.

I nodded my head at him. "I will. I'll let Agent Garlinger find the killer." I couldn't tell if he believed me or not. "In fact, I have to phone her and let her know about Jared Jones. She wanted to keep this as quiet as possible, not let the media have a field day. Especially not have them make the connection to a serial killer and sensationalize it."

"Jude...?" The fact that he didn't believe me was obvious in the skepticism I heard in that one word.

I leaned across the table and took his hand. "Honest. I won't get caught in the middle of this."

I got up and waited until he stood, as well. "Thanks for lunch. I better let you get back to the kitchen."

Before I headed back downstairs, I stopped at the coffee machine in the service area. When I picked up a cup from the shelf above, a coaster fell off and landed on the floor. *What's that doing here?* I wondered. As I bent to pick it up, I saw it held a crude drawing of a knife with red drops that looked like blood splattered over it. My breath caught in my throat and heat flashed through my body.

The killer had left me another warning. One I couldn't ignore.

I was shaking all over as I sat at my desk, picked up my cell, and called Agent Garlinger. I had information to give her. She needed to know about this latest threat to my life. And she needed to do something to stop it.

Chapter Fourteen

er machine picked up and I left a message. I launched into a hysterical tirade about the coaster, asking when were they going to catch this madman, how could she let this happen, and what was she going to do about it. She was responsible for my safety, wasn't she?

My words sounded strident and disconnected, and I knew the fear had started me ranting. I took a few deep breaths and relayed it all again in what I hoped was a more rational tone.

I finally remembered the original reason I was going to call her and explained about Jared Jones. I asked her to call me back. I wanted to know if she could actually keep the press away or if The Lounge would be under siege from reporters. Most of all, I wanted to find out more about the killer's victims and the odds that I would be his next one.

When I thought about the men this killer had taken, I couldn't overlook the fact their bodies had all ended up here in my hood. Manhattan was a large borough, in both size and population. He could have left the bodies anywhere. While the Lower East Side wasn't necessarily his only hunting ground, it was definitely his dumping ground. At least that we knew of for now. His 'comfort zone,' Agent Garlinger had called it.

Two victims had gone missing near Times Square and two from right nearby. What did they have in common? What if anything, other than their appearance, had marked them as targets? Maybe if I could figure that out, I'd be able to tie the murders together, solve the case, uncover the killer, and...

Jeez, Jude! What are you, Nancy Drew, girl detective? I brought myself up short with a deep sigh. Not ten minutes ago I'd practically promised Pete

I'd leave the detecting to the professionals and here I was jumping right in, even after being scared half to death by the killer's latest note. Some people—yes, I mean me—never learn. You'd think I didn't have anything else on my plate, like running a business and enjoying a loving relationship with Eric. But still, what harm could it do to do a little digging just to satisfy my own curiosity and maybe save my life? Looking into the victims wasn't the same as stalking the killer, was it? It was just information, right? Right. I'd just have to keep it on the down-low so he wouldn't twig to what I was doing.

I turned to my computer and was just about to type in the name of the first victim, Lukas Janssen, when I noticed the time. Social Hour was about to start, and I needed to go back upstairs to the bar and compose myself until I spoke with Agent Garlinger. My research would have to keep until tomorrow when I'd have the whole day to spend surfing the web for information.

In the meantime, a low bass thump from the sound system floated down to the office along with the hum of end-of-the-week conversations from happy patrons reminding me I had to get to work—not to mention Molly buzzing downstairs for help. Murder would just have to wait while there were drinks to be poured.

Upstairs, the bar and lounge area was full with the after-work crowd blowing off steam from their nine-to-five gigs. People were still in the holiday spirit and The Lounge was packed.

Sully was at his usual spot at the bar, a Jameson neat in front of him. He was speaking with Jim Deems who'd taken the next stool over. They had their heads together chatting animatedly. They looked up and both greeted me then went back to their discussion, Jim taking off his red baseball cap, which he knew I didn't allow in the bar.

"S-s-sorry, Jude," he stammered, giving me one of his sheepish looks. He hadn't stuttered this much in a while. Something was making him nervous. Then, I heard the words "Rangers," "Devils," and "hat trick." They were speaking about hockey and I tuned out.

At least they're not talking about the murder, I thought as I began to edge away before they could get on my case about not having a TV at the bar so they could watch the game.

Jim stopped by most often of the 10th Street Irregulars and generally plopped down next to Sully. Maybe it was a male bonding thing since, of all the men in the group, he was the closest to Sully in age. His garage was around the corner on Avenue A. Every time I passed by, I thought about how dilapidated it looked, kind of like Jim himself in his almost worn-out clothes and oil-stained cap. He'd already been a resident of the neighborhood when Sully bought his buildings and moved in soon after. He'd helped out Pete once or twice when his old clunker of a car needed servicing. Big and solid with the ginger hair and bushy eyebrows of his Scottish ancestors, all he'd wanted in return was for The Lounge to add haggis and mashed turnips to its menu. As if that would ever happen. Just thinking about the dish made with sheep's offal, suet, and beef intestines made me shudder.

Jim stopped my progress toward the other end of the bar with a raised glass he wiggled in front of me. "I'll have another, t-t-hanks." I took the glass from him and began to pull a beer from the tap. His eyes were a little unfocused and he was slurring his words. He must have started earlier, somewhere else, and I'd have to watch how much I served him.

"Sully told me what happened today with that reporter. Did the guy know any details, like how Michael was killed with that big, fancy knife?" he asked, leaning in conspiratorially.

Before I could tell him I didn't want to discuss it, especially in front of a bar full of people, he patted Sully on the back. "Anyway, you were lucky this guy was here to help you out," he added, smirking, "or you might have had to t-t-take him out yourself."

I gave Sully the stink eye and frowned. He'd told Jim details about the murder and filled him in on Jared Jones on purpose, knowing he wouldn't be able to keep from goading me just a little. Even though he seemed meek and mild mannered, Deems was one of those people who liked to push your buttons.

That was fine with me, I liked to push right back. "Sure you got that right?" I asked. "After all, Sully was protecting his property, his tenants, and my customers, like you, from the press. Wouldn't want them to be poking their noses in *your* business now, would you? Who knows what they might find?" I gave him a wicked smile. I knew a lot of his business at the garage was off the books.

"Yeah, yeah, marines l-l-landing with boots on the ground, and all that." His expression turned dark, then he laughed uneasily. Jim drained his beer and pulled out his credit card to pay. He signed the slip and left with a wave and a "Got to get going."

"Was it something I said?" I asked Sully. Deems usually hung around for a little while longer trying to make eye contact with the women at the bar. So far, that hadn't worked out for him. I wonder why?

"Isn't it always?" he replied.

I ignored his remark and asked another question. "Why did you discuss the murder and Jared Jones with him? The more people who know about this, the more chance of it becoming public. And Agent Gar—"

He stopped me with a slice of his hand in front of my face. "Jim lives here. He's got a right to know what's going on right outside his door."

Maybe he already does, I thought, going back to my feeling that it had to be someone from the neighborhood. Of course, I didn't say any of this to Sully. He'd made it abundantly clear what he thought of my theory, which I was more determined than ever to discuss with Elaine Garlinger. Too bad I hadn't had a chance to feel out Jim without Sully being around. Even if he could be ruled out as a suspect, he might know something that could help her with the case. After all, he'd been living and working in the neighborhood for more than twenty years.

I'd been looking down at the bar, unconsciously rubbing my hands along the gleaming polished wood while these thoughts went through my mind. When I looked up, Sully was staring past me at the mirror over the back bar, his eyes focused on something only he could see. *What's he up to?* I wondered. I cleared my throat and it brought him back to the present.

"I gotta go." He turned his glass over on the coaster and rapped his knuckles on the bar, his usual signal that he was done. Then he was gone.

I watched him leave, troubled by our last exchange and wanting to call him back to smooth things out. I started to say his name when my cell beeped. I looked at the caller ID. It was Agent Garlinger returning my call. I turned my back on the crowd at the bar and answered. We agreed to meet the next day at my apartment to discuss the ramifications of my latest note and Jared Jones showing up. So far, the story hadn't appeared on TV or on the station's website. She must have persuaded them to hold it for now.

I should have been elated that she was taking me seriously. Instead, I felt let down, like the world as I knew it was about to fall to pieces.

Chapter Fifteen

A sliver of sunlight peeking through the bedroom curtains woke me up early on Saturday. I slipped out of bed quietly, not wanting to disturb Eric. He'd still been up when I arrived home at two a.m. Usually, he was happily snoring away by then. And I always teased him that I'd taken a picture of him, mouth agape, drool dripping on his pillow and posted it on social media. Of course, I'd never do that. I could be mean but not to him.

After I'd assured him last night I'd have an FBI agent for company, he decided I could be trusted on my own while he headed into his office in Mount Vernon for a meeting with his partners. They were working on landing a big, new account and needed to put in the hours. Not that he hadn't been doing that already.

Honestly, I was happy he'd be out of the apartment when Agent Garlinger arrived. I couldn't tell him about the coaster and its message. He would not have taken it well. Even though I assured him we were just going to discuss the media—a.k.a. Jared Jones and company—and how to deal with them if, or when, they showed up again. I knew he didn't believe me. Well, not entirely.

When I finally heard him stirring, I brought him in a steaming cup of Café Bustelo with one sugar and sat on the bed while he drank it.

"You're the best," he said taking a sip of the rich, dark brew. "I couldn't live without you," he added, taking another sip.

"Really?" I raised my eyebrow in mock surprise. "Give the guy a coffee and he'll tell you anything. Doesn't take much, does it?"

He put the cup down on our nightstand—a vintage mid-century piece he'd bought for me after we'd been dating a while—and pulled me close.

I cuddled into his body, still warm from sleep, and mentally pinched myself. How did I get so lucky?

"Jude, are you sure you should be meeting with Garlinger? What if the killer finds out and thinks you actually saw him?" He squeezed me tight. "It's too dangerous." A frown creased his gorgeous face and his dark brown eyes went even darker.

"He's not going to find out. No one knows she's coming here." I paused. "Not even Sully."

"What? You didn't tell him his old crush was going to be in the house? You're slipping." The frown was replaced by a grin.

"I just didn't get around to it." Forget that he practically flew out of The Lounge last night. I'd tell him later, much later, after she left and I had a better idea of how she planned to handle things.

"So, what time are you picking up your parents?" I asked, changing the subject. Eric's parents, Cecelia and Roberto Ramirez, lived in Mount Vernon, near Eric's office and his apartment. They hadn't been to the city in a while and I wanted to treat them to dinner at The Lounge, although he'd joined them on New Year's Day, I knew they missed Eric, who they didn't see often enough, even though he lived a few blocks away from them. They enjoyed any time they could spend with him.

"I'll get them about six thirty and if there's no traffic, we should be here by seven, in time to park." Parking rules in Manhattan were brutal, and if you didn't follow the signs you could get a hefty fine or even be towed away.

"Sounds good. Pete is preparing a special dish for tonight. And before you ask, he refuses to tell me what it is."

Eric stretched and got out of bed. "I have to get going," he tossed over his shoulder as he headed for the shower. I sat and watched him walk away. It was quite a nice view.

After Eric left, I took my shower and dressed so I'd be ready for when Agent Garlinger arrived. As I munched away on a bowl of cereal and sipped a mug of coffee, I opened my laptop and resumed the search I'd had to abort the previous afternoon.

Typing in the name Lukas Janssen brought up fewer articles than I would have expected. Here from Denmark on a holiday, 22-year-old Lukas, his girlfriend, and another couple were planning to welcome the new year in Times Square. While waiting for the ball to drop, Lukas went off to purchase a souvenir for his sister and never returned to his friends. Frantic, they sought out the police who ultimately began an exhaustive search of the area.

I stopped reading and thought about Lukas's disappearance. Back in the late 90s, New York's reputation for being unsafe had done a one-eighty and tourism was thriving. To have a tourist disappear like that was totally unacceptable to the city leaders.

The police pulled out all the stops. They conducted a massive search all across the city. They enlisted the help of the public with flyers showing his photo and description and a hotline number to call, staffed by volunteers and police personnel. They offered a reward for any information. Thousands of flyers were posted. And, while there were hundreds of tips and sightings, all of them proved to be false.

I shook my head. It was incredible that not even one person had spotted him.

Finally, three days later, a bunch of kids playing in Tompkins Square Park noticed a glove sticking out of a pile of snow. They went over to pull it and realized there was a hand inside. They'd found Lukas Janssen.

Those poor kids. I shook my head. Was Lukas actually the killer's first victim? Or had he started long before and managed to stay under the radar?

My doorbell ringing brought me out of my reverie. Agent Garlinger was downstairs. I buzzed her in and waited for her to reach my apartment. When she knocked lightly on my door, I greeted her and let her in.

Today, she was dressed more casually in black jeans and a soft, baby-blue cashmere sweater. Her hair was pulled back in a low ponytail and her face devoid of makeup. I could see why Sully would still be attracted to her. She was a beautiful forty-something-year-old woman with a few laugh lines around her eyes and a winning smile. She must have been a stunner when she was younger.

"Coffee?" I asked, holding up a mug.

"Yes, black thanks," she replied as she took a seat on my couch.

I poured her a mug of coffee, handed it over, grabbed my own, and sat opposite her.

"So…" we both began at the same time.

"You first, please." I nodded for her to go on.

"The coaster. You found it in the bar?"

I nodded. "Yes, back by the coffee machine. Anyone could have put it there. It's in the passage that leads to the restrooms and there's a lot of traffic." I paused and handed her the coaster, which I'd placed in a zip lock bag. This was getting to be a habit.

She looked at it and shook her head. "Quite the artist, isn't he? I'll send it for prints and DNA, but I'm pretty sure we won't find anything. She sat back and pinned me with her eyes. "Jude, you have to protect yourself.

"You know, you could be in real danger, don't you? The coaster and that note you received? He might think you actually saw him and can somehow identify him."

"But I didn't see anything really." *Not counting Michael's dead body,* I thought.

She leaned forward, resting her elbows on her knees and winding her fingers together. "The killer doesn't know that for sure. In his mind, you're a witness. If he even suspects you're looking for him…"

She didn't have to finish her thought. A ripple of fear went through my body. Her words had made the fear feel more real. I swallowed it and I nodded. "I'll be careful. I will."

"Now, to Jared Jones." She said his name with a sardonic laugh. "You know he won't stop poking around. He sees himself as a truth teller, but he's really a shark and the rest of the population are the minnows he swallows up along the way."

"But there hasn't been anything on the news, online, or in the paper." I placed my coffee on the table as I spoke. "How did you manage that?"

"My boss in D.C., Hughie Mack, who oversees all the BAU units, called Jones's boss, Roger Armistade, the head of the station, and cashed in a favor.

They go back a ways, play golf together. You know, the old boy network." She lifted her eyebrows. "He also promised to give WVEX an exclusive on the story when we're ready to go public. I don't know how long we can keep the murder contained or prevent Jones from uncovering the other New Year's murders and coming up with a serial killer." I could hear the disgust in her voice.

"This might be a stupid question." I shrugged. "But I'll ask it anyway. Would it be better to let it slip about the other three murders, get ahead of the press?"

"Your instincts are good, Jude." A small smile turned up the corners of her mouth. Hughie and I were discussing that last night, but we decided to wait a few more days to try and corner the killer.

"Sully told me about your theory…that it could be someone from the neighborhood."

"Oh, so you spoke to him?" I asked, trying to keep my voice even. "He didn't agree with me, so why would he bother to tell you?" I could feel some of my anger slipping through my words. I didn't want that to happen. It wasn't her fault that Sully ratted me out. Talk about 'the old boy network.'

"Well, for starters he's concerned about you. He said…umm…you can be extremely stubborn when you decide to do something."

I bet he didn't exactly put it that way.

Agent Garlinger continued. "He also thinks you could be right."

"What?" I could feel the blood rushing to my face. "Then why is he giving me such a hard time?"

Agent Garlinger just looked at me. We both knew the answer.

"Here's what we're going to do." She sat back and raised her eyes to mine, a stern expression on her face. "You need to stop detecting and watch out for yourself and your business. If we don't have a suspect within the next forty-eight hours, my unit will release the information that we have a serial killer on the prowl, along with the details of the three previous murders.

"We'll announce a massive man hunt and get the media involved. They'll be all over the story…and possibly your restaurant, as well." She paused and watched for my reaction.

I kept my face neutral, although I was churning inside at the idea of an army of Jared Jones-like clones stalking me and The Lounge.

"Please take this seriously, Jude. You have to behave as if you do not know a thing; that you did not see anything, or anyone—which is true, correct?"

All I could do was nod.

She put her hand on my arm. "This is a brutal murderer we're speaking about, someone who would not hesitate to kill you, too, if you got in his way."

I gulped. I knew she was right, but all I'd planned to do was to ask a few questions. Not lasso and hog-tie a killer. "I understand," I replied, "but what about Sully?"

She looked surprised at my question. "What about him?"

My anger was coming back now. "Is it alright if he goes off looking for the killer? He's got a vested interest in clearing this up, as well."

"He is not going to do that." Her tone was adamant. "Sully is going to leave the manhunt to the law enforcement officials." She shook her head. "He won't get involved."

I bit my tongue. I'd seen the look on Sully's face last night at the bar. He was up to something. Bet he hadn't told Lanie that part.

She stood up to leave. "Well, thanks for the coffee, Jude." She slipped into her coat, then offered her hand. "I will keep you in the loop as much as I can. I promise. And I'll try to minimize the media's presence."

She turned to leave and looked over her shoulder at me. "Please stay out of the investigation. I don't want to see you get hurt."

Her last words rankled me. I knew it wasn't a threat, but it sure sounded like one.

Chapter Sixteen

The meeting had not gone at all the way I expected. It was stupid to think she'd let me be part of the investigation, or sign off on my plan, and I was totally annoyed with Sully for telling her about my idea to ferret out the killer.

The kicker was that I felt conflicted and I didn't know why. I hadn't promised Agent Garlinger that I would cease and desist, but my silence before she left implied it. I knew Sully would be watching me like a hawk to see if I was behaving. I'd have to be very sneaky if I wanted to keep on questioning the 10th Street Irregulars. I smiled. Sneaky I could do.

I looked out the window, waiting for Agent Garlinger to appear on the street below and slip into her car. After about five minutes she was still a no-show. I figured she'd gone upstairs to Sully's place. Colluding with the enemy is how I thought of it.

I sat down and opened my laptop. The cursor was blinking on the article I'd been reading about Lukas Janssen. He deserved so much more than to be found buried in the snow in the park. So did the other victims. Stabbed in the heart was a terrible way to die, not that any way was good. I typed in the name of the other men the killer murdered: Peter Finley who was found in John V. Lindsay Park off the FDR Drive, and Jake Hammity who'd been found at the New York City Free Municipal Baths.

There were several articles about each of them, which I planned to read. My meeting with Elaine Garlinger had given me a headache. I needed aspirin and fresh air.

The day was cold and gloomy, so I bundled up in my new, long, velvet coat, wrapped my big, wooly scarf around my neck, and headed out.

I must have made an unconscious decision, because before I knew it, I'd crossed over the 10th Street pedestrian bridge and was at John V. Lindsay Park on the East River Drive, viewing the spot where Peter Finley had been found behind the comfort station. Honestly, I didn't know what I expected to find there among its ball fields and tennis courts, certainly not the killer revisiting the scene of his crime all these years later. There were a few couples walking arm-in-arm and some kids on skateboards going up and down the wide path bordering the river. Two groups of twenty-somethings were playing a pickup game of basketball, oblivious to the temperature. To say this was a cold case would be putting it mildly.

I rested my arms on the railing that separated the path from the river and looked into its murky depths. The currents in the East River, while calm-looking on the surface, ran fast and treacherous. Fall in and you'd be gone in an instant. Today, the water was gray and uninviting, reflecting the dull sky above, a sign of winter that made me feel morose.

I don't know how long I stood there, but suddenly I felt a tingling at the back of my neck. I gulped and swallowed hard. My instinct was to turn and run, but I was frozen in place. *You're being stupid, Jude,* I told myself, and took a deep breath. I slowly turned my head to the left and pretended I was watching the skateboard kids further down the path. I let my eyes drift toward the comfort station and the bare trees behind it. Nothing moved. No one was there ready to jump out at me, although I could swear that's what was going to happen.

My hands were shaking, and I adjusted my scarf in an attempt to still them. Maybe Agent Garlinger was right and I should stop nosing around. I decided to leave and passed the restrooms and stand of trees around them as I headed for the exit. I noticed large footprints that appeared to be from a man's work boots, sunk down about an inch into a patch of leftover snow behind the trees. It was crusty and dusted over with dirt and would probably stay that way until April. The prints stood out like a tourist in front of Macy's store windows, a set facing the path where I'd been standing and one toward the park's exit. The gnarled trunks of the oak trees in front of them were thick and could easily have concealed someone from my sight.

Moving quickly, I began to walk home, imagining the man who'd made those footprints lurking in a doorway, ready to lunge at me. I resisted the impulse to look back and walked a little faster.

Fear made me tense and wary. I was jumping at shadows and eyeballing anyone who passed close to me, my hands were clutched into fists ready to strike. All these signs were like a bright orange light flashing at me. A warning that maybe I should stop my investigation and let the cops take care of it. That's what a normal, sane person would do. Yet, even through my panic, I knew I couldn't cave in to fear. It had me in its grip last year more than once and I wouldn't let that happen again. I pulled my shoulders back and decided. I had to find out why four men had been murdered. I could no more give this up than a lion would give up its kill.

Ten minutes later, I was back at The Lounge, calmer and more resolute. I convinced myself I'd be careful; that I wouldn't run off without thinking about the consequences and, if I had legitimate suspicions, I'd relay them to Agent Garlinger. Having settled that with myself, I felt calmer and in control.

I couldn't resist poking my head into the bar where Molly was mixing pitchers of mimosas for the brunch crowd. The tables in the dining room were filled, and a few people were dining at the bar. I waved at her as I made my way to the kitchen.

Pete was working quickly, but methodically, to get all the brunch orders out on time. He looked up at me and shook his head. "Not now, Jude."

Jeez. I wasn't planning to settle in for a long chat. I just wanted to ask about the special dinner he was cooking for Eric's parents tonight. I guessed I'd be surprised, too.

I went out the back door, trying to avoid looking at the dumpster, even as it drew my gaze right to it. Once again, I wondered what kind of monster would kill someone in such a brutal way. And why? I thought about some of what Agent Garlinger had told me about serial killers. They were *not* the evil geniuses the press often made them out to be or people who made mistakes on purpose because they wanted to get caught. What they were was psychotic. At least I thought so.

I'd bet The Lounge this killer wasn't any different. Maybe he was tired of lingering in the shadows, wanted to make a name for himself and be up there with the likes of Dahmer, Gacy, and Bundy and was taunting us by killing close to home. Daring us to catch him. It had been a long time since his last kill—five years. Was that too much time to wait for satisfaction? Could he be missing the attention the media would offer and the secret knowledge that they got it, and him, all wrong?

My head was spinning again as I walked into my building; the headache I'd had earlier was back with a vengeance. I started to unbutton my coat and unravel my scarf as I walked down the hallway and pushed the button for the elevator. Closing my eyes, I massaged my temples as I waited. When the elevator finally dinged its presence, I started to enter and was one step in when I realized someone was behind me. I began to turn to say hello but didn't get very far. Gloved hands grabbed my scarf from behind and started to pull the ends tight around my neck while a raspy voice whispered in my ear. *"You bitch."*

I struggled to get loose, but his grip was too strong and the scarf was getting tighter. "I warned you to keep out of my business." His hands gave a final pull. "Now you're gonna get what you deserve."

My self-defense training kicked in. I went slack, surprising him, then pushed my elbow hard into his ribs. He backed off for a second allowing me to take a breath.

But it wasn't enough. He kneed me in the kidney and the pain was excruciating. He was so close I could smell the stink of his sweat coming at me. I was suffocating. I needed air right now. I struggled harder, trying to rake his face with my nails, but he'd covered it with some sort of mask. With one last effort, I moved into him and reached behind my left shoulder with my right hand to grab his arm and flip him. But he was ready for me and angled away, pulling tighter on my scarf. I began grasping at it, wedging in my fingers and trying to loosen his grip. My breath was nearly gone. My lungs, on fire, felt like they were bursting and I felt myself fading. Oh god, I was going to die and I couldn't do anything to stop it. My struggling was as useless as an ant fighting an elephant.

Through the mist that was enfolding me, I heard footsteps coming toward us and a voice calling out, "Hey! What the hell are you doing?"

My attacker heard it, too, and panicked. He let go of my scarf and flung me to the elevator floor as he fled toward the back of the hallway and its door to the yard beyond. The footsteps I'd heard were next to me now and a voice I recognized was calling my name. It was Tony Napoli.

"Jude. Jude. Are you alright?" he asked, helping me to sit. "Don't move. Let me look at you, okay?" He gently moved my hands from where I was still clutching my scarf and placed them in my lap.

I was gasping for air and shaking like a leaf. All I could do was nod.

"Stay here," he commanded and took off down the hall.

I wanted to call out, but my voice wouldn't work. To tell him to be careful, to let it go.

Slowly, I rose until I could stand. My legs wobbled like they were made of Jell-O and my throat ached, raw and scratchy.

Tony returned a few minutes later and pulled out his cell phone. "He's gone. I couldn't catch him. Must have hopped over one of the fences." He shook his head. "We should call the police," he said, "report this."

"No." I coughed. "Please…no police." I was bent over nearly double with the effort of speaking.

"But, Jude—"

I held up a hand. "No police." My voice was slowly coming back. "I'll be okay in a few minutes."

"You sure?" He had his cell phone in his hand ready to punch in 9-1-1.

I nodded. "Yes. I'll talk to them later, when I'm more myself." I stopped then to catch my breath again. "Thank…thank you. If you hadn't come in when you did, I don't know what would have happened."

I could tell from Tony's somber face that he did. "Yeah, well," he brushed off my thanks, his cool guy persona coming out. "I was just going to check on Art, see how he's doing."

"Did you see the guy's face?" he asked. "Recognize him?"

"No. He was wearing something over it. It was a little scratchy, like one of those wool balaclavas. And I think he had on a hoodie. I could feel the fabric against my skin when he spoke to me." Remembering the hiss of his words and the pull of his hands made me start shivering all over and I wrapped my arms around my middle as if I were freezing. "And, he smelled bad, sour and dank."

"Are you sure you're okay?" Tony asked again, concern clouding his dark brown eyes. "Do you want me to get someone from the restaurant, or Sully?"

"No." I practically shouted, and from the look Tony gave me I knew I sounded shrill. "Really, I'm fine." I forced myself to give him a small smile. "I'm just going to go up to my apartment and rest for a while." I took his hand and squeezed it tight. "Thank you, Tony, really. You saved my life." We both knew what would have happened if he hadn't turned up when he did. "Please don't mention this to anyone, okay? I don't want people worrying about me." He knew I meant Eric and Sully.

He nodded his assent, but I could tell he didn't agree, although he didn't argue with me. He waited until I got back in the elevator and the doors closed. He probably stood there until it reached my floor.

Upstairs, I sank into my couch, coat and scarf still on, and put my head back. My throat was sore, and I was sure I'd have some bruising around my neck. Even though he'd used it as a weapon, my scarf was soft enough that it hadn't cut into my skin like a rope or wire would have.

The killer had meant every word of his warning. Somehow, he must have imagined I recognized something about him. I hadn't and couldn't think what that could be. Maybe it would come to me when I was doing something else.

A thought suddenly struck me: What if he believed I'd somehow figure out who he was, that I'd tell the cops? Wouldn't that make him try again to get me out of the way? My heart was hammering so hard it felt like it would fly out of my chest. I was having trouble breathing. Was this what PTSD felt like? I tried to calm myself with slow, deep yoga breaths. It took a while but when my breathing finally returned to normal, I tried to think about the attack more objectively.

The killer followed me to the park, but there were too many people around to attack me there in broad daylight, so he trailed me home.

Jude, I told myself, *you're not making this up.* I wasn't jumping at shadows. My imagination wasn't working overtime. This bastard was a real threat. If I told Eric what happened he'd make me swear I'd stop meddling in the investigation. He'd be right to insist considering our past trouble. But now, the killer had made it personal and I couldn't just quit.

I got up, took a breath, tossed my scarf on the couch, and slipped out of my coat. I put on the kettle for a cup of tea then approached the mirror with trepidation. It was time to check on the damage. I looked into our hallway mirror and at least I didn't scream. It wasn't as bad as it could have been. My skin looked pasty. Who knew lack of oxygen coupled with fear could actually drain the blood from your face? I hadn't until today.

I had some black and blue patches on my neck that I could cover with makeup to help the outside me look normal. The tea would help the inner me and soothe my throat. By the time Eric arrived with his parents, I'd be good to go, as Sully would say.

Thinking of Sully made me pray that Tony wouldn't blab to him about what happened. Sully might be at Art's place and Tony had said that's where he was going. I hoped he could keep my brush with a madman just between us, at least for now.

I would report the attack, though. To Agent Garlinger, rather than the police. I didn't tell Tony about her or our meeting. He'd probably hear about it from Sully anyway. Spill to one of the 10th Street Irregulars, and you've spilled to all.

I peeled off my clothes and headed for the shower. It was only later as the hot, reviving water poured over my body that I realized Tony said he was on his way to visit Art. So why didn't he get in the elevator with me and go up to six?

Chapter Seventeen

I planned to meet Eric and his parents downstairs at seven. Cecelia and Roberto were wonderful people and caring parents and I enjoyed spending time with them. When Eric and I started dating, they accepted me into their warm and generous family and made me feel like I belonged there. They never blamed me for what happened, even though I'd felt somehow responsible for the death of their other son, George, Eric's twin. I knew it wasn't really my fault, that events had spiraled out of control, and George had gotten caught in the middle. But still, I felt guilty.

I put these thoughts out of my mind along with what had happened this afternoon. Tonight, I wanted to enjoy the evening, talk and laugh over delicious wine and Pete's amazing food. Looking miserable and dwelling on the past wouldn't help.

Besides, it would only make Eric suspicious. Instead, I decided to focus on looking my best. I went into my bedroom and opened my closet. I needed something chic yet fun to wear to dinner.

I went through my clothing hanger by hanger until I came to one of my favorite pieces: a silk charmeuse ivory jumpsuit from the 1940s. With its shoulder pads, nipped-in waist, and flowing, flared pants, it could have been made for Lauren Bacall, who I channeled as I did my makeup. I kept the look soft and smoky, and even though I didn't have Bacall's long hair to drape over one eye, I thought I looked seductively vampy. And, like her, I knew how to whistle.

I added some open-toed platform sandals in gold and I was ready. Believe me, I hadn't forgotten that I'd been attacked. I just wasn't going to let it paralyze me. I knew the memory would rear its ugly head later, no matter how much I tried to subdue it. I'd tell Agent Garlinger about it in the morning, that is if she hadn't already heard about it through the 10th Street Irregulars grapevine. I didn't know how much I could trust Tony to keep from blabbing to Sully and Sully from passing on the information. Anyway, I was sure to find out who knew what when I went downstairs to The Lounge if any of The Irregulars were at the bar.

I left for The Lounge at about six thirty and slipped in through the back door. When I looked into the kitchen, it was a lot calmer than it had been at brunch. The dinner rush wouldn't start for a while and Pete, his crew, and the wait staff were going over tonight's menu specials and the wine suggestions to pair with them. They had just finished the daily family dinner and were sitting around the big kitchen counter listening intently as Pete spoke. A few people were taking notes, and some were asking questions, which he answered easily.

Pete was a perfectionist and he expected our staff to be the same. There was no room for error in the kitchen. Not knowing how a dish was prepared or putting in an order for the wrong entrée was wasteful and time consuming. Definitely not the best way to please our diners or get the four-star reviews we were aiming for.

I walked off to the bar before anyone noticed I'd been peeping and took a seat at the service end. Dean had come on at five for his shift. He nodded to let me know he'd seen me and finished mixing a drink for the woman in front of him who was seated facing the door. When she turned to pick up her drink from the bar, I saw that it was Elaine Garlinger.

What was she doing here? Was she meeting Sully? I looked past her but didn't see him in his regular seat. Of course not. If she was here, he'd be sitting right next to her. She must have felt me watching her because she turned all the way around, noticed me, and gave me a little wave.

Screw me, I thought. *And damn Tony. He must have given me up.* I smiled and wiggled my fingers back at her. I'd have to speak with her. It would seem odd if I didn't. Taking a deep breath, I walked down the bar and took the empty stool on her left side.

"Agent Garlinger, twice in one day. I'm surprised to see you here."

"Please, it's Elaine." She gestured with her hand. "I'm off duty." She smiled and her face lit up. "Sully invited me for dinner." She checked her watch. Of course, it was designer like the rest of her wardrobe. "He should be here any minute."

"Great." I hoped the sarcasm in my voice hadn't leaked out.

Dean came over then and saved me from making the stupid remark that was on the tip of my tongue. "Red wine?" he asked, and I nodded yes.

"About earlier today," she began.

Oh no. My heart started pounding for the third time today. *She knows what happened in the elevator.*

"I'm sorry if I left on a sour note…"

She didn't know. Tony hadn't ratted me out. Relief poured through me. I felt like a yo-yo, my emotions going up and down.

"But I just wanted to remind you again how dangerous this guy is." She paused and toyed with her drink. "But you saw that for yourself, didn't you?"

My confusion must have shown on my face. If she wasn't aware of the attack…

Of course, she sensed it instantly, her eyes probing into mine as she spoke. "Michael Bevins," she added. I nodded and sipped the Rosso di Montepulciano Dean had placed in front of me. I could see why she was so good at her job. She had killer instincts and had gotten her point across again, all with a smile on her face and a drink in her hand.

"Listen, Elaine…" I began, but I was interrupted by Sully walking into the bar. Her face lit up when she saw him and vice versa. I coughed to get her attention before he reached us. "There's something I need to tell you," I said. Sully had arrived at the bar and passed by his regular stool and took the one on Elaine's other side. *Oh boy, changing stools, it must be serious,* I thought.

"Hi, Sully." I gave him a smirk—just a small one—as I cut my eyes from him to Elaine. He gave me a hard glare and a grunt as a reply.

Then I brought my mind back to the conversation I was having with Elaine. It was to be continued, but not in front of Sully "But it can wait until tomorrow."

She nodded absently at me as she turned her full attention to Sully. "Sure, Jude. That's fine."

I watched them for a few minutes as they settled in and ordered a drink. I tamped down the urge to eavesdrop, but I couldn't help peeking at them. They were speaking softly, their faces inches apart, eyes riveted on each other. I was sure Sully was going to kiss her, but he moved back slightly. He must have realized they weren't alone and, of course, people—including me—were watching. I turned away smiling to myself. Sully had it bad. I hoped he wouldn't get hurt.

Chapter Eighteen

Cecelia, Roberto, and Eric arrived at seven on the dot. It was their first time at The Lounge. They oohed and aahed over the restaurant, which made me beam. To me, it always looked classier at night, with soft light from the wall sconces playing off the pearl gray and silver-accented walls. I was proud of the décor, the way a mother is of her gifted child—willing to let everyone tell you how special he or she was. I didn't go that far but I loved the old wooden bar, which I'd rescued from a century old tear-down, and the back bar with its antique mirrors and glass shelves. The Lounge was elegant yet comfortable, chic yet homey. Loaded with style, just like me. In my opinion anyway.

Eric's parents were a good-looking couple. Cecelia was petite with softly-rounded curves and dark blond hair that gleamed with a few streaks of golden highlights. Her toffee-colored eyes contained hints of gold, and she had a wide and generous smile.

Roberto, on the other hand, was tall and muscular, his dark hair and deep, brown eyes exactly the same as Eric's. His face—with its high, sharp cheekbones—was striking and added to his charm.

Dinner was amazing. Not only was the company wonderful, but also the meal.

Cecelia and Roberto couldn't say enough about Pete's *arroz con guisantes y cerdo asado con aguacate*—yellow rice with pigeon peas and roast pork with avocado. Everything was delicious and I'm sure I went up at least a notch in their estimation. Maybe their son hadn't made a mistake falling for a crazy woman. We enjoyed a bottle of luscious, ruby red Artadi Vina El Pison Rioja wine with our meal and finished off with flan and espresso.

Every once in a while, I surreptitiously glanced over at the bar. Oscar and Jim had joined Elaine and Sully. The last time I looked, Elaine and Sully were gone, replaced by Tony. I must have gulped aloud, and Eric raised his eyebrow in a questioning look. I shrugged and he let it go.

After our meal, the Ramirezes asked if they could stop in the kitchen to thank Pete for the special meal he'd cooked for them. I was about to say I'd escort them, when Eric called out to Jon, our waiter, and asked if he'd please escort his parents to the kitchen.

After they left the table, I gave Eric my 'What's that all about?' look. "I was going to introduce them to Pete."

"I know, but I wanted to speak with you privately." Eric leaned in closer.

Damn. I was busted. But how could he know? Now I was going to get the 'I told you so' speech. Something must have given me away. "Eric—"

He cut me off before I could continue. "You know that big deal we've been working on?" I nodded and he continued. "We got it, Jude! We sent in the last of the paperwork this morning and they got right back to us. I wanted to tell you first." His words were spilling out and he was bursting with excitement.

"Oh my God, that's great." I moved closer and gave him a kiss. "I'm so proud of you. I know how much effort you put into landing the business." I pulled back and looked at him, "You have to tell your parents. They'll be over the moon."

He nodded. "Of course, I will. But Jude," his voice had gone soft and his eyes focused on mine as he continued, "you're the most important person in the world to me. You know that, don't you? Whatever I do, I want to share it with you. I'd never hold back or leave you out of anything that was important."

I pulled my gaze away and looked down at my hands. "I…I know" was all I could manage to utter. I felt horrible, ashamed. Here was this wonderful man in my life, willing to do anything for me while I was sneaking around him and hiding things, things I'd let him believe I wouldn't do.

Cecelia and Roberto returned to the table and I was saved from more self-recriminations. Cecelia's eyes were gleaming with the thrill of meeting the chef who'd cooked a special dinner just for them.

Roberto placed his arm around her shoulder. "You know what your mother did, Eric?" He shook his head at his wife. "She told Pete she was going to send him some of *her* special recipes to try. Can you believe it?"

Of course, all this was said with affection, the kind that comes when two people love and respect each other.

I took in their exchange and smiled as best as I could. "I think Eric has something he wants to share with you, and it calls for a bottle of champagne!"

I rose from the table and walked to the bar. I asked Dean to pull out a bottle of Cristal from the cooler and open it for me. I snuck a look at Oscar, Jim, and Tony. Tony was looking at me intensely. Had he told the others? I couldn't tell from their expressions. I was getting paranoid and needed to stop it.

I turned my attention back to Eric and watched as he told his parents his good news. I could see from the hugs, kisses, and the smiles on their faces they were overjoyed for him. He glanced my way and smiled, his gorgeous face filled with delight. He'd made his parents' evening and it gave him pleasure to do so. This was probably the happiest they'd been since George had been killed.

I picked up the Cristal and four champagne flutes and walked back to the table. I felt like a phony. I hadn't lied, but I had let Eric believe that I wasn't going to involve myself in the serial killer investigation again. Yet, somehow, I hadn't managed to keep away.

The only thing for me to do was to quit poking around or come clean. I was torn, because neither option appealed to me. I thought of my namesake, Saint Jude, again. Didn't he realize I was desperate? So where was he when I needed him?

Maybe if I prayed hard enough, I'd get a sign from above to tell me which way to go.

Chapter Nineteen

I woke up and sleepily turned to the side of the bed Eric slept on. My hand slid out and found an empty space where I was expecting him to be. My eyes opened wide, and for a moment, I wondered why I was alone. Then I remembered he had slept at his own apartment last night.

He was staying over more and more often, and I knew he wanted to make it permanent. I was dodging the issue. I cared about him deeply, but something was holding me back. Something I didn't want to name. If I got too close to him would something happen to make it all go wrong? With my history, it could easily come to pass and that would break my heart.

Cecelia and Roberto had wanted to take an Uber home to Mount Vernon, but Eric wouldn't have it. He insisted on driving them home and planned to drive back to the city.

His parents told him it was too much. Especially since he was expected at his office in the morning to finish all the paperwork on that new account we'd just been celebrating.

I agreed and told him it made more sense for him to sleep at his own place rather than make the trip twice. So now I was alone.

I stretched and got out of bed. I thought about calling Sully and getting together for Sunday breakfast. We hadn't really talked for a few days and I wanted to feel out how much, if anything, he knew about yesterday. Then I remembered his date last night and smiled. He looked happier than he had in a long while.

Far be it from me to intrude. Actually, I'd love to, just to see the expression on his face when I showed up at his door. But it would be tacky, even for me, in case Agent Garlinger had stayed over. I didn't mind embarrassing *him*, but I didn't want to embarrass *her*, and besides, I needed her on my side.

I wasn't working until later in the evening, so I flopped back on my pillow, tucked my hands behind my head, elbows extended like wings, crossed my ankles, and gazed up at the ceiling.

I used to do this on Saturday mornings when I was a kid and had stuff to figure out. All that angst that came with being young—boys, school, being totally misunderstood. Usually my mom made me get up to do my chores before I got very far.

Of course, thinking about Saturday mornings and my mom brought back memories of the boating accident that killed her and my younger brother. A boat I would have been on if I hadn't gotten so angry at Aiden, stomped off, and told him I wished he'd die. Which he had, along with my mom, when a sudden storm capsized their small sailboat.

Going down memory lane where guilt was hiding behind every bush and tree waiting to jump out at me wasn't helping with my current dilemma. Did I give up the hunt or continue? I knew I had to speak with Elaine Garlinger. I wanted to inform her about the attacker and Tony's timely intervention. Then what? I sighed and slipped out of bed, imagining my mom making a racket with her pots and pans to get me up. She'd smile when I sleepwalked into the kitchen, complaining that the noise was enough to wake the dead.

If only it could.

Chapter Twenty

gent Garlinger answered on the first ring as though she'd been expecting my call. "I see," she replied in a voice that sounded vaguely annoyed—and anything but understanding—after I told her about my attack.

"Look, I tried to tell you at The Lounge, but Sully arrived before I could finish." I didn't say what I really meant, that she totally dismissed me the moment he walked in the door.

"Did you speak to anyone about the attack?

"No, of course not. I wanted to talk to—"

Garlinger cut me off. "What about Tony?"

"No. He promised not to mention it to anyone." Except, maybe he'd told Sully, who passed it on to her.

"Well, someone let it slip to the press." She paused. "The BAU has been getting calls all morning about *both attacks* at your place. The media know about the murder, the knife through the heart, the dumpster." She paused. "They're not stupid. They'll figure out soon enough it was the work of the New Year's Eve Killer. They also know you were attacked personally. Nearly strangled." Her anger was coming over the phone in waves like a tsunami crashing against the shore. "We can't keep it under wraps any longer. We have to respond."

"But who—"

"That's the million-dollar question, isn't it?"

I was stunned. I could see how the Michael Bevins murder could have leaked. There were a lot of people around on New Year's Day. But my attack?

No one else knew but Tony, and I didn't believe he'd called the press.

"The only other person who could know all of this is the killer." As soon as the words tumbled from my mouth, I knew they were true.

"You may be right." Her reply was hesitant, but—

"I am right and you know it." My whole body was trembling with anger. "He's toying with us, altering the press to get the attention he craves. Of course, they'll put it together." I was practically yelling now. "You've got to make this stop. I...I can't deal with the press, the Jared Joneses of the world. I didn't call the police because I was counting on you. Maybe I was wrong. But this guy...he's upping the ante. Taunting me...and you. He'll come after me again, you know that, and maybe next time Tony won't be around to help me." I knew I was ranting but couldn't stop myself.

"Please, calm down, Jude. We're doing everything we can to find this guy. You know that." Her tone was reasonable and cajoling, the way someone speaks when they're desperate to convince you they're right. I wasn't buying it. "We can give you protection or move you to a safe house until we catch him."

I barked out a bitter laugh. "I can't just walk away from my business. Besides, you haven't been able to catch him in twenty years, what makes you think you'll get him now?"

There was silence on the other end of the phone. I knew it was a low blow, but I couldn't help it.

"Please, think about my offer. I can protect you."

"I doubt it," I said, then hung up.

I was pacing the apartment, looking out the window every few minutes to see if the media had shown up. They didn't disappoint. Soon there were trucks from the major stations and a gaggle of reporters crowding around the entrance to The Lounge. I wanted to open my window and scream at them to get the hell away.

I took a few cleansing breaths, not that it helped all that much, then punched in Eltee's number. When he answered, I quickly explained what was happening and asked him to come in to work as soon as possible.

His response made me feel even worse. "Boy, Jude girl, you sure got yourself in it this time." I could almost see him shaking his head. "I'll be there as soon as I can." His sigh was heavy and loud. "You stay away from those sharks, okay?"

I agreed and punched off. I was just about to call Eric when my cell beeped, making me jump and drop the phone. I quickly retrieved it. It was Eric. He must have read my mind. I took another deep breath before answering.

"Hi, Eric. I'm so glad—"

He didn't let me finish before he started speaking. "I have to leave town tonight, Jude." I could hear the excitement in his voice. He traveled often, so I was surprised he sounded so keyed up. "Our new client, PSS Industries, wants Dominic and I to come up to Buffalo for a few days to become familiar with their business."

"Okay," I replied. "That's good. Great. You guys really earned this, but there's—"

"I know I must sound like a kid on Christmas morning. I can't help it. They're a really big client." He paused for a second "God, what am I thinking. If you need me with you, Dom can go on his own."

"I'm fine. I'll be fine." I hoped I sounded convincing. If Eric thought something was off, he would never go away. "This is the new business you guys have been working for. You need to be there. Don't worry about me."

"If you're sure." I could hear a tinge of relief in his voice. "I should be back by Wednesday night."

"I am. Besides, if I need any help, I've got Sully and Agent Garlinger to call on." *If only*, I thought.

I'd done it again. Side-stepped my chance to tell Eric everything. Avoided the anger he'd feel for not informing him yesterday. He'd also cancel his trip. I couldn't let that happen. The relationship with a new client is always fragile and I didn't want to be the cause of it being strained.

"Listen," I said, "the press has found out about Michael Bevins and put it together with the other three murders. There will probably be some awful stuff on the news or in the paper. Stuff about The Lounge, too. Please, don't get upset if you see it. You know how they like to sensationalize everything.

Who knows what they'll say?" I hoped, if they reported my attack, Eric would think it was just made up garbage.

"Jude, I can cancel this trip. You need me to be with you."

"No. Please, don't do that." I made my voice easy and light. "Agent Garlinger is going to take care of it. She's coming over now to deal with the press." Well, she would be. I'd make sure of that as soon as I called her.

"Please, Eric, go on your trip. I'll keep you posted. Honest."

He reluctantly agreed and we clicked off. I knew I was pushing this relationship right to the edge. I hoped I wouldn't push it over. I promised myself I'd explain everything to Eric when he got back from Buffalo.

I'd call Elaine Garlinger back, apologize, and ask her to get over here and deal with these people. Sully, too. He needed to know what was happening on his property.

The attack yesterday finally registered in my subconscious. I felt wrung out and scared. I gazed out the window again. The media crews were still there. I knew they'd camp out until they got the information they were looking for—a sound bite for the evening news or a provocative *New York Star* headline. I could see it now. "Knife at the Heart of Serial Killer Murder" or something equally lurid. I shuddered. Then I picked up my cell and punched in a number.

Elaine answered on the first ring. "Jude. Has something happened?"

"No, but I'm afraid it will. Can you to come to The Lounge right now? I need you to speak with the media." I paused. "And I think I'd like that protection you offered."

Chapter Twenty-One

Sully knocked on my door just five minutes later and gave me a big bear hug as he entered. Elaine must have called him and told him to hustle down to my apartment.

"Where's The Guy?" he asked. He liked giving pet names to my boyfriends. Roger had been, "The Boy." Obviously, Eric rated higher. I knew Sully liked him better. He hated Roger, so liking Eric more, even a little, wasn't hard. Someday, he might even get to be "The Man."

"The Guy is on his way to Buffalo to spend some time with his new big client."

"Buffalo?" Sully shook his head. "They don't have accountants of their own up there? They have to poach one of ours? Does Eric know how cold he's going to be?"

"We didn't discuss it," I replied. "Mostly we talked about Michael's murder and how Agent Garlinger is going to handle the press." I paused. "As soon as she gets here."

"She's on her way." Sully took my hand and led me to my couch. "Sit," he ordered. "I'm making you coffee." He looked over at me. "Decaf," he added with a nod.

"Did she tell you what happened yesterday afternoon?" I bit my lip and looked up at him.

"Very briefly, but I got the gist." He fiddled with the coffee maker and continued. "Did you happen to mention this to Eric?"

"Not exactly. He really didn't give me a chance. He was so excited about Buffalo. I'll tell him soon."

"You'd better." He gave me the marine drill sergeant look and tone when he spoke: focused and pointed, making sure I'd pay attention. "He's not going to be happy that you 'forgot' to mention it. By the way, neither am I. Why didn't you tell me yourself?"

"I...I was angry—at you, at myself, at everyone—for what was happening." I leaned forward, put my elbows on my knees, and cupped my hands around my face.

"You're lucky that Tony showed up when he did."

"Believe me, I know." I had a flashback to those big, gloved hands pulling my scarf tighter and tighter.

Sully handed me a mug of steaming black coffee and sat in the chair across from me. "Still think Tony could be the New Year's Eve Killer?" he asked.

I shook my head. "Not after yesterday, unless he has the power to clone himself and be in two places at once."

"Good. I'm glad we got that settled. Now you can go back to serving drinks without third-degreeing your customers."

"Just because Tony helped me—"

My doorbell rang.

"That must be Lanie. I'll get it." Sully rose to answer the door.

I watched him as he walked toward it. He really didn't want me to keep looking into The Irregulars. That much was obvious. He made his comment sound casual, but his eyes had given him away. They'd turned steely and cold. There was something going on that he didn't want me, or anyone, to know about. Well, we'd see about that.

Agent Garlinger joined us along with two other agents from her office, Special Agent Rita Samuelson and Special Agent Ari Maguire. Agent Samuelson was here to help control the press and the flow of information that was passed along. Agent Maguire was to be my 'minder' making sure Sully and I stayed out of it. That was fine with me as long as the media didn't feel free to accost the restaurant's patrons or Sully and myself. I mentioned Eltee was inside and manning the door. He wouldn't be easy to get around and wouldn't let any of the press slip through.

She'd also sent another agent to keep watch over Art Bevins who certainly didn't need to have the press corps on his back asking a million questions as he was getting ready to bring Michael's body home to Ohio.

Art could be a little bit full of himself. He didn't often let you forget he was a "successful" TV writer and some of his so-called funny remarks could be snide, especially when he spoke to Jim Deems. I think he enjoyed making him stutter. But still, having your younger brother murdered by a serial killer wasn't something anyone deserved.

Elaine Garlinger showed us the statement she was going to give to the media. It was straightforward and factual. I wasn't sure they'd settle for these bits of information, but it was all they were going to get.

She read it aloud to Sully and me.

"Good afternoon. I'm Special Agent in Charge, Elaine Garlinger, of the FBI's Behavioral Analysis Unit in New York City. On Thursday, January first, the body of a young male was found behind the premises of 340 East 10th Street. We believe this is the work of a serial killer who has been stalking the East Village for over twenty years and is also responsible for three other deaths, beginning in 1999.

Additionally, we believe the same perpetrator attacked one of the tenants of the building yesterday. The FBI will be relentless in pursuit of this individual and employ all of our resources to ensure his capture.

No other details will be released at this time. We will provide more information as the case develops. If you have any information regarding these incidents, please call the FBI office at Federal Plaza.

I would like to remind you that this building, the adjacent one, and the space behind it are private property. Please respect that. My colleague, Special Agent Samuelson will be taking questions. Thank you."

It sounded pretty good to me, but knowing how the press operated, I wasn't sure they'd keep their distance. I could hear their questions in my head and see them holding their smartphones horizontally to capture every word: *Is it the New Year's Eve Killer? Do you have a person of interest? Are you close to making an arrest? Who was the other person attacked?* And so on.

When Agent Garlinger returned to my apartment, I asked a question of my own. "Do you have any idea at all of who might have killed Michael Bevins and attacked me?"

She hesitated for a moment and lowered her eyes before she replied. Was she going to lie? "Actually, we are looking at a person of interest, but I'm not at liberty to divulge their identity at this time." She paused. "You know that's how this works, Jude."

"What?" My voice went up an octave. "Never mind how it works. The bastard almost killed me." I moved closer and got right in her face. "I think you owe me an answer."

She shook her head. "I need more information before I act on this. I'm sorry."

"Sorry? You think sorry's enough? Well it isn't. I want to—"

"Jude, give it a rest," Sully weighed in. "Elaine is doing everything she can to catch this guy."

"Oh, are you on the FBI team, now?" I knew I sounded bitchy, maybe even a little resentful, but I was furious. I stomped away from them and went to the window. I could see Agent Samuelson fielding the reporters' questions. No one looked happy at her answers. I understood why.

Chapter Twenty-Two

The FBI agents and Sully left—except for Agent Maguire—who was going to protect me, even if it killed me to have him around. My apartment isn't all that big, and it felt crowded with Maguire, a wedge of a guy, sucking up the air and taking up my space. Of course, he was polite. The FBI probably included sensitivity training as one of their courses. No matter what I asked him, he smiled a 'no comment' smile and deflected the questions.

I needed to get ready for my shift, but first I figured I better call Eric. I told Maguire I'd be in my bedroom and would scream for help if anyone tried to rappel down from the roof. I don't think he found it amusing.

Eric probably wasn't going to be amused either when I fessed up about my attack. But I took a deep breath, picked up the cell, and punched in his number. For once, I was hoping that it would go to voicemail.

No such luck. He answered on the first ring. "Hi, honey. How are you?"

"Great," I replied. There I was, fibbing already. "How was your flight?"

"Fine. It takes longer to get out to Kennedy than it does to fly to Buffalo. Dominic and I are meeting with the big guns from PSS for an early dinner." He paused, and I read an awful lot into it. "So, what's going on, Jude? I didn't expect to hear from you today."

"I wanted to talk to you. It's important." I could hear him breathing on the other end, waiting for me to continue. "You remember how I mentioned the press might elaborate on Michael's murder and make up stuff?"

"Jude, wha—"

"Please, just let me finish. On Saturday, while you were up in Mount

Vernon with your parents, I took a walk to John V. Lindsay Park to—"

"Oh, Jude, why did you go there?" His voice was measured and a little exasperated. I imagined him shaking his head at me.

"I wanted to see where the second body was found." I paused. It sounded macabre, even to me. "Someone followed me home and…attacked me in our hallway."

"What? Why the hell didn't you tell me?" His anger burst through like a sudden storm. It was filled with more vitriol than was warranted, and I thought maybe he'd been holding it in for a long time. "You carried on as if nothing happened. Dinner…my parents. What's wrong with you?"

That was a fair question. "I didn't want to alarm you. Tony Napoli walked in while the guy was threatening me and scared him away before he could hurt me." Almost the whole truth.

There was silence on the other end of the phone. "I'm sorry, Eric. I should have told you, but I didn't want to spoil the evening for you and your parents. And then, you announced your good news and—"

"Do you love me?"

The question seemed to come out of nowhere. So unexpected it startled me and I needed a moment before I could reply. "I…I do." I'd never said the words to him, but I suddenly realized it was true. "Very much."

"Then it might be time to show me. I know you have a mind of your own and do whatever you want. But we…we're in this together. Or I thought we were. So, either you start trusting me or this is never going to work. I hope you understand that." Then he was gone.

I gaped at my phone, Eric's smiling face beaming up at me from its screensaver belied the words he'd just spoken. I hadn't had to explain myself or my actions to anyone for a long time. I wasn't sure it was even in my DNA to behave that way—to ask for someone's approval. Maybe it was time to change—to be a real partner in this relationship and not take Eric for granted.

I looked down at my phone again and noticed the screen was wet. The tears that slid from my eyes had dropped down on it like rain falling from a leaf at the start of a storm, a slow plop, plop that finally grew into a deluge.

I wiped the tears from my face with the back of my hand, but I couldn't wipe away the memory of Eric's words. *Have I lost him?* I wondered. *Have I finally screwed up the best thing that ever happened to me?* I looked in the mirror and shook my head. Please God, no, I told my reflection. Don't let me lose him, too.

Chapter Twenty-Three

The Lounge was busy for a Sunday night. The dining room was nearly full and there weren't too many open seats at the bar. I tucked Maguire at a table where he could see me at all times and told him to have dinner on the house. I recommended Pete's sirloin—a big steak for a big guy—with gorgonzola mashed potatoes and a frisée salad with lardons and croutons. It was the least he deserved after my surly behavior all afternoon.

I should have been happy that business was good, but even though the vibe was subdued, I wondered how many people were here because of the murder. People like to act like they're appalled by violence, especially death, but I believe they get a vicarious thrill from being close to it. They wouldn't if they'd ever found a dead body.

Eltee had done a good job of keeping the reporters at bay. Most of them, including Jared Jones and his cameraman, had left. But there were still a few diehards out front. If they thought their press passes and smartphones would help them get past Eltee, they were mistaken. At six foot three and two seventy-five, he was a mountain they were never going to scale.

I knew there'd be late-night features on all the network and local stations. I was happy the media hadn't gotten a photo of me to go along with it. It was bad enough the exterior of The Lounge would be front and center in their reports, I didn't need to be identified as the attack victim. Especially if Eric saw it, he'd be twice as worried about me, and probably twice as angry.

I mixed drinks and pulled beers from the tap, trying to smile at my customers as I worked. It was hard going. I wanted to be upstairs canoodling with Eric and listening to him tell me he loved me over and over. Fat chance. He'd probably stay in Buffalo and tell me he never wanted to see me again.

"Why the long face?" The question came from a voice at the service end of the bar. When I looked in that direction, Oscar Lupe leaned forward and peeked around the guy sitting next to him. He hadn't been in much since the murder.

I pasted a smile on my face and poured him a shot of Cuervo Gold, his drink of choice. "On the house," I said as put it on the coaster in front of him with a salt shaker and a slice of lime.

"Thanks," he replied then bit into the lime, sprinkled salt on his hand, licked it, and downed the shot. "But you still didn't answer my question," he persisted and tipped his head to one side.

He's fishing for more gossip he'll spread around the neighborhood, I thought. Working for the local cable company, he overheard lots of private conversations and didn't always keep them to himself. I was usually careful about what I said in front of him. I decided to play it nonchalant. "Just post-New Year's blues." I shrugged. "You know how it goes. All the hype for the holidays and then they're over in a flash. Plus, of course, this year…"

"Yeah, I get it." He held up his hand as if to ward off trouble. "Terrible thing that happened to Art's kid brother." His eyes went far away for a second, then focused back on me. "Did the cops find out anything yet? Have any leads?"

"The FBI took over the case and they're still 'making inquiries.'" I made air quotes around the last words. "That's all I know." Well, I did know a little more, but I wasn't going to give out any information, especially to him. But maybe I could get some.

"Hmmm," Oscar replied and lifted his shot glass for a refill. "I'll have another."

Oscar was a small man with short, sandy hair and pale-blue eyes. He was the quietest of the 10th Street Irregulars and he didn't drink more than one or two shots whenever he came to The Lounge. It seemed to me when the group was together at the bar, he mostly took it all in, although he obviously thrived on asking me questions. Of course, with Sully around, it could be hard to get a word in, never mind a whole sentence.

"I've been thinking about that night," I leaned in close so the guy next to Oscar wouldn't hear, "and I can't imagine how that happened. Can you?"

"No." He answered quickly, shaking his head. "I've been thinking about it, too. Jeez, that poor kid. He seemed nice, and Art was so proud of him."

"I know." My voice oozed with sympathy. "Did you happen to notice when he left here?" I asked.

"Not really. We were all talking and laughing, and I think he came over and said goodbye and then just left." He looked up at the ceiling, as if he were visualizing the bar as it looked that night. "Actually, maybe I saw him go downstairs to the restroom after that, but I'm not sure. It could have been earlier. All I remember was that, at some point, he was gone."

He placed his empty shot glass on the bar. "Speaking of which, I've got to go. Work tomorrow." He pulled out a couple of bills and left them under the coaster. "Thanks, Jude. See you during the week."

It was going on eight o'clock. I smiled to myself. Most people were just sitting down to dinner, not slipping into bed. I said good night and watched as Oscar left. No one else had mentioned Michael going downstairs to the restroom before heading out. Maybe someone followed him and struck up a conversation, told him they were a friend of Art's and invited him to meet up for another party later. I wished we'd installed security cameras like Pete and I talked about a while ago. It would have made figuring out where everyone had been so much easier.

If my theory was right, it would mean someone from The Lounge was the killer and my attacker. It was warm in the bar, but suddenly I felt cold and clammy all over. I knew I couldn't remember who else might have gone downstairs when Michael did. It had been too crowded. I'd ask Dean tomorrow when he came on for his shift.

There was a lull at the bar, and I began polishing glasses while I thought about that night. I wondered if Sully had noticed. He was used to surveilling the territory and storing away the details. Of course, he'd been drinking and not paying attention. There was only one way to find out. I picked up my cell and hit speed dial.

Sully came in at about nine and took his usual seat at the bar. I grabbed a bottle from the back bar, poured him a Jameson neat, plunked it down, and stared at him. He stared back.

I blinked first. "Thanks for coming."

"You're welcome." He nodded his head politely. "Why did you summon me?" he asked.

"Oscar was in and he—"

"You gave him the third degree, didn't you?" He shook his head at me. "Jude, you have to let this go and let Lanie—"

"Whoa! I didn't interrogate him. He brought it up himself." Sully gave me the fish eye. "Honestly." I crossed myself over my heart.

"Okay." Sully was still skeptical. "So?"

"So, he remembered seeing Michael heading downstairs to the restroom. He thinks it was after he said goodbye to all of you right before he left here." Sully was tapping the bar, waiting for more. "Maybe someone followed Michael and approached him, somehow got him to agree to meet up later." *And killed him,* I added to myself.

Sully's expression was intense. "Did you happen to notice anyone going downstairs at the same time?" I asked.

He toyed with his Jameson, spinning the glass around and I could tell he was thinking. "We all used the restroom at some point during the night…and I don't just mean The Irregulars." He picked up his glass and took a long sip. "Let me think on it a bit."

Well, at least he wasn't rejecting my idea as quickly as usual. "This has made me decide that we need to install security cameras. I wish we'd done it before." I looked around the restaurant. All was peaceful and fairly quiet.

"Not a bad idea." Sully followed my gaze. "A little late, but still, it wouldn't hurt. The customers wouldn't even notice. And I'm sure Eric would feel better when you're closing up on your own."

Leave it to him to push my buttons, even unknowingly. "Yeah, well, about Eric—"

"What did you do now?" He sighed in exasperation and shook his head at me.

"It's so nice to see you have such confidence in me." He couldn't miss the sarcasm in my words. Why did he always assume things were my fault? "It's not something I did." I sighed. "It's more what I didn't do."

"Oh? Are you sure of that?" he asked, warming up for a lecture. "You—"

He left off speaking as his cell beeped. He'd placed it on the bar when he sat down, unusual for him, and I wondered if he was expecting a call. He looked at the screen. "It's Lanie." He answered, got up, and moved away to a quiet corner.

I got back to my glass polishing. It was a distraction to keep me busy while Sully was speaking with the FBI agent. I glanced over at him while I was working. He'd gone beet red, a color I'd only observed a few times before and associated with his Irish temper. Either Lanie was breaking up with him—*not a nice thought*—I told myself, or she had some pretty intense news to share.

Sully hung up, walked back to the bar and handed me his half empty glass. "Fill it up, and follow me," he commanded and began to walk off toward a table in the back of the dining room.

"What? No please or thank…" I started to say, but a quick look at his face, still suffused with fury, shut me down quick. I nodded my assent and moved out from behind the bar. I asked one of the waitresses to keep an eye on it and marched through my dining room like a good little trooper.

Maguire started to rise from his table to follow. A slight shake of my head and he sat back down. He was already punching in a number on his cell by the time I reached Sully. Most likely calling the boss.

"So, what's going on?" I asked. I'd rarely seen him looking this distressed. It was bad, and scary.

"That was Lanie," he replied, "with some news." He picked up the Jameson and downed it in one gulp and was squeezing the glass so hard I thought he'd break it.

I already knew who called, I wanted to say, but I kept quiet and let him go on.

"She, or rather the FBI, has been told to back off the case and let the NYPD do their job."

I snorted. "Like Ortiz and Delmonico could catch a serial killer even if he pounded on the precinct door screaming, "I did it! Let me in. Arrest me.""

"I'm serious, Jude. It seems the detectives complained to the police commissioner that the FBI was stealing their case—a case of murder on their turf. The commissioner then called the new mayor who called the head of the BAU in D.C."

Sully was pacing like a caged tiger. "The mayor is trying to make a point about his campaign promise of wielding an 'iron fist' to fight crime in the city." He stopped his pacing and leaned forward, placing both hands flat on a table. His voice was a hiss that reminded me of a den of cobras getting ready to strike. "He also has the ear and the backing of the president, his very close and personal friend, whom he helped get elected. Are you getting the drift?"

I was and I couldn't believe what I was hearing. "It's all political bull isn't it? What about the men who were murdered?"

"It's a new regime all around. None of them were in their positions when the other three murders occurred. They're saying involving the NYPD is a more practical way to get the job done. They know the territory, have the manpower, yada, yada."

I was shaking my head. "Wait a minute. Doesn't the FBI always handle these kinds of cases? They have the resources and the manpower, right? Didn't our new mayor ever watch *Criminal Minds*?"

Sully plopped himself down in a chair and I took the one opposite. "The mayor isn't totally stupid. He's hedging his bets. He got the commissioner to agree to let the FBI *assist* the NYPD with their investigation."

I could only imagine what Elaine Garlinger thought of that. "What is Elaine going to do?" I asked.

"She said she'd turn over what she has to the NYPD and liaise with them. Let Ortiz and Delmonico get up to speed on all the evidence." I didn't miss the smirk in his voice.

"Okay, so what's she really going to do?" I asked again, wondering if she'd actually let the detectives fumble their way through.

Sully smiled, his first since Elaine Garlinger's phone call. "Solve Michael's murder and catch a serial killer," he replied. "Now, can I please have another

CHAPTER TWENTY-THREE

Jameson?" He wiggled his empty glass at me.

I nodded as we walked back to the bar. "Yes, but only because you asked so politely."

Chapter Twenty-Four

The next few days were quiet. It felt like people had post-holiday depression after too much shopping, eating, and drinking and were holed up at home. Sully stopped by in the afternoons when he got home from his volunteer job at the Big City Food Bank. He filled me in on what was going on there and kept me company while I set up the bar. And, for once, he had the tact not to ask about Eric.

I hadn't heard from Eric since our phone conversation on Sunday, two days previous. He was due back in the city tomorrow and I had no idea if I'd see him then, or ever again. I hated that we hadn't had a chance to talk things through, and I was afraid it was just too late.

I wasn't going to call him. Maybe I was being stubborn, but he was the one who hung up on me. Every time I thought about not seeing him again, my eyes filled with tears. I was an emotional wreck. Something had to change.

A little voice inside said maybe that something was me. I was the one who needed to commit to the relationship in an honest and open way. Jeez, I thought. I'm sounding like Dr. Phil, not Jude Dillane.

A touch on my shoulder brought me out of my reverie. I nearly jumped as high as the bar. It was Dean who tapped me, not the boogeyman.

"Where were you?" he asked, his baby blues crinkling into a frown.

"Nowhere you'd want to go." I replied and attempted a smile.

"I've been thinking on what you asked me about New Year's Eve and I just can't remember if I saw anyone follow Michael down to the restrooms." He lifted his hands to the sky. "It was so busy…"

"Thanks for trying." Dean walked to the other end of the bar and started chatting with the customers sitting there.

I'd just finished putting away a few bottles of wine in the cooler under the bar when I straightened up and did a double take. My friend Jamila—the one friend I'd made from my undercover stint at the Big City Food Coop—was sliding onto the barstool in front of me.

"Hey there, girlfriend. I sure miss seeing you at Big City." She flashed the big, happy smile I remembered, her head shaking from side to side, causing her dangly earrings to sway back and forth.

I leaned over the bar and gave her hug. "I can't believe it's you. What are you doing here?"

"Slumming," she replied with a sparkle in her eye. "You know I'm used to those classy places in the Bronx, but I thought I'd give your place a chance to impress me."

I hadn't realized how much I missed Jamila until now. She'd been the one bright spot in the gloomy confines of the Big City Food Coop, not just because of her wild, multi-hued outfits, but also for her sunny disposition. We'd spoken a few times but had never managed to get together until now. I missed her gossip, her fashion sense, and her take on life that everything would turn out okay.

Here, amongst my customers with their chic and trendy clothing—mostly in black—she was a supernova you couldn't miss. And no one did. Especially Dean.

He was over in a New York minute, smiling like the movie star he planned to be. I almost expected one of those movie-magic, twinkling-star effects to appear on his front teeth. "Hi, I'm Dean." He held out his hand.

Jamila slipped her hand in his. "Jamila. Nice to meet you," she replied, breaking into the widest grin I'd ever seen.

They stayed that way for a little longer than necessary until I cleared my throat.

"Dean, I think someone needs you," I jutted my chin toward the other end of the bar.

"Later," he said to Jamila and I knew he meant it.

"Who is *that*?" she asked as though Prince Harry had just appeared out of thin air, forsaking Meagan and begging Jamila to be his new American princess.

Oh boy, this was not going to be good. Jamila was beautiful, with caramel-colored skin and deep, brown eyes that were usually wide with excitement. She was fun, clever, and a little naive. Not a match for 'women fall all over me' Dean.

"So, what's been happening at work?" I asked, trying to turn her attention away from Dean.

"Doesn't Sully tell you anything?" She laughed. "All the old management has been replaced except for the accountants Sue and Danny. New faces, same old same old," she replied, shrugging one shoulder to allow her fuchsia, boatneck cashmere sweater to slip a little, while glancing toward the other end of the bar. This from the woman who viewed gossip as a contact sport.

"Really?" I asked in an incredulous tone. "That's it?"

"Well," she said, finally turning to face me. "I don't know if you heard, but Lydia is getting married again to someone with even more money than her ex." She fished in the oversized bag she had plopped down on the stool next to her and pulled out a copy of *The Star*. It was already open to the gossip page with a photo of a beaming Lydia sporting a rock the size of an ice cube and cuddling up to Arthur Kleinman III, heir to a New York shipping fortune.

I couldn't help myself. I burst out laughing. Leave it to Lydia Johnson Schuyler to overcome a very public divorce, *plus* losing her position as director of Big City over a huge financial scandal, and still come out on top. *Wait 'til I tell Eric,* I thought. *He won't believe it.*

"What's so funny?" Dean had ambled over to my end of the bar, speaking to me but looking at Jamila with those bedroom eyes of his.

They started chatting and I realized it would be easier to stop two stars from colliding than stopping these two from getting together. I moved over to Dean's station and left them to it. Dean was already making her one of his famous cocktails. I hoped Jamila had Ubered to the city. Any more than one of those drinks and she wouldn't be able to drive home.

Jamila's gossip about Lydia made me miss Eric even more. Even Lydia with all her hubris got a second chance. If he didn't call me tomorrow when he returned, I didn't know what I'd do.

To make matters worse, Sully walked in. Catching sight of Jamila, he made a beeline for her, with barely a hello for me. Were all the men in my life deserting me?

A little while later, the rest of The Irregulars drifted in and Sully called them over to meet Jamila. He introduced Mike, Oscar, and Jim. Now I really felt left out, maybe even a little jealous. Not an emotion I was used to experiencing.

I must have looked more forlorn than I thought, because Sully left the group and sat down in front of me. "A surprise, huh?" He tilted his head toward Jamila who was eating up the compliments as fast as The Irregulars were dishing them out.

"How's Art doing?" I asked. He was the only one missing from the group.

"He's still in Ohio with his family. His parents and sister are devastated. They can't believe Mikey is gone. Art didn't think he should leave them on their own." A sadness filled his words and the eyes that met mine were clouded with anger. "They're desperate for the police to find the killer." He sat up even straighter than usual, as if he knew he had to be strong, and slammed his hand on the bar again and again. I reached over and stilled it.

"Have you spoken to Elaine today?" I asked.

He nodded slowly. "She turned over the file to Ortiz and Delmonico. They've had time to review it and she'll be meeting with them tomorrow."

I hesitated before asking my next question. "Did she give you any hint as to who her person of interest might be?" I figured she might have relented and told Sully even if she didn't want to tell me.

"No. She can't do that, Jude." He took the hand I'd placed over his and gave it a squeeze. "She promised she'd keep us in the loop as much as possible, but she can't divulge the guy's name. Not yet. Not until there's more evidence."

She'd said "guy" to Sully. Not that it was really any surprise the killer was a man. It would take one mean and nasty woman to kill in such a way. "Okay, I guess." I shrugged and looked around the bar. The Irregulars had moved to a table and were ordering food.

Sully got up to join them. They were drinking and laughing and having a great time.

Was I crazy to think one of them was the serial killer? Letting my imagination run wild? Every once in a while, one of them would glance over at the bar. They all looked envious of Dean, who was still chatting with Jamila—especially Jim Deems, who couldn't stop watching them with his greedy eyes. *Good luck with that.* Seriously, if he kept this up, I'd have to remind him he was way too old for her.

An hour or so later, Jamila said goodbye to Dean with a small kiss on his cheek and waved to The Irregulars who were still sneaking glances. She gathered up her things and came down to my end of the bar.

So," I said with a smile, "did The Lounge impress you?"

She glanced toward Dean who was finally paying attention to his other customers. "Well, it's not too shabby." She laughed. "I think I might be back real soon."

"I'll look forward to it. It was really good to see you."

After Jamila was out the door, I called Dean over. When he reached my end of the bar, I bent close and whispered in his ear, "I want you to understand something. Jamila is very special to me. If you hurt that woman, I will make you regret it. So. Do. Not. Screw. With. Her. Understand?"

His answer surprised me. "I won't. I swear. I like her. We really hit it off. I don't want to mess this up." Then he sauntered away and back to his spot while I stood there with my mouth hanging open.

Chapter Twenty-Five

I t was finally Wednesday. For me, it seemed like a day of reckoning, not the hump day most people looked forward to.

I wasn't working until later in the evening, and I didn't want to spend the day worrying if Eric would call. Of course, that didn't stop me from looking at the clock every ten minutes. My emotions over the last week had been like that crazy Thunderbolt rollercoaster at Coney Island. Straight up for two hundred feet at ninety degrees, then a heart-stopping drop into twists, turns, and upside down loops. I couldn't take much more.

I'd sent Agent Maguire back to FBI headquarters. I explained I planned to stay in until my shift at the bar and I was sure there were better things he could do with his time than watch me straighten out my closet or clean the kitchen. I told him if he was still on babysitting duty, he should come to The Lounge at seven. He could enjoy another dinner while he minded me.

Okay, it was kind of a bribe, but he left the apartment with a smile on his face. I suspected Agent Garlinger would not be as happy with my decision. But I really didn't care.

I fully intended to stay in for the day, but by the time I finished my chores, I needed a break. I felt like I was suffocating in my apartment and wanted to get out and breathe.

I tossed on a puffy parka, warm boots, tucked my spiky hair into a watch cap, and slung my bag over my shoulder. It was a cold day with sunny skies that were deceiving in their promise of warmth.

The wind whipping through the park from the river sent chills through my body. I pulled the hood of my parka over my cap and tucked it tight against my chin. It was the current look in my neighborhood. It covered up the telltale basics and was androgynous enough that I didn't think anyone would recognize me unless they stared at my face. I felt safe enough being on my own.

I wandered around for a while absorbing the vibe of the Lower East Side and letting it calm me until my stomach started to rumble.

Chinatown wasn't too far away, and I headed in that direction thinking of crab soup dumplings from Shanghai Joe's. As usual, the restaurant was packed and people who didn't seem to mind the cold were waiting on the sidewalk out front.

Since I was alone, I was lucky and snagged a small table of my own. The restaurant was warm and toasty. There were lots of locals speaking Chinese, tourists confused over the extensive menu, and some of the jury duty people from the courthouses nearby who were out for a long lunch. It was loud in the restaurant, but in a good way, with clinking cutlery and undertones of happy, satisfied diners enjoying their meals.

I watched as waiters brought out heaping plates of fragrant dishes for the big parties seated around circular tables, each of which contained a large rotating tray in its center to make it easy to share their choices.

Finally, my lunch arrived: a pot of tea and a wicker basket of steaming dumplings filled with hot soup and crab meat. The smell alone made me smile. It was just what I needed. I polished them off in no time, paid my bill, tucked my fortune cookie into my pocket, and headed out again taking a different route home. I was in no hurry to return to my apartment and I wandered for a while looking into all the produce and fish markets on Grand and Essex Streets before walking toward the river.

As I passed the gorgeous old building that housed the Seward Park branch of New York Public Library on East Broadway, I stopped short. It was one of the gems of the neighborhood, built in the Italian Renaissance Revival style and commissioned by Andrew Carnegie who was also responsible for the main library on Fifth Avenue. Better yet, it housed the archives of years and years of newspapers on microfiche—the perfect way to do some research the old-fashioned way and find out more about the New Year's Killer murders.

I'd already Googled all the victims and knew I could use the internet for the rest of the research I had in mind, but those threaded spools with images from faded, sepia-toned newspaper pages seemed more real to me. We'd learned how to use them when I was in grammar school and one of our teachers took us on an afternoon visit to our local branch of the library. I wanted to check the coverage of the murders of the first three victims, Lukas Janssen, Jake Hammity, and Peter Finley.

To begin, I requested the microfiche spools from *The New York Times*, *The Daily News*, and *The New York Post from* January 2000. When the librarian delivered them to me, I loaded in the first reel and got busy searching, my small notebook and pen by my side so I could take notes as I read.

I'd already looked up Lukas Janssen online, and although I wasn't expecting to uncover much more, I found a few stories and photos about his murder, including pictures of his family when they'd come to New York to claim his body that hadn't been on the internet. It was gruesome—their faces snapshots of horror, rage and sadness. Right then, my lunch didn't seem like such a great idea as I felt my stomach lurching around threatening to expel it.

Lukas's parents had mentioned he'd been wearing a silver cross pendant made of two intersecting replicas of Thor's hammer. They claimed he never took the necklace off and wore it as a protective amulet he believed would bring him luck and give him confidence. The papers all had a shot of Lukas wearing it, his smile wide and inviting. It was a beautiful, intricate piece and I'd never seen one like it before.

Someone had stolen that smile from him as well as his cross. It wasn't with his effects that were turned over to his family. The police searched for it in both Times Square and the park but never found it. They thought it might have been lost during his attack. I thought the killer had kept it.

Lukas, a tourist, didn't have anything to do with the Lower East Side or the other victims, so it wasn't likely I'd find anything else to add to my research.

I returned the spools I'd just viewed to the front desk and asked for the same newspaper files from 2007. Hopefully, they would serve up more information on Peter Finley. I loaded the first reel and studied it carefully.

Again, there were a few stories about his murder I hadn't seen on the internet. I shuddered at the black and white shots of the cold and wintry John V. Lindsay Park where his body had been found, and from where someone had followed me home on Saturday.

No one ever said it was going to be easy, I reminded myself and got down to business. Peter disappeared on his way home from a party at a bar and restaurant in Times Square that he'd attended with his colleagues from North Star Bank. That much I already knew.

I continued to scroll and read and found that he, his wife, and their new baby had moved downtown to the financial district shortly before Peter's murder. On the night of his disappearance, when he wasn't home by four a.m., Amanda, his wife, became worried. She called around to some of his pals who told her he'd left for home around one a.m., and then, finally, the police, who explained they couldn't start a missing person file on Peter until twenty-four hours had passed. By then, she was so distraught she called a family friend who was a lawyer and got her involved. This seemed to prompt the police to begin investigating.

I sat back and rubbed my eyes. Taking all this in was hard going. I shook my head, looked up at the ceiling, and asked myself why I was doing this. Were my motives as pure as I liked to think they were, or was I trying to make amends for past failures?

I was crossing my own Rubicon, committing to this search for a killer for reasons I really didn't fully understand. Would history repeat itself and would I start something I'd regret for a long time?

Okay, Jude, enough soul-searching. Get back to work. I refocused on the newsprint in front of me and started reading again.

In one statement to the press, the distraught woman kept blaming herself. It seems their babysitter had cancelled at the last minute and she encouraged Peter to meet his friends while she stayed at home with their infant. "It's all my fault," she said over and over again. "If I had gone with him, this never would have happened." A photo of her tear-stained face with its vacant expression and dulled eyes accompanied her words. Somewhere toward the bottom of the article, she also mentioned that Peter's ring from Fordham

CHAPTER TWENTY-FIVE

University was missing.

I sat up straight at that. That tidbit hadn't been in any of the reports online. Had the police been trying to keep it quiet, one of their discreet facts that only the killer would know if he'd taken the ring? Well, now I knew it, too. I made a note about it and added it to the info I'd jotted down on Lukas's murder. I was beginning to see a pattern.

Souvenirs were his thing. Find them tucked away somewhere and you'd find the killer.

I wondered if Amanda Finley still lived in Manhattan. It had been twelve years since Peter's death, and she may have moved on. If not, I'd try to find her and reach out. There might be something else that could help my investigation.

There you go again, I told myself. *It's not your 'investigation.'*

I know, I replied. *I'll tell Agent Garlinger about everything I've found.*

Good, I said.

But just her, not those two dickhead detectives.

Okay, I get it.

I felt better now that I talked it through, even if it was to myself. I checked the time and realized I should be getting back home and getting ready for work. Looking into Jake Hammity would have to wait for another day.

The time had passed quickly, but not swiftly enough for me to realize I still hadn't heard from Eric. That added another layer to the sadness reading about the murders had caused.

I gathered up my microfiche rolls, brought them to the front desk, and thanked the librarian for her help. I looked outside, past one of the library's graceful arched front windows, and realized that dusk had fallen and the day had turned gloomy and sullen.

Redressing for the cold, I bundled into my parka and cap, pulled up my hood, and prepared to go into the darkening evening anonymously as I made my way home. I stuck my hand in my pocket to retrieve my gloves and pulled out my fortune cookie with them. I tore open the cellophane that covered it, broke it open, and read the message it contained.

All day, I'd been wishing that something would happen to shake things loose. Maybe it was the cosmos at work, but my fortune seemed to align with my thoughts. The message was simple: "Be careful what you wish for, lest it come true."

And here I thought it might be something about winning the lottery.

Chapter Twenty-Six

I'd no sooner opened the door to The Lounge than Dean rushed out from behind the bar to meet me, hands flying, his movie star face crunched into a very un-starlike frown.

"What? What happened?" I asked, already thinking the worst, that Eric had had an accident, or Sully suffered a heart attack.

"I've been trying to reach you. You didn't answer your phone." His words were tumbling out one over the other like ice cube piling into a glass.

"I had it shut off." I put my hands on his arms and spoke slowly as I eased him away from the front door and the bar toward the back of the restaurant. The few customers already at the bar didn't need to hear our conversation. "Please, tell me why you're so upset."

He nodded and I let go of his arms. "The police were here and they took Pete in for questioning."

I was shaking my head as I spoke. "Why? No. That can't be."

"It was about the knife…the one that killed Art's brother…Michael." He paused, his mouth forming one tight line as if he didn't want to utter the next words. "They escorted him out to the street and shoved him into their car."

Could this really be happening? "Was it Ortiz and Delmonico?" I asked.

Dean knew who they were. He nodded. "Yeah, the detectives were here along with a couple of patrolmen." His eyes looked up to the ceiling before he continued. "Listen, when I couldn't reach you, I called Sully. I know he was with you when you guys discovered the body. I hope that was okay."

"Where is he now?" I looked around the restaurant and finally took in the people at the bar who were trying not to gawk and not making a very good job of it. I moved Dean further back into the room.

"He just stepped into the kitchen to check with Alain. See if he heard anything when they came for Pete."

"Okay. You go back behind the bar." I tossed a don't-even-mess-with-me look at the bar and the oglers looked down at their drinks. "And keep it on the down low." I jutted my chin in customers' direction. "There's been enough gossip already. I'll go speak with Sully and Alain."

The kitchen was as silent and still as I'd ever seen it. Alain and Sully were huddled together in the small space at the rear that passed for Pete's office. The prep cooks, bus people, and dishwasher were standing around speaking softly to each other.

I threw them a different kind of look as I passed by. One that said, *Get your butts in gear, we're open for business.*

I squeezed in next to Alain and planted myself on the corner of the counter Pete used for his computer. "What happened? Did you talk to Elaine?" I addressed my questions to Sully.

"Yeah. She's on her way to the precinct. She'll get those two pathetic Ds to spring Pete loose." His voice was filled with anger. "You know what this is, don't you?" he asked, then answered his own question. "It's payback time for the last time we tangled with them and for Lanie grabbing their case."

"But the Mayor and Police Commissioner gave it back to them."

"With the proviso that the FBI remains involved." Sully's mouth twisted into a sneer. "They felt like they were dissed."

I turned to Alain. "When did they come for Pete? Did you hear what they told him before they took him away?" Saying the words made me imagine how pissed off Pete must have felt. I gulped, hoping he didn't do or say anything rash.

Alain was nodding at me. "It was about a half hour ago. They said they needed to speak with him down at the station. When Pete asked why, they told him his fingerprints were on the knife used to murder Michael Bevins."

"Jeez, they already knew that," Sully interjected.

Alain continued. "Pete said he'd gone over this with them before. That the knife was from here and had been stolen sometime after closing on New Year's Eve. He said it was in the statement he'd given at the time."

"Yeah, the one that Lanie got then." If Sully kept interrupting, I'd never get the whole story.

"So?" I asked. "They took him in anyway." I realized my hands were balled into fists. "When they should be out looking for the real killer." My anger was rising, and I was boiling mad.

Sully's voice was conciliatory, which I knew was costing him. "Listen, Jude. Lanie's going to get Pete out and bring him back here." He put his hand on my shoulder. "She's got it."

I started to bark out, "Yeah, right," but thought better of it. Sully wasn't the enemy. Neither was Agent Garlinger. I didn't want to have another argument to add to the list.

"Okay," I said at last. "Alain you're in charge until Pete returns."

"No problem. We're already prepped for dinner. There are just a few more items to prepare." He nodded at me slowly. "We'll handle it."

"Good. I'll be outside if you need anything," I replied, then turned and left the kitchen with Sully.

"I just don't get it. What did Ortiz and Delmonico think they were going to achieve by hauling Pete in?" I knew if the news got out we'd have the media all over the place again, after we just managed to get rid of them. Believe me, that old saying that any publicity is good publicity was a load of bull.

"They know they can harass you under the guise of investigating and get away with it. But we won't let them. Lanie also called in a favor from a lawyer she used to work with, Samantha 'The Shark' Vitale."

"Jeez, she sounds like a member of the Mafia."

A smile lit up his cool, gray eyes. "She's the best. A killer who goes for the jugular. She's meeting Lanie at the precinct. Those two dummies won't know what hit them."

"Okay, good." Sully's words had calmed me down and I took a deep breath.

"So, where were you and why was your phone off?" he asked.

"I'll tell you if you promise not to go all war zone marine on me."

He gave me a piercing look that said, *This better be good.* "Let's hear it."

I filled him in on my impromptu visit to the library and what I'd learned about the first two victims and their missing pieces of jewelry. "And I'm planning to share all this information with Agent Garlinger as soon as I see her."

I could tell Sully was bursting to reprimand me for not following orders to butt out. To give him credit, he just gave me a terse nod and changed the subject to one fraught with even more peril: Eric.

"Have you heard from Eric? Didn't you say he was due back today?"

I nodded. "He is, or at least I think so." I looked down at the ground. "He hasn't called." I hadn't told Sully all the details of our argument, but he knew enough to use his imagination to fill them in.

"Maybe you should call him," he said gently.

I shook my head. "No. I can't." Then I put a smile on my face. "Let's leave it at that, okay?"

For once, he didn't push for more. "Why don't you go get ready for your shift and I'll stay down here with Dean and wait to hear from Lanie." He patted me on the arm. "If The Shark lives up to her rep, Pete should be back any minute and those two detectives should be chum."

I looked in my bar's beautiful back mirror and realized I was still dressed in all my outdoor gear, hood included. "I'll see you in a few," I said and made for the door.

"And, Jude, turn your phone on. You never know who might be trying to reach you."

Chapter Twenty-Seven

I showered, changed into my black turtleneck and jeans, put on some makeup, and sat looking at my phone. Eric was not going to call. And I couldn't call him. Well, I could, but I wouldn't. Call it pride, some might say stupidity, but that's the way I felt. After ten more minutes of willing my cell to ring, I gave up and shoved it in the back pocket of my jeans and left for the bar.

It had filled up with the after-work crowd, and the dining room had some early patrons. Things looked normal on the outside, but I knew better. Dean seemed tense and less upbeat than usual, his ready smile hidden under tight lips. I gave him a nod and gestured toward the kitchen. I peeked in, not wanting to disturb Alain, and saw that things appeared to be running smoothly. Everyone was at their stations doing what they were supposed to be doing. Except Pete.

I went back to the bar and slipped behind it, ready to work. "Dean, thanks for holding things together today." I smiled at him, hoping he'd return it. "Why don't you go have some dinner." I realized with all the craziness surrounding Pete's abduction by the police, family dinner never happened.

When he was gone, I walked over to Sully who was in his usual seat, cell phone out on the bar. "Anything from Elaine?" I asked.

He picked up his cell and showed me the message: "Pete being released now. Coming back to work. Tell Jude."

I let out a long, slow breath, realizing how happy it made me to see those words. "Guess The Shark did a good job." I smiled at Sully. "And Lanie. Is she going to be in trouble for doing this?"

"Hey, she's still the FBI and that trumps the NYPD." He paused and took a gulp of the Jameson he'd been nursing. "At least in my book."

"Is she coming by? I'd like to speak with her," I said. "You know, fill her in on what I found out today."

"I spoke to her when she got to the precinct. Ortiz and Delmonico were pretty pissed off to see her. She told me she planned to have a talk with them about procedure, which I'm sure they'll love. Then she said she'd stop by here. So, yeah, you'll get a chance to talk to her."

I picked up a bottle of Jameson and refilled Sully's glass. "Thanks for pitching in before. Dean looked freaked out." I gazed over at my head bartender who was now tucking into a juicy cheeseburger with fries as he texted on his cell. He finally looked happy. Watching him eat made my stomach start rumbling and I figured I'd grab something when Dean came back. In the meantime, I poured myself a glass of Chianti.

"Did Dean say if they cuffed Pete when they took him out?" I was afraid of how he might have reacted if they had.

"No. And they walked him out the back." A flash of anger flew across his face. "Which again leads me to believe they were just being bastards looking to make trouble."

I had no answer to that. It seemed petty and a waste of time. "What about you?" I asked Sully.

"What do you mean?" he replied.

"The other night, you seemed like you had an idea about something to do with Michael's murder."

"Naw. You're mistaken. I was just thinking, that's all. There was nothing."

I knew he was lying. Like most people, Sully had a tell, a sign that gave him away. Although he'd deny it, his was swiping his right index finger next to his nose when he was stalling or lying. He did that now. He didn't want to share what he'd been trying to work out, although he knew exactly what I was talking about.

I was just about to call him on it when the door opened and Pete walked in. He did not look like a happy camper. I rushed out from behind the bar to give him a hug. He barely squeezed me back. "This has got to stop," he whispered in my ear and moved away from me toward the kitchen. "We'll talk later. Now, I need to get back to work." He held up his hands as if to ward me off.

I gulped and just stood there trying to understand what happened. Had this all gone too far? Was Pete thinking of leaving the business? I looked over at Sully who'd caught it all. He reached out a hand and I took it, like someone going under for the third time in a tempestuous sea.

I wish I could say that Eric had come into The Lounge, got down on bended knee and told me he couldn't live without me. But happy endings like that only happen in romance novels, not real life.

Agent Garlinger, however, did stop by, looking more pissed off than I'd ever seen her. Thankfully, this time it wasn't directed at me.

"I had to lay it out for Ortiz and Delmonico that, since they wanted the investigation to stay within the NYPD, it would be more beneficial to keep looking for the suspect than to harass people they knew to be innocent." She let out a deep sigh. "What a pair. I hope your partner isn't too rattled. They shouldn't be bothering him again."

"I'll drink to that," Sully piped in, holding his glass aloft.

I remembered Pete's look from a few hours before. He was more than rattled, but it wouldn't do any good to mention it. Instead, I said, "Thanks for helping out. Please tell Samantha Vitale to send her bill to me."

Garlinger waved it away. "No bill is due. Believe it or not, taking on those two was more like fun than work for her. She loved every minute and she made sure they never booked him."

"So there's no official record of Pete being brought in?" I asked.

"I checked that there wasn't before Samantha arrived. They never processed him. She just reminded the detectives of what would happen if somehow Pete's questioning leaked to the press." Elaine smiled. "It wasn't a pretty sight."

Sully was making a shark fin with his hand and mouthing the opening music to the movie *Jaws* behind Garlinger's back. I gave him a look that said he better quit it.

A lawyer who didn't want to get paid? That was rare in my book. "Well, at least tell her I owe her a dinner at The Lounge. You, too."

"You got it." She lifted the glass of Maker's Mark I'd poured her and tilted it in my direction. Now that she seemed calmer, I thought I could mention my library research from earlier today.

"There's something I wanted to discuss with you," I began. Then, with Sully listening in, I proceeded to tell her what I'd learned about the first two victims.

"Damn." She slammed her glass down on the bar. "Of course, the FBI knew about the jewelry, the cross and the school ring, but they purposely held back those details." She shook her head at me. "I'm not happy you were able to find that so easily."

I wanted to say, "Hey, it wasn't easy!" Instead, I told her I'd never tell anyone about it. I wondered if the killer had taken something from Jake Hammity, as well, but I held my question.

I cleared my throat. "Agent Garlinger…Elaine, I did want to ask you about Peter Finley's wife and child."

"Okay." Her voice was wary. "Go ahead. I'll answer if I can."

"Do you know if they're still living in the city, down in the financial district?"

"Why do you need to know?" she asked, her tone now in the frostier professional zone.

"Just curious," I replied. "I thought it might have been hard to stay in the city where your husband was murdered and bring up a child there."

I watched her carefully as she took a sip of her drink before replying. "I believe they left."

She turned to Sully, effectively ending the conversation. "It's late and I have to be up early tomorrow, so I'm going to get going."

"Okay, let me walk you out." He turned over his glass and rapped on the bar, signaling he was done. "See you tomorrow, Jude."

"Thanks again for helping Pete out, Elaine. I really appreciate it."

She gave me a long look before she spoke. "I think it would be best if you didn't dig any deeper into these murders." She reached over and put her hand on mine. "I'm already concerned about your safety. So, don't make me worry anymore."

Her touch was warm, but it gave me a chill. I nodded numbly and said goodnight. Then they were gone into the cold winter evening. I stood behind the bar and wondered why she'd lied to me when I asked about Peter Finley's wife. I'd bet anything they hadn't "left." And, I was going to find out if I was right.

Chapter Twenty-Eight

It'd been four days without Eric, but who was counting? I should be savoring my newfound boyfriend-less freedom, I thought—going places, seeing friends, having fun. Well, at least I was going places—downstairs to my office to take care of my paperwork and ordering.

Pete was barely speaking to me, which I didn't understand. It wasn't my doing that got Ortiz and Delmonico to roust him and bring him in. Every time I tried to chat with him, he said he was too busy, had a *kitchen to run*. A not-so-subtle way of letting me know I had a *bar to take care of*, as well.

I knew we'd talk about this soon. We had to. I didn't want Pete to be so unhappy that he might actually think about selling his share of the business.

He hated the fact that we were involved in this serial killer murder, especially the idea that I was poking my nose in it to the detriment of our business, not to mention my well-being. Somehow, I'd have to reassure him that everything was okay.

I had my babysitter back today. If nothing else, that should keep Pete calm. Agent Maguire knocked on my door earlier that morning and told me Agent Garlinger had insisted on it. Now, he was sitting at a table in the dining room, drinking coffee and reading the papers while I was downstairs slaving away.

Maguire would keep me company until Eltee showed up. The big guy would stay in The Lounge until closing, then walk me upstairs to my apartment. I was definitely protected from harm, self-inflicted or by others.

Schedule done for the weekend and ordering complete, I logged on to the internet for a little poking-around time. I typed Amanda Finley's name into one of those people-finder search sites, paid twenty-nine dollars, and came up with a phone number and address for an Amanda Finley residing at 41 River Terrace in Battery Park City. It also listed a Chloe Finley living there.

I thought about just heading over and ringing her doorbell, surprising her. But I knew that would be a terrible thing to do. And it certainly wouldn't prompt her to speak with me.

I decided to call her and explain my interest in her husband's death. She still might not want to talk, but maybe I could convince her.

I had no idea if Amanda Finley worked or not, or what her profession might be. I figured it would be best to wait until dinnertime to call when I'd have a better chance of getting her instead of her voicemail.

I powered down the computer and trudged upstairs where I found Dean pacing in front of the bar. When he saw me, he stopped and pulled his shoulders back. I sensed an ambush coming. He looked like he wanted something, something I might object to.

"Jude, I need to speak with you. Got a minute?"

I nodded yes and took a stool in front of the bar. "What's up?" I asked.

His face was a mask of anxiety flashing on and off before he spoke. "I know it's kind of short notice, but can I have Saturday afternoon off?"

"Saturday?" I asked with a bit of annoyance I couldn't hide. "Dean. You know how busy Saturdays can be." I lifted a hand toward the bar and waited for him to speak again.

"I know, but Kara said she could cover for me." He paused. "I want to take Jamila to the holiday market in Bryant Park. It's the last day it's open. She's never been, and they're closing down Saturday night."

"So, you want time off so you can have a date?" I asked. He looked so serious, I almost laughed, my previous annoyance gone. "With Jamila?" I added.

"I'll be back by seven to take over from Kara. Don't worry about the bourbon sampling. I'll work it."

Damn, with everything that was going on, I'd forgotten all about the event at The Lounge. Dean had been planning a new event every few months. For post-holidays it was a bourbon sampling, a full-bodied whiskey perfect for cold weather.

A new, small batch, artisanal bourbon company had approached us about doing a tasting event. They were giving us several bottles of their bourbon. The idea was to offer each bar customer a shot or mixed drink on the house. If they wanted another, it would go on their tab. We'd printed up table cards with all the details and our customers were looking forward to the event.

Pete was planning to prepare food that complemented the bourbon's flavor: smoked riblets glazed with maple syrup, grilled peach slices wrapped in bacon, and sweet potato tarts topped with pecans and brown sugar. They would be our special bar appetizers, that's if Pete was still cooking for us—especially since the entire event had slipped my mind.

"Okay, you can take the afternoon off." I paused, then asked, "Is Jamila meeting you here?"

He nodded. "She's taking the train down from the Bronx and we'll leave from my apartment. It's going to be fun."

"I bet," I said with just a touch of sarcasm. "Just be back on time, okay. And bring Jamila along if you like."

"I will, no worries." He was all smiles now as he went back to the station behind the bar.

Oh right, I thought as I headed to the kitchen to have a chat with Pete.

"They brought me into the station like a common criminal." Pete was wielding a cleaver and pounding a steak with such force, bloody juices were splattering the counter.

"I know. I'm so sorry," I replied. "I had no idea..." My words failed me. Nothing I could say would make this better.

Pete kept pounding, his face mottled with anger. *That's it. It's over.* I was sure he'd decide to leave the business, worried about the danger of a serial killer hanging over us.

He put down the cleaver and nodded to his tiny office. Our staff was nervous enough after the murder and they didn't need to hear our conversation. "Having those creepy reporters hanging around isn't doing our reputation any good. We can't afford to lose customers."

He was right. The restaurant business was a delicate balancing act. It was hours and hours of hard work to offer appealing food that would bring in the people. And success depended on not just the food, but also things like ambiance and great service.

Pete glanced at the kitchen. "Our people are getting nervous, afraid we'll close and they'll be out of work."

I understood what he was telling me. I had been preoccupied with this killing. And, he reminded me, it wasn't the first time. I assured him that our business came first. I meant it. It did, and I would never put it in jeopardy. We hugged. He gave me some mac 'n' cheese for dinner and told me to get my butt back to the bar.

Chapter Twenty-Nine

Thursday night came and still no Eric. Even Pete's mac 'n' cheese didn't work its usual magic of cheering me up. I tried to keep busy and not think about it. But each time the door opened, my heart would jump into my throat and I'd look up expecting to see him. I'd screwed this up royally. But, hey, that's life in the Jude Dillane lane.

We were busier than usual with people who like to start the weekend early, and the bar was three deep through social hour and beyond. Eltee spent most of his time at the door letting people in as others left. All that was missing was the velvet rope, not that we were so discriminating. We were a neighborhood bar and restaurant, after all. And Eltee's job was usually fairly simple since our customers weren't particularly rowdy. They didn't need too much watching over, unless you counted Sully and The Irregulars.

They arrived *en masse* at about nine thirty, looking a little bit the worse for wear. Art was with them. He'd just returned from Ohio, and they were determined to lift his spirits with the alcoholic kind. It wasn't working. *Grief had a funny way of catching you unawares*, I thought. Or as an old friend of mine would say, "Just when you thought it was safe."

They took a table in the cocktail lounge away from the noisy bar and settled in. I stepped out from behind the bar and went over to the group. I nodded hello at all of them and took Art's hand in mine. "I'm glad to see you back home. What happened was horrific and nothing I can say will make it any better." I squeezed his hand. "Just know everyone's doing all they possibly can to find this bastard. And, they will."

Art looked annoyed, taking back his hand quickly and giving me a weird half-smile, which felt put-on. For the briefest moment, anger flashed in his eyes. I took a step back not understanding what I'd said to make him so incensed. Then he turned to Jim, who'd been watching the exchange between us. "You look like a slob." Jim hung his head and muttered something I didn't catch.

Whoa. I gave Sully a 'what the hell' look and he interrupted, which for once was a good thing. "How about some drinks over here!"

I stared at him and waited a beat, regaining my composure. "Looks like you may have already had a few."

He waved that away like he was swatting a fly. "Naw. We're good."

There was no need to take their orders. I already knew what each of them drank. They were a predictable lot, rarely changing. Except for tonight. Jim came over to the bar and switched out his usual beer for a margarita, catching me off guard. I put away the mug I was just about to fill and grabbed the cocktail shaker instead.

"Branching out?" I asked, trying to defuse the embarrassment Art had caused, as I filled the shaker with ice, tequila and our special house margarita mix.

He looked uncomfortable. "I had one that Dean made the other day," he glanced at Dean who was at the other end of the bar, "and it was really good. Hope yours can match it." He smiled in Dean's direction as I shook his drink. "Never too late to try something new, is it?" His voice was snippy, and he said it like a challenge that he expected me to refute.

Had I just been dissed? By Jim, of all people. I shrugged it off. "Go for it," I said as I poured the drink into a margarita glass I'd rimmed with salt and handed it over. "Hope it lives up to your high standards."

My Irregulars were all acting strange. It had to be the murder, I thought as I finished pouring the rest of their drinks. I called over Rashid, our cocktail lounge waiter, who delivered them to the table.

About ten minutes later, Tony walked up to the bar with his glass in hand. He nodded at me and waited until I finished with the couple I was serving.

"Want another?" I asked.

"Sure, why not?" He replied with a devilish grin on his face as he drained the glass. "Might as well live it up."

I poured him a fresh Johnnie Walker Black and handed it over. When I looked up at him, his grin was gone and his expression had turned serious. "How are you, Jude?"

"I'm fine, really." I tried to smile but I was sure it looked more like a grimace. "No one's tried to come after me again. Plus, I have my own FBI guy looking after me."

"You need to be careful, Jude. I mean it." His dark-brown eyes turned serious.

I didn't know how to respond. His words had almost sounded like a warning, but Tony was the one who'd saved me from my attacker. Finally, I replied. "I will be." I nodded. "It's a promise."

Tony smiled at my words and his whole face changed back to its usual pleasant appearance. "Glad to hear that."

I handed him his drink. "On the house. And thanks."

He lifted it towards me in a silent toast, then walked back to his pals who seemed to be having a great time. When I looked over, Art pinned me with his eyes, then grinned and licked his lips. Was he leering at me? It was creepy and I turned away.

Art, Oscar, Jim, and Tony all left together about an hour later as the Thursday night scene got louder and crazier. It was too much for their older sensibilities. Sully stayed behind, moved to the bar, and watched the show from his regular seat. A few times I caught him glancing my way.

"What?" I asked as walked over and stood in front of him.

"Don't take this the wrong way—"

"That's a great way to open a conversation. Just spit it out, why don't you."

"Right now, I think you're being your own worst enemy."

"And by that you mean?" I wasn't angry or upset at what Sully was saying, just curious. Maybe on some level I knew he was right. I was stubborn and proud and hated to lose.

"Call Eric. Apologize if you have to. Tell him how you feel. He'll come around."

I picked up my bar mop and twisted it in my hands. "Maybe," I replied and shrugged.

Sully pulled out his wallet and put some money on the bar. He turned over his glass and rapped on the bar. With that, he was gone.

Sleep didn't come easy. I tossed and turned and woke up several times reaching out for Eric. I missed him more than I ever thought I would. I told myself I'd take Sully's advice. I'd call Eric in the morning and ask him to forgive me, beg him if I had to.

Sighing, I got out of bed and headed for the kitchen. It was useless to try to get back to sleep. I'd make some tea and try to relax. As my bare feet hit the cold wooden floor, I shivered and looked around for my slippers, remembering I'd left them in the living room.

Walking to retrieve them, I stopped dead. Out of the corner of my eye, I noticed a white envelope halfway under my front door, almost glowing in the otherwise total darkness, calling out to me with its stark brightness.

I felt immobilized and stood there watching it, sweat breaking out on my body. I don't know how long I stayed that way. Finally, I moved toward it, knowing something that arrived like it had in the middle of the night wouldn't contain anything good. I bent down, my hand reluctantly reaching out to slide the envelope toward me. Inch by inch, I moved it closer. When the whole envelope was inside my apartment, I took a step back and stared at it as if whatever was inside was going to jump out at me.

Now, I was shaking all over, a hot mess of fear and terror. Taking a deep breath, I lifted the envelope from the floor and held it at arm's length. Reminding myself over and over that it was just an envelope, I walked to the couch and sat down, placing the bright, white rectangle on the coffee table.

I could tell there was something inside from a small rise in its middle. With trembling hands, I lifted it up and slid a finger under the flap. I pulled out the folded sheet of paper it contained and unfolded it. It was a note in the killer's block print, along with a lock of blond hair tied with string. I dropped both on the coffee table as if they were snakes about to strike and pushed back into my couch as far as I could. The note was to the point:

THIS IS YOUR LAST WARNING.

STAY AWAY OR I'LL KILL YOU TOO.

I heard a buzzing in my ears and felt my head filling with panic. My body was spiraling, and it seemed like I was falling from a great height with the earth rushing up to meet me.

That's all I remembered when I came to. I pushed myself up into a sitting position on the couch and came back to reality slowly. I had fainted and now I was awake, the note and hair still where I'd left them. I scooted back into my couch curling into a ball, as if the paper and hair actually had the power to hurt me.

I took a deep breath and snatched up my cell phone. He answered on the first ring. "Please can you come over. I need you," was all I said. Then, I sat back and waited, the note and bundle of hair never out of sight.

Chapter Thirty

Eric used his key to let himself in, calling my name so I wouldn't be frightened. I sprang from the couch and ran to him. My arms flew around him and I was holding on for all I was worth. He hugged me back and kept hold of me until I stopped shaking. "I'm sorry for everything. Can you forgive me?" I asked.

He leaned down and gently wiped the tears from my face. Then he kissed me. "I forgive you and I love you." He took a step back, still holding on to me. "What happened to make you this scared?" he asked.

"I'll show you." I took his hand and led him toward the living room where I'd left the note and the hair. We both sat down on the couch and Eric looked at both without touching them.

I realized he didn't want to add his fingerprints to the note. "Did you call the FBI?" he asked.

I shook my head. "Not yet. I'll call Agent Garlinger and let her handle it." I realized Eric didn't know that she was now sharing Michael's case with the NYPD. "So much has happened since you've been gone."

I told Eric about all that had occurred since he left on Sunday. He listened without commenting, his face a blank canvas devoid of emotions.

"Jude, are you done with this?" He gestured at the note, but I knew he meant the whole investigation.

"I…I'm not sure. Agent Garlinger lied to me when I asked if Peter Finley's family was still living in New York. I just—"

He stood up so quickly, the coffee table almost turned over. "When are you going to learn? Can you tell me?" He picked up the note and shook it in front of my face, adding his fingerprints all but forgotten. "Isn't this enough to make you stop? Do you want to end up dead, too?"

"Eric, wait." I put up my hand to stop him speaking. "I was hoping that you could help me," I continued before he could interrupt. "You know, have my back. All I want to do is speak with Peter Finley's wife. Ask her if she remembers anything about that night that could help Agent Garlinger with the investigation." I looked up at him with my tear-stained eyes, pleading. "You could just come with me."

He placed the note back on the table. "If I do that, and I mean *if*, will you stop looking into all of this?"

We were still staring into each other's eyes and I could see the love and the fear in his. Were mine showing him the same thing? I nodded. "Yes, Eric. If you'll help me this one time, I promise I will."

We sat up talking until dawn turned into daylight and the sun streamed into my apartment. Eric told me about his new client and his time in Buffalo. Everything had gone smoothly, and he and Dominic had shown PPS they could handle their business with integrity and competence.

I filled him in on what had been happening at the bar, mostly about Pete being hauled off for questioning by Ortiz and Delmonico just for a show of power and how Elaine Garlinger's lawyer friend, Samantha "The Shark" Vitale, took them down a few notches.

"Can you spend Saturday with me at The Lounge, or do you have to work?"

"I'm good for Saturday. What's happening?"

I explained about the upcoming bourbon event, which I thought he'd enjoy. I also told him how smitten Dean was with Jamila, whom Eric knew from the Big City Food Bank. "He asked for Saturday afternoon off to take her to the holiday market in Bryant Park. I warned him not to mess with her." I made my stern face and Eric laughed. "But I think they really like each other. Go figure."

We had some breakfast and then it was time to call Agent Garlinger and tell her about the latest threat I'd received. I couldn't know for sure, but I suspected the blond hair was Michael's.

I reached her at her office, and she said she'd be over in an hour with Agent Maguire.

Then I did the hard part and called Sully to tell him someone had gotten into his building again and left me another surprise.

Chapter Thirty-One

We all gathered in The Lounge over steaming cups of coffee. At this stage of the game, we'd drunk enough coffee to send everyone's nerves into the red zone.

Sully was in a full-on "heads will roll" rant, fuming about the "break-in," as he called it, and was planning updates to the building's "defenses," including security cameras in critical positions.

Eric sat close to me in protective mode, ready to jump in at the slightest provocation.

Agent Maguire sat there taking it all in while Agent Garlinger questioned me.

Everybody was on edge and tempers were close to the boiling point.

"I don't know what else I can add." I gazed down at the note and bundle of hair, both now in separate evidence bags. "I woke up, saw the envelope, and opened it. I was scared, so I called Eric and asked him to come over. Then I called you. That's it."

I left out the part about how freaked out I was until Eric arrived and how thunderstruck I'd been that the killer had gotten so close to me again.

"Do you think that's Michael's hair?" I asked.

"It will have to be tested, but it most likely is his." Agent Garlinger held up the evidence bag. "The killer is baiting you. I believe he wants you to know he can reach you anytime. Using Michael's hair is part of that."

"It's interesting that he gave it up."

Agent Garlinger looked at me across the table. "What do you mean?"

I thought about Lukas Janssen's cross and Peter Finley's ring. "Well, he likes souvenirs, doesn't he? So why would he send this to me, unless he has something else of Michael's to gloat over?" I asked.

Sully had stopped ranting and Eric and Agent Maguire were totally silent. "He does, doesn't he?"

She drummed her fingers on the table before answering. "Yes, you know he does."

"So, I'm right." I leaned in toward her, the Chanel fragrance she was wearing wafting past the end of my nose. "He does have something else that belonged to Michael."

Garlinger nodded. "The sterling silver bracelet he was wearing." She toyed with the coffee cup in front of her. "It was a high school graduation gift from Art, and Michael never took it off." She gave me a cold, hard stare. "We couldn't find it anywhere. So, yes, we're pretty sure the killer has it."

Sometimes, it's horrible to be right. I stood up and walked toward the window, looking out onto 10th Street. That the killer had desecrated Michael's body even more, made me ill. He was a monster. Not the kind that came out from under the bed at night to scare little children, but a real one straight from hell. I turned back to the group. Each person was looking at me, as if wondering where I was going with this. "Maybe we shouldn't tell Art about my gift from the killer." *Especially given how weird he was behaving last night.*

Agent Garlinger nodded her agreement. "There's no need for him to know about this."

We discussed the break-in for a while longer, not coming up with anything new. Agent Garlinger was leaving and taking the evidence back to the FBI lab—the NYPD had agreed the FBI crime scene techs could process the evidence more thoroughly. She took one parting shot at me before she left. "This is it, Jude. No more investigating, or meddling, or whatever you want to call it. Stay out of this investigation before you get hurt, or before I have to put you in protective custody." Her eyes bored straight into mine. "I mean it."

Then she walked out of The Lounge.

Sully was glowering. "I have something to take care of, then I'll be back.

Be here, Jude."

Then, he turned and followed Agent Garlinger out the door, tossing me dirty looks over his shoulder and shaking his head.

That nagging feeling scratching at me that Sully knew more than he was letting on was back. There wasn't much I could do at the moment, but I'd find out what he was up to one way or another.

In the meantime, I focused on Eric and Agent Maguire, who was back on full-time guard duty. "So, boys, are we having fun yet?" I asked. Of course, I didn't expect an answer.

I left Agent Maguire reading the paper and eating the breakfast I'd ordered for him while Eric and I went upstairs. I assured him Eric would protect me if the killer showed up, and he reluctantly agreed.

Once in my apartment, I locked and double locked the door. Eric took a nap while I showered. Usually, being in the shower eased away my tension, but not this morning. I was a bundle of nerves, still jumping at every unfamiliar sound or errant creak.

I was afraid something else, even worse than Michael's murder, would happen. I couldn't help it. It was genetic. I inherited it from mom's Italian Catholic family who were the most superstitious people you'd ever meet.

My mom's aunts and my grandmother went to mass every day. They made novenas like clockwork, doing nine days of penance and prayer at least once a month as they implored various saints to grant them special favors.

If you had a headache, it wasn't just a headache. It was the *malocchio*—slang for evil eye—that someone had cast on you. The cure was almost as bad as the headache: a handkerchief tied around your temple while three drops of oil were dropped into a bowl of water to send that evil packing. When you asked them about it, they'd roll their eyes at you as if you were from a foreign country and didn't understand English. "We're unique," Aunt Carmela once told me, "You know, different," she added, sounding a lot like her husband's favorite baseball player, Yogi Berra.

In my family, it wasn't good things that came in threes. It was the opposite. So, counting my three notes from the killer and his attack on me, it's no wonder that, even though I'd had more than my three strikes, I knew it wouldn't be over until it was over.

Chapter Thirty-Two

Saturday morning, Agent Maguire knocked on my door at ten. I was awake but not in the mood to have a minder trailing behind me all day.

"Are they paying you overtime to be my bodyguard?" I asked.

"Uh, yeah. Why are you asking?" I could see I'd caught him off guard.

I nodded. "Good. You're going to earn it. Come with me."

Two minutes later I was unlocking the door to The Lounge and shutting off the alarm. "This is your lucky day. You're going to learn the bar business from the ground up." I tossed him an apron. "And I wouldn't want you to get your nice clothes all dirty."

I put on Cyndi Lauper's "Girls Just Want to Have Fun" and let the playlist of my favorite women singers blast through the bar for the next few hours as we took inventory. I had Agent Maguire pull out the bottles of liquor from behind the bar as I measured the amounts left in each one and wrote the numbers on a notepad so I could reconcile the bar sales and figure out the percentage of cost. Well, Eric would help with that.

As each shelf was emptied, I had Agent Maguire clean the glass while I went down to the stockroom for the replacements I needed. I usually did this task on my own, but having a helper, even a reluctant one, made it so much easier. Besides, it was fun to boss around an FBI agent.

As fit and strong as he seemed, it was obvious he wasn't used to this kind of work. "Think of the bending and stretching as a warm-up for the gym," I told him. "Help keep you in shape for running after the bad guys."

After about another hour, we were done. The shelves were gleaming and the bar was fully stocked.

My stomach started rumbling, signaling it was time for food. I called up to Eric and told him to join us for lunch. We had talked until late into the night and I was feeling much better about our relationship. So, I hoped, was he.

I decided to invade Pete's kitchen and make lunch. Since I really didn't cook much, I raided the refrigerator for some cold cuts and whipped up prosciutto and fresh mozzarella sandwiches on rosemary focaccia bread with a hint of pesto. Over the sandwiches, which were delicious, I tried to pump Maguire for information about the case.

"No dice, Ms. Dillane. Agent Garlinger would kick my butt out of the Bureau."

"It's Jude," I replied, turning on the charm and looking into his eyes.

He started to laugh. "Not going to work, Ms....Jude. I like you and all, but I value my job...and my life more." He got up and poured himself more coffee, gesturing with the carafe to check if Eric or I wanted any. We both declined. I poked Eric in the ribs and whispered, "Think that last gibe was meant for me?"

When Agent Maguire sat back down, I tried again. "Will you just answer one question?" He let out a sigh and gave me the look my mom used to use when she was so fed up with me that she'd just give in. I took it as a yes. "So," I asked, placing my elbows on the table and resting my chin in my palms, "Does Agent Garlinger have a real suspect yet? And, if she does, is it someone from around here?"

"That's two questions and you know I can't answer either one, but I give you props for trying."

I made a face and sat back in my chair. "Okay. I give up." He smiled in relief. "For now," I added.

With that, Pete walked into the kitchen. "Did I hear right? Jude Dillane is giving up? Is the earth standing still?" As if the sarcasm wasn't enough, he poked a finger in his ear and shook it like he was clearing it out so he could hear better.

I tossed a grape from a bowl on the counter at him. He caught it and popped it into his mouth.

"We were just leaving." I stood up. "Let's give Pete space to do his prep work." I tossed another grape at my partner. "And, Pete, make sure there's no ear wax in tonight's specials."

Back out by the bar, I told Agent Maguire he could leave. Eric was going to stay with me and there was no need to worry. I'd be safe.

His desire to dump me outweighed his fear of getting caught out by Agent Garlinger. Eric and I both promised I'd be good as we shooed him out the door. Also, now I'd have something to hold over him.

"Well now," Eric said as he nuzzled my neck from behind me and wrapped his strong arms around my waist, "what would you like to do with the rest of the afternoon?"

I took his hand. "Follow me," I purred in my most seductive voice as I led him out of the back of the restaurant, nodding to Pete that we were leaving.

Outside, the air was frigid, wind blowing hard and howling, whipping up swirls of dust and detritus in the alleyway. There was nothing as gloomy as a cloud-laden, single-digit day in January. The overbearing sky brought New Year's Day crashing back into my mind, reminding me of how cold Michael's body must have been in the dumpster—not that he'd felt it after the knife had been plunged into his heart. I shivered, and Eric pulled me in to him, misunderstanding my body language as a reaction to the cold.

"Let's take a long weekend somewhere warm, Miami or the Bahamas. Get away from the cold. We could both use a break."

I murmured something non-committal as we pushed open the door to my building. *If only*, I thought.

When the elevator crawled its way past my floor, Eric let go of my hand. "Where are we going?" he asked.

"Just to Sully's for a few minutes. He's been acting all secret service on me and I want to find out why."

"I thought you agree—"

I cut him off with a kiss. "This isn't meddling. It's...just a chat among friends. You know, to find out where things stand." *Especially since Agent*

Maguire was a dead end, I thought. I took back Eric's hand and squeezed it. "And you're with me, so full disclosure, right?"

Two minutes later, I was knocking on Sully's door waiting for his usual command to enter. Instead, I saw the cover over the peephole slide back and imagined Sully looking through. A second later, I heard the lock click open and Sully let us in to the apartment. As always, it was pristine. No dust would dare show itself on Sully's shelves or dirt leave its mark on his floors. Even the sun cooperated, peeking out through the clouds and casting a soft glow over the living room. I sighed, thinking again of the chaos in my place—once again filled with Eric's things, as well.

"Hey, how are you?" He asked, directing his question at Eric. "Some of us were feeling a little antsy while you were away. Poking around and getting into trouble."

"I'm good," Eric replied, ignoring Sully's crack. "It's nice to be home." He gave my shoulder a little squeeze. A warning not to react to Sully's little jibe.

"Yeah, well, thank God you're back to keep an eye on this one." He tipped his head toward me.

"Don't talk about me like I'm not here." I tossed a nasty look at Sully and took a step closer. "I have questions." I glowered at him. "And I want answers."

Sully turned and walked toward his liquor cabinet. He opened it and took out a bottle of Jameson and held it up in our direction. Both of us shook our heads no and Sully poured himself a small shot. "Sit," he said, more a command than an invitation.

"Before you start in on me, you should know Lanie hasn't told me anything." He took a good sip of his whiskey. "God knows I've asked."

"Okay, I'll buy that." I hadn't gotten much out of Agent Maguire, either. "But you're up to something, I know it."

"I was thinking about your idea that one of The 10th Street Irregulars could be the killer." Sully paused. "You might be right." Then he downed the rest of his drink.

I was in shock, unable to move or speak. Finally, my brain started working again and I croaked out, "What? What are you talking about?"

"Let me explain." Sully started pacing with his hand behind his back, in true military fashion. He got to the end of the room, then turned, marched halfway back, and faced Eric and me.

"Lanie let me look at the files on the other cases." He held up his hand. "Before you go ballistic, she wouldn't let me see anything at all on Michael's murder, no matter how hard I pushed.

"The more I looked at the intel, the surer I was that the killer was from around here." He stopped speaking and a look of fury filled his eyes. "On New Year's Eve, the only people Michael spent time with before he left The Lounge were The Irregulars. Art mentioned they came down to the bar just after Michael arrived at his apartment."

I already knew that, which was what led me to my suspicions about The Irregulars in the first place. I started to speak, but Sully held out his hand toward me. "I know I scoffed at your idea, but the more I thought about it…well, I believe you could be right."

Sully resumed his pacing, his words coming to us like a ping-pong ball bouncing back and forth. "I started doing some recon on the guys, and I've discovered some unsettling information."

I'd been quiet while Sully explained his "operation," but I couldn't wait a moment longer. I jumped off the couch and stopped him as he was making another turn toward us.

"Jesus, Sully, who the hell do you think it is?"

"Tony Napoli."

I started shaking my head before he even finished saying Tony's name. The words flew out of my mouth like a barrage of gunfire splattering in every direction. "No. You're wrong. Not Tony. Tony's the one who saved me from the killer. He's not the guy. Can't be."

"Jude," Eric reached out to me from the couch, "sit down. Let Sully finish."

I turned on him as quick as a snake striking. "There's nothing to finish." Then I looked up at Sully. "You're wrong."

Sully took a seat opposite the couch and raised his hands in supplication. "Hear me out, okay? Just listen for…"

His words petered out. I knew he was going to add "once" but thought better of it.

"Okay," I agreed, "but you're wrong." I sat back and crossed my arms around my middle, waiting.

Sully ran his hand through his silvery hair, leaving little trails across his scalp. "I spent some time following each of The Irregulars, trying to get a feel for who they are."

I interrupted. "You know who they are. Your friends."

Sully nodded. "You're right to a point. I do know each of them, but we're more drinking buddies than friends." He leaned forward, his posture letting us know he was serious, deciding how he was going to explain what he'd done.

I did some research on Oscar, Jim, and Tony. When I searched online, the usual info came up. Oscar's address and his job, his Facebook info. Jim's garage and the website for that, as well as a professional association." He paused for a moment. "But there was nothing at all on Tony. He could have been a ghost."

I had been suspicious of Tony at first. Never using a credit card and not revealing much about himself had deepened my doubts. But I'd changed my mind.

I looked up at Sully. "Nothing?" I asked. "No address, or business info, Facebook, Twitter?" Sully shook his head. "How can that be possible? Everyone is out there somewhere," I ventured.

"Not if you're not who you say you are." Sully let that hang in the air for a moment. "Believe me, I searched hard. I even called in a favor from a private detective I know. It's like Tony Napoli was never born."

Eric had been quiet up until this point. "So, you think he's hiding who he really is?"

"I do." Sully sat back. "It made me suspicious, so I followed him."

I was still stunned by Sully's revelation. If Tony Napoli didn't exist, who was the man using that name? Was it possible he'd been responsible for the attack on me?

Questions filled my head, and my voice stuck in my throat as I started to speak. "When you followed him, what did you find out?"

"Not enough to seal the deal." Sully's marine-perfect posture gave way and he slumped back into the chair. "He met with a nasty-looking character over on 11th Street and it looked like they made some sort of exchange."

"Could have been drugs," Eric said.

"That's what I thought," Sully replied, "so I stuck to him. He went into one of those abandoned tenements on 13th Street and stayed in there for quite a while. When he came out, he walked over to 11th again, sat on the steps of the old Free Municipal Baths, then got up and walked home."

A shiver inched its way down my spine. "That's where Jake Hammity—"

"—Was found." Sully finished my thought.

Had Tony returned to the scene of his crime, I wondered?

"Guys," Eric said holding up his hand, "this is pure speculation. It's not evidence of anything, let alone murder." He was laying out his arguments the way he'd lay out a spreadsheet. "Using a false name is not a crime. Lots of people change their names for a number of reasons. Especially people who might want to get away from tricky situations, or who want to start over.

"Also, he's the one who helped Jude and ran after the guy who attacked her. He couldn't be doing both things at the same time."

"But what if it was a setup? What if the guy I saw him meet attacked Jude so Tony could 'save' her?" I could see Sully wanted a way to make his supposition real.

Neither Eric or Sully had been with me when my attacker struck. If it was a setup, he'd gone way beyond playing a role. If Tony hadn't shown up when he did, I might be dead.

"And what about Art?" I asked. "Did you do 'research' on him, as well?" I remembered how strange Art had been in the bar the other night. Sully had upset me, accusing Tony without any real proof.

"Art?" he said. Derision colored his voice. "Michael was his *brother*. How could you even think such a thing?"

I stood up from the couch. It was time to end this conversation. "All we're doing is second-guessing each other. I need to think about this." I watched Sully, trying to judge his mood. "Please don't go off half-cocked and do something stupid."

Sully snorted at me, obviously still annoyed at my mentioning Art. "Words of wisdom from Ms. Impetuous."

I ignored his remark and patted him on the shoulder, then grabbed Eric's hand. It was time to go. "Come by tonight. It's Dean's bourbon event. I know you wouldn't want to miss it."

Chapter Thirty-Three

Eric and I went back to my apartment and began to pick over what Sully had told us. I shook my head back and forth like it was attached to a rag doll instead of my body. "He's wrong. It's not Tony."

"Maybe you should call Agent Garlinger," Eric suggested, "and tell her what Sully's thinking. You said she had a person of interest in mind, so she could at least steer him clear of Tony and let him know he's off base."

"And he'd stop nosing around Tony." I smiled up at Eric. "That's not a bad idea. I knew I kept you around for a reason."

I had just jumped out of the shower when my cell rang. "This better not be Sully," I muttered under my breath, not wanting to disturb Eric, who was napping.

"Jude! It's Kara. You've got to come in right now. There's a hysterical woman named Jamila here insisting on seeing you."

"Who? Jamila?" She was supposed to be on a date with Dean. What was she doing at the bar?

"Are you sure?" I asked.

"Yes, and I can't get her to calm down. Please hurry."

I jumped into my work clothes, shook Eric awake, and hurried down to the bar. Jamila was a lot of things: colorful, vivacious, excitable—but I'd never seen her hysterical. My stomach was in knots as I entered The Lounge, wondering what had happened to cause this outburst in my friend. If Dean had done something, I'd…

The thought flew out of my mind when I saw her. She looked ashen and dull, as if all the color had been leeched out of her. Even her bright, blue sweater looked faded.

I rushed to her. "Jamila, what's wrong? What happened?"

She bit back a sob and grabbed my hand. "It's Dean. He's gone."

The breath whooshed out of my chest and my vision went blurry. I grabbed on to the back of a barstool to keep myself from falling. "Gone?" I rasped, my thoughts racing ahead to the worst-case scenario. "Did he have an accident?" She shook her head. "Well, what happened? What do you mean gone? Jamila—"

Eric walked in right then, took one look at us, and steered us to a table in the back of the dining room. "What's going on?" he asked, concern clouding his expression.

At his words, Jamila started sobbing harder. "I…don't know…I'm not sure but, Dean…he's gone."

Every time she said the word "gone," my heart jumped. "Please, Jamila, start from the beginning, okay?" I tried to keep my voice calm as I looked at Eric, who I was sure could see the panic in my eyes.

"I met Dean at his apartment like we'd agreed on," she began. "We went out to lunch at a place around the corner from his house and then we took a cab to Bryant Park. Dean said it's the last day the booths would be open. It was very crowded."

She paused, and I signaled to Eric to go to the bar and get her a drink. He nodded, and a few moments later, he handed Jamila a snifter of brandy.

"Take a sip of that," I gestured to the glass in her hand, "then tell me the rest."

Jamila's hand was trembling as she lifted the glass to her lips and sipped, but the fiery liquid seemed to calm her almost immediately. "It was so pretty there. The holiday lights were still up, and all the stores were having sales. We walked from booth to booth looking at everything. There was even an ice-skating rink, which looked like fun."

I could sense the old Jamila coming back, riffing on the people and things she saw. I interrupted her with a soft, "Um hum. And then?"

Her face sagged as she realized she'd strayed from the real story. "I wanted to buy a gift for my little sister, a pair of earrings I'd seen in one of the booths we'd passed. Dean said he'd get us some apple cider while I did my shopping and meet me at the jewelry booth."

She paused and took another small sip of the brandy, which seemed to fortify her, bringing a little bit of color to her face. "I finished up and was waiting for Dean to come back, as we'd agreed." A tear slipped down her face. "I stood there for a while, thinking maybe I'd misunderstood and he'd said to meet him at the cider place. Finally, I went looking and couldn't find him.

"Oh, Jude, I looked everywhere. First, I thought he might just have left me on my own, but then I realized he wouldn't do that." She shook her head. "I thought something had happened to him and I checked with the information booth and the first aid station. But he'd hadn't been there, either. Then, I thought maybe he'd gone back to his apartment for some reason and I decided I'd go see if he was there. If he'd dumped me in the middle of the park, I was going to let him have it." The edge of a smile appeared at the corner of her mouth, until it started trembling along with the rest of her.

"When I got there, I found this on his door."

She held out her hand, which held a crumpled piece of paper, and pushed it toward me. "It was addressed to you. I thought that was weird. Why would a note to you be on Dean's door? I rang the bell and could hear it echo inside the apartment. Dean wasn't there. I didn't know what to do. I looked at the note taped to the door and decided to open it." A sob caught in her throat. "I was sorry I did the second I read it." Her tears were flowing freely now. "I'm scared, Jude."

I took the paper from her, just as afraid as she was to read it. My hand was trembling as I smoothed it out, and a part of me already knew what I was going to find.

Eric walked up behind me and put his hand on my shoulder. I held the paper a little higher so we could both read it together. it's wrinkles and creases seemed to make the words wavy and hard to make out. Or maybe it was the tears spilling from my eyes. The message, printed just like the first one I'd received, chilled me to the bone.

I WARNED YOU TO STAY OUT OF MY BUSINESS.
BUT YOU COULDN'T, COULD YOU? NOW, YOU'LL PAY
THE PRICE. I HAVE SOMEONE CLOSE TO YOU
AND I'M GOING TO KILL HIM—OR MAYBE I'LL
KEEP HIM ALIVE FOR A LITTLE WHILE LONGER,
JUST TO MAKE YOU SUFFER BITCH.

I didn't realize that my breath was coming in raspy gulps until Eric gripped my shoulder tighter. "He's got Dean." I said to Eric through my tears. I turned around and looked up into his face, all rational thought deserting me. "He's going to kill him, like he killed Michael and those other men. He's going to kill…"

I could hear my voice rising, ratcheting up from panic to true hysteria. Eric's pleas to calm down fell on deaf ears. I kept repeating the words "He's going to kill him," over and over until Eric finally shook me hard enough to bring me back to the present.

Jamila gawked at both of us, eyes as wide as a scared doe's, taking this all in. She didn't know about the murders this killer had committed, but she'd read the note and knew Dean was in terrible danger. "Who is this from?" she asked. "Why would this…this crazy person take Dean?"

When neither of us answered her, she started pleading. "Please, Jude, why does some maniac want to kill Dean?"

How could I tell her the truth? That Dean was in a madman's clutches because of me. I started to explain, but the words wouldn't come. My throat closed in pain each time I tried to force the sounds out. Finally, Eric took over and, for once, I was happy—eager even—to have someone speak for me.

When he was finished, fresh tears were pouring down Jamila's face. I reached out my hand and held onto hers, trying to comfort the both of us.

Eric looked at me, then at his watch. I'd lost all track of time. It was time for The Lounge to open for business. My first thought was to close for the day, to send everyone home until…until what? Until we found Dean? We weren't going to find him so quickly, not on our own. I sighed and gazed at Eric. I willed myself to calm down and be professional, for the staff and the business, and for Dean.

Letting out a deep breath, I spoke to Eric. "Why don't you and Jamila go upstairs. I'll tell Kara to watch the bar while I speak to Pete. Then I'll come right up and we'll call Agent Garlinger and Sully."

Eric agreed and took Jamila out the back and around to the building's entrance. I had a quick chat with Kara, explaining that Dean was ill and couldn't make it in. She'd seen the state Jamila was in and she knew there was more to the story than I was letting on, but she could tell from my face that asking questions would be useless. I asked her to stay put until I could get back and help and told her to ask one of the wait staff to pitch in at the service bar if she got jammed up.

Then I went in search of Pete. One look at my face and he knew something was wrong. He didn't question me when I crooked my finger at him to follow. We moved from the kitchen to my office downstairs and I told him everything Jamila had relayed about the afternoon. Then I showed him the note addressed to me.

"I don't know how much more of this I can take, Jude." His face was a mask of icy control as he spoke, handing the note back to me. "What if this guy kills Dean?" he asked. "I mean we don't even know if Dean is alive, or if the maniac stabbed him to death already.

"You and The Lounge are in his crosshairs and I don't think he's going to stop until—"

"Until he gets me?" I asked, my voice devoid of all emotion.

"I didn't mean that, but he's out for more blood. And, if this gets in the papers—about Dean, I mean—our business will suffer." Pete was more upset and agitated than I'd ever seen him. "We talked about this before, Jude, and you know how I feel." He shook his head. "All this unwelcome and sensational publicity. The blowback could end us."

Of course, he was right. First, a murder outside our back door and, God forbid, another one with Dean as the victim, would be nothing but bad publicity, something The Lounge might not survive. It would be like a pariah in the restaurant community.

"Think about what you're doing, Jude," Pete added in a tone that held more meaning than the words implied. After the body in our dumpster and being dragged in by the police, I understood how he felt.

I nodded and we walked back upstairs. We left it at that for the moment, and I went up to my apartment to call in the troops. I'd already wasted enough time. We had to find Dean.

If the killer had wanted me to suffer, he was getting his wish. My heart was cracking in pieces and all I could think about was Dean, drugged and bound somewhere waiting for the inevitable.

Because no matter what he'd written, with its slight promise of the hope of keeping Dean alive, if Dean had seen the man who grabbed him, the killer would have no choice but to end his life.

Chapter Thirty-Four

My talk with Pete had taken longer than I expected, and Sully was in my apartment when I arrived. Eric had called him, and he came down immediately. In turn, Sully had called Elaine Garlinger and she was on her way with reinforcements. Probably Agents Maguire and Samuelson, among them.

I hoped she wasn't going to shut me out, because this time, no matter what she said, I wasn't leaving. I had skin in the game. There wasn't any way I was going to be sidelined.

Of course, Eric and Sully wouldn't see it that way, so now wasn't the time to push it. I'd listen to what Garlinger had to say, then take it from there.

She arrived a few minutes later as did Ortiz and Delmonico. Fortunately, Garlinger took charge of the situation. She asked the detectives to escort Jamila to the station and look after her. There was no mistaking what she meant: they were to take her statement and treat her well. She was not a suspect, just an innocent bystander. What happened that afternoon was a lot for her to process, and anything—even the smallest detail of what she'd seen and heard—could help the investigation.

The two detectives didn't look happy. Big surprise. But they agreed to do as she asked.

Eric volunteered to go with Jamila. He knew she was scared and confused and would be better off with someone she knew to look after her. He would bring her back to The Lounge after she spoke with the detectives. She could stay with us or Eric would make sure she got home. He told me all this in a whisper, and I agreed it was a good idea. Something she told the police might make more sense to Eric than to them. Agent Garlinger had agreed and made sure the detectives understood that Eric was to stay with Jamila the whole time.

When the detectives left with Jamila and Eric, Sully and I sat down with the agents. Garlinger dispatched Maguire to the BAU forensic lab with the note Jamila had found. Probably, the only fingerprints on it would be mine and Jamila's. She sent Samuelson and two other CSIs to join the NYPD who were processing Eric's apartment. Then she turned to me.

"This is not your fault. I know you think it is, but this guy, he's showing off, mocking and provoking all of us. Saying 'just try and catch me.'" She balled her hands into fists, and I could feel the heat coming from her in waves of frustration. "Dean was…is," she corrected herself, "a crime of revenge. He's pissed off and he wants to show us he's in charge. Killing on New Year's Eve isn't important anymore." She shook her head. "Taunting you is. And he's raised the stakes. He won't get away with it. We'll find him and stop him."

"Before he kills Dean?" I asked, my anger rising and superseding my fear. I stared into her dark eyes, challenging her to answer. She met my gaze and held it. Finally, I was the one to look away.

"Yes," she replied softly, not rising to take my bait.

"Is it Sully's suspect? Tony Napoli?" I watched her carefully as I asked my question. Her eyes flicked toward Sully, but she didn't react and her face remained calm. "Or, didn't he tell you about his conclusion that Tony is the killer?"

"Jude," Sully broke in, "stop."

"What's this about Tony Napoli?" Garlinger asked, whipping around so fast her long, dark hair covered her face for moment. "What the hell is wrong with the two of you?" Her words hit us hard and heavy.

She pointed at Sully accusingly. "Do you want to get yourself killed, as well? Because it seems the both of you," she swept her hand around to include me, "are doing everything you can to make that happen."

She rose from the chair she was sitting in and leaned in toward us. "Listen to me. Stop this right now. We," her voice crackled with heat as her temper rose and her face turned red, "have a person of interest we're looking at."

She held up a hand. "And before you ask for the tenth time, I cannot tell you who that is.

"You want us to find Dean? While he's still alive? Then stay out of this investigation. Both of you." She grabbed her coat and bag and headed for the door. "Jude, go downstairs and do what you're supposed to do: run your bar and restaurant. Sully, you come with me. I'm not finished with you yet."

We both stared at her open-mouth. Sully had a look on his face I'd never seen before, one of meek submission. Then he sighed and followed her into the hallway.

I, on the other hand, hadn't been told off like this since Sister Mary Margaret overheard me saying "the disgusting F word," as she described it. I had detention for a month, and she sent me right off to confess my sins to Father Colapietro.

I wondered what she'd do if she heard me now as I banged around my apartment, punching pillows and tossing magazines and clothes around while I used every four-letter word I could think of.

Chapter Thirty-Five

Trying to hold it together, I marched downstairs to The Lounge and took my place behind the bar. Kara moved to the service end while I worked the front. I kept my phone out on the back bar, so I wouldn't miss Eric when he called. I imagined they'd be at the station for a while, as Jamila told and retold the events of this afternoon. As angry as I'd been with Agent Garlinger, I knew she was doing Jamila a favor by allowing Eric to be with her. I just wished he'd let me know what was happening.

At around seven, several customers asked about Dean and the bourbon tasting he'd invited them to. I had to tell them it was off for tonight and we'd reschedule. I added that Dean wasn't feeling well and would be disappointed if we went ahead without him.

Since Pete had already prepared the dishes that were to accompany the tasting, I served the smoked riblets, grilled peach slices in bacon, and sweet potato tarts as freebee bar snacks to our customers who decided to hang out anyway and stay for a drink or two. The customers loved them, even without the bourbon. It crossed my mind that these might be some of the last dishes Pete prepared for The Corner Lounge and that brought my mood even lower.

A little while later, Sully came in and took his usual place at the bar. He looked even worse than I felt—drawn and dull-eyed, shoulders sagging.

"Well, at least you're still alive," I said as I slid a coaster in front of him and poured his usual shot of Jameson.

"Barely," he replied, knocking back the drink in one gulp. "Another, if you don't mind."

I raised one eyebrow as I poured a hefty shot into his glass. "So, what did she say?"

"You mean before or after she practically eviscerated me for acting like one of the Hardy Boys?"

I had to smile at this. "Both," I replied.

"Lanie reminded me that she was in charge of the investigation. Not me, or you." He gave me a pointed look to make sure I got the drift. "She said we were only making things harder for the team by meddling."

"Ok. I heard that before. What else?"

"Then she reamed me out for encouraging you in this 'foolhardy investigation' you're conducting on your own." He held up his hand. "Her words, not mine."

"But you didn't…aren't," I protested.

Sully toyed with his glass. "I know that, and I told her, but Lanie doesn't believe me." He took a good sip of his Irish. "And, last but not least, she told me to forget Tony Napoli or anyone else I might suspect."

"So, it isn't Tony, then. I was right."

"Are you even listening?" The frustration was pouring from his voice like lava from an active volcano. "We need to be done with this. Let her do her job and, if we're very lucky, find Dean while he's still alive."

At that we both went silent, me looking down at the bar, thinking about my friend, and Sully gazing into the depths of his drink.

This pointless introspection didn't last long. The front door opened, and the rest of The Irregulars poured into The Lounge with Tony leading the way. The temperature had dropped into the teens and the men brought the frigid air in with them, blowing on their hands and stomping their feet.

"Speak of the devil," I dipped my chin toward the group. "Don't mention what happened to Dean, especially to Art." *Something told me he didn't need to know about this, or how worried we were,*

Tony, Jim, Oscar, and Art gathered around Sully, shouting out greetings. They'd obviously had a nip or two elsewhere before heading to The Lounge. Jim had left on his red baseball cap with its "Deems Automotive" logo embroidered on the top. I gave him a stern look and he removed it immediately. He knew my no hats rule. The Lounge was a classy place, after all.

"So, what's with the bourbon tasting?" Oscar asked. "Where's Dean?"

"He's not feeling well. I postponed it." I kept the explanation as matter-of-fact as possible.

"Yeah, right," piped in Jim. He gave me a cocky wink. "He's probably playing hooky with that cute little Jamila girl he's running all over town with."

"Don't be so jealous," Tony snickered. "You're way too old for her, pal."

They all laughed as I poured their drinks, except Sully, who was scrutinizing his friends like he could read their minds. They were too busy chowing down on the bar snacks to notice.

"What's with you?" I whispered to him. "Thought we were going to act normal. Don't you think you should join them?" I added as the group moved to a table in the cocktail lounge.

"I don't know. Something's off." he glanced over at the guys.

"Are you still focusing on Tony?" I cut my eyes toward the group.

Sully shook his head. "Naw. It's…I don't know."

Just then Oscar called out, "C'mon, Sully, we need your opinion on older men dating younger women." They all started hooting at Jim again.

Sully snatched up his drink, rapped on the bar, and got up to join them, a scowl on his face. He put some money down, then moved toward their table, a smile now firmly in place. "Well, let me tell you about that," he said with bravado as he swaggered away.

Couldn't they hear how false he sounded? He'd been fine until The Irregulars had come in. Something they said had put him on alert. I thought about the conversation and couldn't find anything off. I didn't know what was bugging Sully, but I was going to find out as soon as possible.

I didn't get the opportunity that evening. About a half hour later, he left the group and the bar, with a curt wave in my direction. *Jeez,* I thought, *what did I do now?* I was too busy to dwell on it and kept pouring drinks and explaining that the bourbon tasting had been postponed.

Dean would have been pleased—I caught myself thinking in the past tense and stopped. *No. He will be pleased to hear that when we find him.* I aimed my thoughts firmly at the future.

Just then, Eric walked in giving me a rueful smile. "I'm sorry I didn't call," he said before I could get a word in. "I thought it would just be better to come home as soon as they let us go." He shrugged out of his coat, hung it on a rack on the side of the bar, and took the seat Sully usually occupied in the corner. Finally settled, he leaned over and gave me a quick kiss. "No Fibbie babysitter for me?" I asked, looking at the entryway.

"I told Garlinger I'd be with you every moment." He smiled. "She practically made me swear on a Bible that I'd keep you out of trouble and in sight at all times."

"She's such a romantic," I said. "How's Jamila?"

"Exhausted. She's upstairs. I thought it would be better if she stayed with us tonight. I made her a cup of tea and turned on the TV." I nodded. That was fine with me. "They made her go over the timeline of this afternoon at least a dozen times."

"Did she remember anything helpful?"

"You know, I'm not exactly sure." A puzzled expression crossed his face. "Agent Garlinger joined us pretty soon after we arrived at the station." *After she let Sully have it,* I thought. "She let the detectives conduct the interview but sat in for most of it." He took a sip of the wine I'd poured for him, then continued. "At one point, Jamila mentioned that Dean thought he saw someone he knew, but in a confused kind of way, surprised this person would be at the holiday market."

"Did Dean mention who it was?"

"No, and she wasn't sure whether it was a man or a woman." Eric leaned his elbows on the bar and scrubbed his face with his hands. He brought them to rest on the bar and I covered them with my own. His eyes were heavy-lidded and the stubble on his cheeks added to his overall look of tiredness. "She looked in the direction Dean was facing but all she saw was a bunch of people bundled up in coats, scarves, and hats." He reached for his wine and swirled it around in the glass. "She didn't see the person, and

Dean kind of shrugged it off."

"Did Garlinger think it was important?" This could be a lead, someone who saw Dean, or, more likely, the person who grabbed him. If it was, in fact, someone Dean knew, he wouldn't have been suspicious.

"Yeah, I think so. But she was pretty cool about it. Asked Jamila more questions about the encounter. Where they were exactly when Dean noticed the person. If Dean saw him or her again. Whether Jamila noticed anyone she recognized. You know, stuff like that. She kept it up for a while, then she excused herself and left the interview."

"What did you think?" My voice trembled as I asked the question.

"Garlinger obviously thought it was important. When she came back into the room, she said we could leave.

"I gotta say Ortiz and Delmonico were pretty easy on Jamila." He frowned. "Not the way I remember them behaving."

"Garlinger must have something on them," I joked, "if they were making nice." I leaned in and gave him a kiss. "Thank you for being with Jamila. I don't think she could have handled this on her own."

Eric shook his head. "Don't underestimate her. She was scared and in shock over what happened. But once she settled down, she got through the interview okay." He gave me a wicked grin. "That girl has *cajones*. After all, she's a Bronx girl, just like you."

Chapter Thirty-Six

Eric hung out with me until I closed the bar, even though I could see he was dead tired. Eltee stayed around, too. We'd filled him in about Dean, and he was devastated at the news. I knew from now on he'd be checking out everyone who came into The Lounge and looking at them as the possible New Year's Eve Killer.

Pete left after he closed the kitchen, giving me a curt goodbye on the way out and a muttered, "See you tomorrow." This was not good. One more thing I'd have to address, and soon.

Upstairs, Jamila had fallen asleep on the couch, her face beautifully calm in repose. I grabbed a quilt from the hall closet and tucked it around her. She hardly knew Dean, yet she was right in the middle of this horror story. I'm sure she felt terrified for him, and maybe even a little bit guilty. There wasn't much I, or anyone, could do to make her feel better, except finding Dean alive and unharmed.

Eric and I went to bed, and I clung to him like he, too, might disappear at any moment. It was irrational, but I couldn't banish the crazy thoughts. I tossed and turned and woke up with the sun. I let Eric sleep, and smiled at his gentle snoring, which usually irritated me to no end. I didn't want to wake Jamila, who was snuggled into a ball on the couch.

I had no such qualms about waking Sully. I washed and dressed quickly, left Eric a note, and hoofed it upstairs.

Of course, Sully was already awake. He'd probably even made his bed—being a marine for twenty-five years would beat the untidiness out of anyone. He let me in and headed to the coffeemaker, which was gurgling away, the aroma it emitted making my senses perk up.

We both spoke at the same time.

"So, what gives?"

"What's going on?"

"You first." Sully waved a hand in my direction.

"Well, Jamila remembered something, although it's not much." I shrugged. "She thought Dean recognized someone at the holiday market, someone he didn't expect to see there."

"Did he tell her who it was?" Sully asked, excitement coloring his words.

"No. He blew it off and didn't mention it again." I sipped my coffee and thought about the person Dean had spotted.

"Think it was the killer?"

"Well, Dean wouldn't just wander off with someone he didn't know," I replied. "Maybe the guy told him some story that led him to leave. Probably thought he'd be back in a few minutes."

Sully was pacing in military precision. "Dean is a big guy. He'd defend himself against a stranger...and probably come out on top." He stopped and balled his hands into fists. "Had to be someone he knew."

I nodded in agreement. *But who?* I wondered.

"Listen, Jude, I know the company that does the security for Bryant Park and the holiday market. A friend of mine works for them. Maybe he can help us."

"How?" I asked, dubious about this connection.

"There are CCTV cameras everywhere in the park. I'm sure the cops asked for yesterday's footage, but the security company may have a backup copy." Sully pulled out his cell. "What time did Dean disappear?"

"I think it was around four o'clock. Jamila was buying a piece of jewelry while he went for apple cider. You think your pal will be able to give you the video from the cameras? Do you know for sure if his company keeps a copy?"

"Not for certain, but I'll find out."

"There's got to be a lot of footage to look through," I said, thinking it would take some time to do this.

Sully was already on the phone, explaining what he wanted and why. I could tell from his end of the conversation that his pal was reluctant, but finally agreed. "Think he'll come through?" I asked as he clicked off.

Sully nodded. "He owes me."

I was sure he did, but I didn't want to ask what for. Instead, I looked at my watch. "I think it's time to wake Eric and Jamila. I'm sure she'll want to get home." I walked around the kitchen counter and put my mug in the sink. "Keep me posted. When you get the footage, let me know and I'll help go through it," I added as I left the apartment.

Sully nodded, and I closed the door behind me. On my way back to my apartment, I realized I'd never asked what he'd found so strange the previous night at The Lounge. I had the feeling he wouldn't have told me anyway.

At home, Eric and Jamila were already awake. She looked marginally better than she had yesterday, her face scrubbed clean of makeup and her mane of dark hair pulled back in a ponytail, but her eyes were like dark pools reflecting her sadness.

"Anything new from Sully?" Eric jutted his chin toward the ceiling.

I flicked my eyes in Jamila's direction and subtly shook my head. "Um, no," I replied, certain Eric would get my message that I didn't want to speak in front of her.

Jamila came over and gave me a hug. "Thanks for taking care of me." She turned her head and included Eric in the big smile that formed on her lips. "I...I don't know what I would have done without you guys." Her voice faltered. "Do you think we'll find Dean before—"

I didn't let her finish her thought. "The FBI And NYPD are doing everything they can to get him back." I squeezed her hand. "I promise we'll let you know the minute we hear anything."

"Eric volunteered to drive me home, but I've been enough trouble. I'll take an Uber."

"Are you sure?" I asked.

Eric piped in. "Really, Jamila. I don't mind." I could see he was as worried about her as I was.

She shook her head. "I need to be on my own. You know," a small smile turned the corners of her mouth upward, "to process what happened, as you might say." She gazed down at her phone. "The car will be here in two minutes. I'd better go downstairs." She grabbed her coat and shrugged into it. "You promise to let me know about…"

Her voice was cracking, and I moved in to hug her again. "Cross my heart and hope to…" I couldn't finish the old adage. The word "die" stuck in my throat.

Eric intervened, "At least let me walk you downstairs."

Jamila nodded and they left the apartment. I was alone for the first time since the day before. As I stared at the closed door, I had to fight to keep the tears from coming. I couldn't just stand there doing nothing, contrary to what Agent Garlinger had commanded.

While I sat there, a plan took shape in my mind. I would contact Amanda Finley. I needed to hear her take on what happened on that long-ago New Year's Eve. I'd give her a call and ask to meet. That's if she didn't hang up on me when I told her what I wanted.

Chapter Thirty-Seven

I was just about to tell Eric my plan when he burst into the apartment looking more pissed off than I'd ever seen him.

"What?" I asked as the door slammed behind him.

"You're not going to like this." He placed his hands on my arms, preparing to tell me something his tone made certain I wouldn't want to hear. "Jared Jones and his crew are parked across the street like vultures waiting to pick over a carcass."

"Damn." I shook off his hands and wrapped my own around my middle. "So, they know about Dean?"

He nodded. "And they were shouting questions to Jamila. Fortunately, I got her into her Uber and on her way before they could do too much damage." He uncrossed my arms and led me to the couch. I pushed the cover I'd given Jamila out of the way and sat down.

In the fifteenth century, people had The Inquisition with their instruments of torture, now we had the press with their mics and smartphones. Neither one would give up until they got the response they wanted. At least Jones and his crew weren't standing in front of The Lounge. Sully must have put the fear of God in him last time.

"How did they find out?" I asked.

"How do you think?" Eric's tone was derisive.

"The cops?" I asked. "You think Ortiz and Delmonico called him?" Garlinger will have their badges if they did. She's trying to keep this out of the press."

Eric was peeking out through the blinds and gazing across the street.

"They're still there." He let the slats fall back into place and turned to me. "I think it was someone else," he said pointedly.

His words hit home, and the penny dropped. "The killer?"

"Seems likely." Eric sat down next to me. "If he's taunting us and looking for attention, what better way than getting the media involved?"

I wanted to say the killer was taunting me, but I let it go. Eric was as involved as I was in bringing this black-hearted murderer to justice.

I picked up my cell to call Sully, hoping that he could scare Jones away again, but there was no answer. "Sully's not picking up." I wondered if he'd gone to see his pal about the video footage. "I better let Garlinger know what's going on."

To say that she was not pleased would be the understatement of the century. "You might be right about the tip coming from the killer himself." She paused, and I could imagine her sitting at her desk in her office thinking. "I don't believe either of the detectives would leak Dean's kidnapping. They may be nasty, but both of them have clean records and good busts."

Not how I saw them, but I kept that to myself.

"We're not going to be able to keep this latest incident out of the press for much longer. Damn. We need to catch this guy."

Too late for that, I thought. *They're already on it.*

She changed subjects abruptly. "Are you and Sully staying out of this like I told you to?"

I took my cell away from my ear and made a face at it. Eric just shook his head at me. "Yes. I'm doing as you asked. And Eric is sticking to me like glue." I smiled sweetly at him and batted my eyelashes. She didn't realize I hadn't spoken for Sully.

"Good. Let's keep it that way. I've got to consider how to handle the media. I think the FBI should issue a press release about Dean's disappearance from the holiday market and ask for anyone with information to call us. We'll keep it as a disappearance, not a kidnapping, for now. No mention of New Year's Eve or the other killings. I'll set up a hotline number to field the calls."

"We already know he's been taken by the killer; won't that piss him off?" I asked. "He'll want the credit for this, won't he?"

"I'm counting on it, and it might help to flush him out. Get him to make a mistake."

I didn't like where she was going with this. This was Dean's life we were talking about. We didn't know how long the killer would keep him alive. And if he became angry, it might push him into killing Dean immediately.

I guess I was silent for too long and Garlinger picked up her end of the conversation as though she knew what I was thinking.

"He's still baiting us, Jude. For whatever twisted reason, he wants you to suffer a little longer. We'll find Dean, I promise you." Then she was gone.

I'd put my cell on speaker for the last part of the conversation, so Eric had heard most of it. "We can't just leave this up to her. You know that, don't you?" My voice was quivering, and my emotions threatened to spill over.

He sat next to me and tipped my face up toward his. There was resignation in his eyes, as well as love. "I know. What is it you want to do?"

So I told him.

Chapter Thirty-Eight

I booted up my computer and went to the information I'd downloaded on Amanda Finley and her daughter Chloe from the search I'd done a few days ago. I stared at her address and number and debated if what I was planning was a good idea. Had she moved on with her life? Was it right to bring up her husband's murder after all this time? Would she even speak with me? I stared at my cell as if it were the Magic 8 ball I had when I was a kid and it would give me the right answer. I took a deep breath, punched in her phone number, and waited as it rang.

I actually jumped when I heard her voice. For some reason, I hadn't expected her to pick up a call from an unknown number.

"Hello?" Her voice was tentative, more of a question than a greeting.

"Hi, Amanda. You don't know me," I said. Then I identified myself quickly. "My name is Jude Dillane, and I was hoping I could speak with you about Peter...and his death." There was a long silence on the other end, and I thought I'd blown it, that she'd hung up.

"Why?" she finally replied. "Who are you? What have you got to do with Peter?" She paused. "If you're looking for a story, there isn't one. Don't call me again."

She had assumed I was a reporter, wanting to pump her for information. The latest New Year's Eve murder had been on TV and in the papers. Even though the BAU had tried to keep the connections to the other deaths low-key, Amanda Finley must have seen the news. It wasn't something she'd overlook.

"Wait," I said. "Please don't hang up. I'm not from the media." I could hear her breathing and I kept going. "I'm…a…a friend of the young man who was killed this New Year's Eve. I was hoping you might remember something, anything, that could help us find…" I'd run out of words and waited for her response.

"I told the police everything I knew when Peter was killed. I'm not sure there's anything I can add." Her voice still held the pain of losing her husband. "Dredging it all up again…well, it's not going to be good for me, or my daughter."

"I understand. But if we could meet, even for a few minutes, it would mean a great deal to me." I didn't want to mention Dean and frighten her even more. She was on the fence and I didn't want her to bolt. "It could really help," I added.

She reluctantly agreed, and we set a time for later that afternoon. I would meet her outside her apartment building in Battery Park City while her daughter was at a dance class. I hoped I'd get something concrete out of this that Agent Garlinger could use to find Dean. That's if she didn't toss me in WITSEC somewhere in Idaho.

I knew speaking with Amanda Finley was a long shot. But, every once in a while, a long shot paid off big. I hope that would happen this time and that I wouldn't be the nag eating dust.

Eric had gone down to The Lounge for brunch and was waiting for me. It wasn't as though he'd really left me alone, but I was sure Agent Garlinger wouldn't agree.

The dining room was full, and people were eating at the bar, as well. Oscar and Tony were chowing down at one end and having their usual animated conversation. Sully was absent and I wondered where he was. He hardly ever missed brunch. *Just as well,* I thought. I wasn't ready to tell him my own plans for the day.

"Hi, honey. I'm here," I said as I slipped into the banquette next to Eric and gave him a bright smile.

"Well?" he asked, raising his eyebrows in expectation.

"She agreed to see me." I looked at my watch. "We're meeting at four in front of her building."

"You persuaded her, huh?"

I shook my head. "It wasn't easy. I could tell she's still hurting and wants to protect her child."

"Did she mention Michael's murder?" he asked.

I shook my head. "No, but I'm certain she knows about it. It would be hard not to, given the circumstances."

Just then Julian, one of our waiters, brought out the truffle and Gouda omelets Eric had ordered for the both of us. They were accompanied by a pile of crisp bacon and perfectly-browned home fries and a basket of homemade seven-grain bread. *It's nice to be boss*, I thought as I tucked into this deliciousness. I kept talking as I chewed. "Did you see Pete?" I mumbled through bites.

Eric nodded. "Just for a minute. The kitchen is really busy."

"How did he look?" I asked as I plunked another piece of bread on my plate.

"Like he always does." Eric shrugged and scrunched up his face at me. "What do you mean?"

"Did he look like he could murder someone, namely me.?" I glanced toward the swinging kitchen door and got a peek at our expeditor calling out the orders. "You saw how he was last night. I was afraid he'd just walk."

"He was just letting off steam." Eric put his hand over the mine, which held another bite of omelet I was raising to my mouth. "He loves this place as much as you do. You know that."

Maybe he used to, but I'm not so sure now. "You're probably right."

"As soon as we finish, I can drive you down to The Battery."

"You know, I was thinking, maybe it'd be better if I went alone."

Eric was already shaking his head before I finished my sentence. "No way. I'm sticking to you this time, just like we promised Garlinger." He gave me one of his crooked grins that made me melt. "Besides, I like this idea of being your bodyguard.

I had to stop myself from laughing. Eric was smart and brave and totally amazing. He'd proven that last year and many times since. He looked so satisfied and content at the idea of protecting me, I didn't have the heart to tell him no.

We reached a compromise—I *was* getting better at this relationship business. Eric would drive me and park where he could keep an eye on both myself and Amanda. If anything or anyone looked squirrely, he'd rush to our defense. He'd done it before, and I had no doubt he'd do it again.

Chapter Thirty-Nine

The Hudson River was steel gray, the water slapping against the retaining wall that bordered the Battery Park City apartment buildings, businesses, schools, and restaurants. People had left the area in droves after 9/11, heartbroken about the terrorist attack—what it meant for their neighborhood—and fearful about the atmosphere that surrounded them.

Now, the area was booming again, with more people than ever living and working in the shadow of the new Freedom Tower.

Eric parked on the left side of the cul-de-sac across from Amanda's building.

A woman was standing in the lobby. A slight figure in a big, puffy coat, she was pacing and looking up at the revolving door every few seconds.

I turned to Eric. "That must be her. She looks nervous." I bit my lower lip. "I hope I'm doing the right thing speaking with her."

"We could always call it off and go home." His voice was tinged with hope that I'd relent. I shook my head and started to open the door. Eric put a hand on my arm. "Be careful, Jude."

I smiled and left the car. By the time I crossed the street, Amanda Finley was out on the sidewalk eyeing me warily. "Amanda?" I asked and held out my hand. "I'm Jude Dillane."

She shook my hand. "Let's walk, if you don't mind. It's too cold to stand in one place."

As we moved off, along the riverfront path, I glanced over my shoulder toward Eric's car. He was already out and jutted his chin toward me, signaling he'd follow us. There were some people out walking dogs and others strolling, looking toward the early sunset in the west. Eric blended in, one more guy getting some bracing, but fresh, air before calling it a day.

Amanda stopped suddenly and turned to face me. "What exactly is it that you want from me, Ms. Dillane?"

"I was hoping you could tell me something about Peter that would help find his killer and the killer of a friend of mine, Michael Bevins." I was certain she'd heard about the latest victim. "He…Michael, was found outside my restaurant, The Corner Lounge." I didn't mention Dean. Talking about Michael was hard enough.

"Did Peter have any enemies, or problems with someone at work?" I knew the police had gone over this with her a hundred times and that her answers would be the same.

She shook her head. "No, Peter got along with everyone." She pulled her scarf tighter around her neck and started walking again.

"Did the police ever locate Peter's ring?" I asked.

Amanda Finley gave me a sharp look. "How did you know about that? It was one of those things the police decided to hold back."

Before I could come up with an answer, she continued. "You know, we were happy with our life. Peter's job was going well, and we were blessed with a new baby girl.

"The night he disappeared I was frantic. When I found out he was murdered, it was devastating. I couldn't go to the party with him because our babysitter cancelled. He wanted to stay home, but I insisted he go celebrate our good fortune. Hubris, huh?" She shook her head. "If only I'd let him stay with us…" Her voice trailed off and I could tell she was remembering every moment of that fateful New Year's Eve.

"I know you and Peter lived on the Lower East Side before you moved down here." I gestured to the wide expanse of the Hudson, magnificent even on this dull winter day.

"You know, we loved living there. Our apartment was on 8th Street and Avenue C. We moved because we needed more room for the baby, and since Peter's job was down here…"

She paused again and I thought I saw tears in her eyes. "I still have our old car." She stopped in front of a late-model Toyota and unlocked the door. "I don't know why I keep it. Parking is a nightmare." She reached inside. "My daughter, Chloe, left a book she needs in the back seat." She smiled slightly. "Kids, right?" Amanda checked her watch. "She'll be home from her dance class soon. I need to get back." She closed and locked the door and checked the parking sign. "I'll move it tomorrow morning. That's one thing I miss about the old neighborhood, not worrying about parking the car."

My surprise showed. "Really? Street parking is horrible there."

"Oh, we didn't park on the street. We used Jim Deems's garage. He had a few spaces he rented out in the lot next to the building and it was a godsend. Is he still in business?"

I nodded. I hadn't known he had space for parking cars. "The garage is still in business. He doesn't park cars as far as I know, just repairs them." Jim never mentioned he'd known Peter Finley, which was odd, especially in light of Michael's murder.

Amanda stopped and faced me. "I know the killer is the same monster who murdered Peter. I feel it in here." She put her hand over her heart. "The police have to find him and stop him. They have to." Her last words were said with such passion they made me shiver.

Of course, I agreed. I wanted that as much as she did, before this maniac killed Dean. "They will," I said with as much conviction as I could muster as we headed back to her apartment building. *If they didn't,* I thought about Dean again, *his loss would trail me like a ghost forever.*

We said our goodbyes and I thanked her for talking to me, especially since I understood how hard reliving the nightmare must have been. I watched as she entered her building and felt even sadder than before, if that were possible.

Eric was waiting for me next to the car, blowing on his hands and stamping his feet to ward off the cold. "So," he asked, "how'd it go?"

"Different than I expected," I said as we entered the car. I relayed the conversation to Eric as we drove uptown. He listened without interrupting until I finished.

"Are you going to speak with Garlinger?" He asked.

"Yeah, in the morning. There's something I have to do first."

"Jude…" His tone held a warning like you might give to a small child about to misbehave again.

"I know. I just want to talk to Oscar first."

"Why?"

"I want to check if he remembered anything else about New Year's Eve. "I looked at my watch. "He's probably at The Lounge right now." I also wanted to poke his memory for information about Peter Finley and Jake Hammity, whom he might have known, but I didn't mention that to Eric. Oscar had worked for the cable company for a long time and knew a lot of people in the neighborhood, and a lot about them. I was sure Eric would accuse me of butting in and I didn't want to argue with him.

Eric didn't say anything else as we made our way home. I could sense his displeasure, which I ignored.

We were fortunate enough to find a parking space a few doors down from The Lounge—an unusual occurrence, as I'd mentioned to Amanda. Her comment had gotten me wondering what else I might have missed when I spoke to The Irregulars. Sully and I hadn't lived in the neighborhood at the time of the first two murders, but Art, Jim, Tony, and Oscar had been there for years.

I'd start with Oscar. He was the most observant of the group, the one who at least tried to remember if he'd seen someone going downstairs to the restroom at the same time as Michael on New Year's Eve. I knew if I could get him to recall anything, about the murders of Peter Finley and Jake Hammity, he'd share.

Chapter Forty

On Sunday nights most of our customers came in for an early dinner, their heads already wrapped around work on Monday. Oscar was at the bar where I'd expected to find him, probably waiting for Sully and the others to join him for a drink to close out the weekend.

I asked Eric to run up to my apartment and bring me my black, cable-knit sweater, which I knew he'd have trouble locating since it was way at the back of my dresser drawer. I knew I was using it as an excuse to get him out of the way, but I wanted to speak to Oscar on my own.

I took the stool next to his. I could see he was nursing his tequila, fiddling with the glass, lime and salt shaker in front of him. I called Kara over and pointed to his drink. "Another one for Oscar on the house and a red wine for me, please."

"Thanks, Jude." He lifted the glass Kara placed in front of him in my direction.

"My pleasure," I replied as he bit into the lime, sprinkled salt on his hand, licked it, and downed half the shot. "So, how was your weekend?" I asked.

He shrugged. "Quiet, as usual." He looked around The Lounge. "Spent a little time here." This time he smiled at me. "Hey," he added, "how's Dean? Feeling any better?"

He caught me off guard with his question, but it gave me the opening I'd been looking for. He obviously hadn't seen Jared Jones and the other reporters outside The Lounge or read anything about Dean's disappearance. I didn't know how much longer it would be until everyone knew.

"Still on the mend," I replied, thinking of the pain he must be suffering at the killer's hands. *Focus, Jude,* I told myself. I had to move this conversation along before Eric came back.

"Before he got sick, Dean and I were talking about New Year's Eve and Michael's murder." I didn't have to pretend to sound sad, I was. "Someone told him that there'd been two other murders like that right here in the neighborhood years ago." I hoped I sounded curious and not pushy.

Oscar nodded, as though recalling the murder. "I knew the first guy, Hammity, from the neighborhood. And, I remember the second one too. The guy—what was his name?" I had to stop myself from blurting out Peter Finley's name. "Something like Franklin or Field." He snapped his fingers trying to remember. "Anyway, he lived around the corner from me but had just moved away."

"Really? Did you know him?" I asked in my most innocent voice.

"Not really, just saw him around. I think he parked his car next to Jim's garage. I'd see him every once in a while when he picked it up."

"Did the police ask you about him?"

"Not until they found the body over in Lindsay Park. Then, they came around and interviewed everyone." He took a swallow of his tequila and continued. "I remember Jim was getting annoyed with all the questions. Since the guy parked at his garage, the cops thought he might have known him better. You know," he gestured with his hand, "maybe heard if anyone had a beef with him." He placed his empty glass on the bar and started to slide off the stool. "I think that's when Jim stopped taking in parking. Too much trouble, he said." Oscar looked at his watch. "Gotta go. Want to catch the game at seven. Tell Dean I expect to see him back behind the bar tomorrow night. We got a bet on the Giants-Packers game I'm hoping to win."

Was Oscar as innocent as he appeared, throwing shade on Jim to ward off suspicion? It seemed odd that Jim would give up the income from his parking spaces. Maybe it really was too much of a hassle. Jim didn't act like he was poor, but he didn't seem to be rolling in dough either.

I was dying to talk this over with Sully. I looked at the door expecting him to appear. Instead, Eric came up from behind and put his hand on my back.

I nearly jumped out of my seat. When I turned, he held up my balled-up sweater

"This was buried under a pile of stuff in one of your drawers." He shook it out and handed it to me. "But you knew that, didn't you?" He glanced at the stool Oscar had just vacated and shook his head sadly. I hope you got what you wanted."

I had nothing to say to that, so I went to my fallback plan and kissed him instead.

Chapter Forty-One

Monday morning, I called Agent Garlinger's office. I'd promised Eric I'd relay all the information I'd gotten from Amanda Finley and what I'd squeezed out of Oscar Lupe. She was out of her office and wasn't expected back anytime soon. I felt like a condemned prisoner granted a reprieve. Only in my case, I knew it wouldn't last long so I intended to make the most of it.

Eric was working from my apartment and, true to his promise, he was sticking like glue. So, I didn't need my FBI minder today. Instead, I hoped Agent Maguire had joined Garlinger and was looking for Dean.

There was one more person I wanted to speak with: Tony Napoli. I didn't believe he had anything to do with Michael's death or Dean's abduction, and he had saved me from the killer. But Sully's surveillance made me wonder about the peeps he hung out with. He might know more than he was letting on.

I was just going to call him when Sully knocked on the door. "Jude, you in there?" His voice boomed out, excited and insistent.

I looked at Eric and shook my head. "Now what?" I mouthed before calling out, "I'm coming."

I no sooner had the door opened than Sully burst in. "They got him!" He took me by the shoulders and shook me so hard I thought my bones would rattle.

It took me a few seconds to process what he was saying. By that time, Eric was by my side and holding on to me, as well.

Sully let go and took in my blank expression. "The killer. Lanie and her team got him early this morning."

I slumped into Eric, my whole body filled with relief. "Oh my God! Who was it? What about Dean? Have they found him…is he alive?" The questions tumbled out, one over the other.

Sully's face fell like a soufflé pulled out of the oven too soon. He shook his head. "They got the guy, someone named Simon Portman, but they haven't found Dean yet."

"What? Why not?" The killer, but not Dean. How could this be possible?

Sully took a breath. "This Portman guy lives over on 13th and Avenue A. He has a record for assault and a long list of violent crimes. He fit the profile and the Feds have been watching him. "They moved in this morning and picked him up at his apartment."

"But what about Dean? Do they know where he is?"

"Not yet. The guy is claiming he's innocent." Sully snorted derisively. "Didn't do any of the murders, didn't kidnap Dean." Sully paused and took a breath, tamping down his anger. "They're also checking out a storage unit he has down by the river. They'll find something that links him to all the killings and Dean. Lanie is sure of it."

I must have looked like I was going to start ranting. Sully locked eyes with me. "Please, Jude. Stay calm. Lanie will find Dean. It's only a matter of time before the guy spills his guts."

"That's not good enough," I replied. "Dean may not have much more time. That's if he's still alive." A sob escaped my lips. I felt like someone who's been transported to another dimension. Nothing seemed to make sense to me.

I composed myself as best as I could. "Did you get to look at the CD from the holiday market? Was this guy, Portman, there? Was he the one Dean may have recognized?"

Sully shook his head. "I didn't get a chance to do that. My pal had to go out of the city yesterday. We were going to meet later today after his shift. He shrugged. "Doesn't seem to be any point to it now."

Sully looked at his watch. "Listen, I've got to go. I have to get up to Big City. There's a shipment going out this morning that's really important and we can't afford to screw up again." He moved closer and gave me a hug. "They'll find Dean. They will."

With that, he was gone—like a tornado swooping in and leaving a gaping void where once solid structures had stood. The only thing that could fill it was bringing Dean back…alive.

Could Agent Garlinger break this Portman guy before it was too late? The alternative was too hard to think about.

Chapter Forty-Two

As soon as Sully left, Eric pulled me close and wrapped his arms around me. He didn't have to say anything. He knew I was hurting. I snuggled into his shoulder and absorbed the warmth of his body. "Love you, babe," I whispered. Looking up, his beautiful brown eyes told me the same.

We stayed that way for a while until I untangled myself. "Coffee?" I asked.

Eric nodded and sat down at his laptop. When I brought him a mug of the steaming liquid, he was frowning over the work emails he was answering. I glanced over his shoulder as he typed with two fingers and smiled, "Now that they got the guy, you don't have to stay here and watch over me." I bent down and kissed the top of his head. "I'm safe." I added.

He turned in his seat and pulled me onto his lap. "Are you sure you'll be okay on your own? Dom could really use me in the office."

I nodded. "Go," I said and made a shooing motion with my hands. "I'll be fine. I was thinking about going to see how Art was doing." He was been acting weird, but maybe it was grief over Michael's death. Sully ran out so fast, I didn't have time to ask him if the FBI had told Art about capturing the killer. He should know. It's only right."

I stood up and Eric closed the computer. "Okay, but I'll be back in time for dinner. I know they got this Portman guy, but take care, alright?"

"I'll be waiting, now go." Eric went to take a shower and I sat down to look up Simon Portman. Now, I wouldn't have to call Tony and my plans to visit Art could wait until a little later.

I booted up and my laptop and my browser opened to the page I'd loaded on Jake Hammity, the local victim from 2013. I'd started looking at his case a few days previous and hadn't gotten back to it.

Since they'd nabbed the killer, it was just my morbid curiosity that made me look further. I scanned the articles I pulled up wondering if there was another hidden clue. There was nothing I didn't already know. Hammity, a bit of a loner, lived in an apartment on 12th Street. He was at a New Year's celebration down the block at a friend from work's apartment and never made it home. Like the other victims, he was stabbed through the heart and his body discarded.

The police interviewed everyone who'd attended the party and canvassed the neighborhood for clues. No one saw or heard anything, and all the partygoers had alibis that stood up.

The media got hold of the story and ran a photo of him taken at the party on New Year's Eve. In it, he was holding up a beer in his left hand and was wearing one of those large Russian Army watches that had been popular about twenty years ago. It had an oversize face with a red star where the number twelve should be and markings around the outside. I noticed the watch because I'd bought one just like in Chinatown when I was a teen. I thought it was cool back then. It was probably still around here somewhere.

Later in the article, there was a photo of him on a stretcher before he was carried away from the old Free Municipal Baths where he'd been found. A photographer must have snuck in when the police weren't looking and grabbed the shot. Jake Hammity's body was covered but his left arm had slipped out and was hanging down from the stretcher. There was no watch on his left wrist. I made the image larger just to check. It was gone. Had disappeared between the time he left the party to when his body was found.

A chill went up my spine. I couldn't prove it, but I was sure the killer had taken it. Another souvenir the authorities had kept quiet about.

If the BAU crime scene investigators found souvenirs from all the victims in Simon Portman's storage unit, it would be the link they needed to tie him to all four murders and the evidence to prove him guilty. I just hoped they'd be able to link him to Dean, as well.

I sat back and tried to connect the dots between everything that happened since New Year's Eve and today. The killer had warned me off almost immediately because he believed I'd seen something that would give him away. I almost wish I had.

I didn't know this Simon Portman and didn't think I'd ever seen him in The Lounge. I'd been almost certain the killer was someone I knew, otherwise why the interest in me? Coming after me just didn't make sense.

I sighed out loud as Eric came back into the living room dressed for work.

"I'm leaving now." He bent down and kissed me, the scent of his aftershave a comforting reminder of the man who wore it. "I meant what I said." He looked over my shoulder at the grainy photo of Jake Hammity's body on the computer screen. His expression became serious and his eyes went dark. "Please be careful today."

"You don't think Simon Portman's the one?" I asked, my question directed as much to myself as to him.

"Maybe. Or maybe he wasn't working alone. So, don't make me worry."

I smiled at his words. "You sound just like my Grandma Marie with her 'Sit down, Jude, and don't move.' She was always afraid something was going to happen to me."

Eric grew more serious. "It already has, and we don't need a repeat performance." He kissed me again, then he was gone.

Chapter Forty-Three

I powered off my computer and stretched. I could feel the kinks in my shoulders and neck pop one by one like bubbles surfacing from the water. My body was telling me I was in desperate need of some exercise. In my bedroom, I found my yoga pants and top under a pile of exercise clothes and chucked them into my exercise bag, blocking out the clutter. I'd straighten up later, I promised myself. After yoga class if I had time. Before my shift, maybe. If I thought about for too long, I'd find ten more excuses to ignore the mess.

It was another frigid, windy day and I bundled up before leaving the apartment.I was about to step outside when I spotted Jared Jones filming a report in front of the alleyway to The Lounge. Unfortunately, he wasn't alone. A whole rat pack of reporters were standing around, as well. So much for hoping my customers wouldn't see the news.

Shit! Now what? I thought as I peeked around the doorframe and strained to listen in.

"We're here outside The Corner Lounge with breaking news," he said as his cameraman panned to take in the building. Jones sounded self-satisfied and important. Of course he did, the little prick. "Behind me," he pointed to the dumpster in the alley, the camera now back on him, "is where the latest victim of the New Year's Eve Killer was found. This reporter has just learned that a suspect, as still unnamed, was arrested by the FBI early this morning and brought in for questioning. It is also thought he may be responsible for the kidnapping of Dean Mason, a bartender who was employed right here, at The Corner Lounge. More on—"

I bolted out of the building, reaching him in about two seconds, and pushed the mic out of his hand before he could finish. It landed on the pavement with a loud clang and ear-splitting screech. How did he know about Dean? No one from the BAU or the police had mentioned kidnapping "Why are you talking about Dean Mason," I demanded. "Tell me."

If my action angered him, he didn't let on. Ignoring my question, he picked up his mic and came at me with an evil glint in his eyes. He moved close, invading my personal space, trying to force me to take a step back. Instead, I held my ground.

"Ms. Dillane, what can you tell me about the disappearance of your bartender, Dean Mason?" he asked, shoving his microphone in my face. Before I could say, "No comment," he was on to his next question. "Is he the latest victim of the New Year's Eve Killer? Has the FBI found his body? Is the man in custody one of your customers?"

The other reporters jumped in and, before I knew it, I was surrounded. I pushed their mics and smartphones out of the way and raced through the crowd. A few, including Jones, followed me for a block, finally giving up when I turned to them and said, "If you want a comment, here it is," and lifted my middle finger right at their cameras. *Let them put that on the air*, I thought. Then, I stalked off toward hot yoga at YogaMondo on 11th Street, trying to calm down and get my zen on before I arrived. It wasn't working. I was still fuming, at Jones and at myself. I was missing something. Something important.

How had these jackals found out about Dean being kidnapped and tied it to the killer? Neither the BAU or the police had let that information out. They'd treated it as a disappearance and played down any misadventure in their statements. And with Simon Portman in custody, this morning's revelation could only have come from one source, the killer himself, grandstanding again. If that were true, it wasn't Portman.

I was shaking all over and my blood felt like it had turned to ice. I was afraid no amount of hot yoga was going to melt it.

Yoga did help a little, if not my mind, at least my body benefited. An hour and a half later, I was back out in the cold, walking fast toward 10th Street when I decided I'd stop by Art's and see if he was at home. As a screenwriter, he worked from his apartment, although I figured he hadn't gotten too much done since Michael's death.

As I slipped into the building, I appreciated the warmth that embraced me immediately. Thankfully, Sully wasn't one of those landlords who stinted on the heat. I rang for the elevator and took it to up to my floor. Inside, I took off my coat and scarf and tossed my damp yoga gear into the laundry bag in the corner of my closet. I'd showered after class, so I was ready to go.

I took the stairs down to the sixth floor and was just about to step from the stairwell into the hallway when I heard raised voices coming from inside Art's apartment. It sounded like an argument, and I didn't want to be caught in the middle. *I'll come back later,* I thought. I was about to quietly retrace my steps when Art's apartment door flew open and Jim Deems came storming out, banging the door behind him. I stood still, peeking through the glass panel in the stairwell door, and watched as Jim punched the elevator button and began pacing and muttering to himself as he waited for it to arrive. Somehow, I knew I should stay hidden. If Jim saw me, he might think I was spying on him, lurking in the stairwell. I was, I realized, as I strained to hear and make sense out of what he was saying. A few words drifted in my direction: "ungrateful," "make it up," "be sorry."

"Whoa," I almost blurted out. What was that all about? The elevator finally came. I waited until Jim stepped in and the doors closed before leaving my hiding place. Jim and Art were buddies. They hung out together at the bar and probably drank together at some of the other local watering places. Jim was often the butt of one of Art's nasty comments. Jim could be nosy and annoying, but I'd never heard him raise his voice before. I shook my head and let it go for the moment.

I reached Art's apartment and knocked. Art pulled opened the door with a scowl on his face.

"What the hell do you want now? I told you to get lost," he spewed out before he noticed it wasn't Jim returning. Before he realized it was me, his face had gone from red-hot angry to full-on furious in a flash. The transformation was so swift and so creepy, I took a step back. Art must have understood. His face changed back to normal before he finished speaking. He knew he'd startled me. "Jude? Hi, how are you? Thought you were someone else. Come in. Come in." Not a word about Jim just having been there.

I walked through to the living room and took in my surroundings. I hadn't been to Art's place before. The living room held a black leather couch and matching arm chair, a low glass coffee table with oversize art books set on top. A glass-and-metal end table was covered with framed family pictures, including several of Michael and Art. The walls were a creamy off-white and the windows were covered with beige and gold sheers that complemented the rest of the room.

I definitely had apartment envy. Art's space was neat, classy, and put together. The only messy area was a paper-strewn desk in the corner that also held a Mac computer, which was open to what looked like a writing program. I nodded in that direction. "Were you working? Did I disturb you?"

He shook his head. "No. Not at all. Come and sit down." He gestured to his couch and I took a seat. "I've been trying to get up to speed with things that I let slide since…" His voice trailed off.

I started to rise. "Listen, if you're busy, I can come back another time."

"No. Stay." He held up his hand like a crossing guard stopping traffic. "I could use a break."

"Okay. If you're sure you're up for company." I knew I was prying, but I was giving him an opening to mention Jim had just been there and wondering why he still hadn't. Maybe he was trying out some script ideas on him. Although, Jim Deems didn't seem to be the type I'd pick as a test critic.

"How about some brandy? I always like a little on a cold afternoon," he said as crossed to a liquor cart under the window.

"That would be lovely," I replied as I settled into his soft, leather couch. "What are you working on?" I asked as he poured our drinks.

He looked up and noticed I was glancing toward the computer. "A thriller for a TV movie." He shrugged. "A bread-and-butter kind of project to pay for my lavish lifestyle." He raised an arm to encompass his apartment, not exactly lavish, but not bad.

"Got a part in it for a tall, striking bartender?" I asked.

His expression slipped for a second and his eyes slid sideways, the way they do when people are stalling. He almost dropped the two brandy snifters he was holding. He recovered quickly and I wouldn't have noticed if I hadn't been staring right at him and seen the smallest flash of menace cross his face. Somehow, he thought I meant Dean and not myself until he realized I was joking. Why would that prompt such a strange reaction, I wondered?

"Not in this script, I'm afraid. It's more like a horror story where everyone gets killed off." He handed me my drink. "I wouldn't want that to happen to you."

Now I was getting seriously creeped out. What was really going on with Art? I gulped down the smoky amber liquid—not in the mood to savor brandy the way you're supposed to—and placed my glass on the coffee table between us. I tamped down the wariness I was feeling and struggled to keep my voice light. "Listen, I just wanted to see how you were doing. I've got to get back and get ready for my shift at the bar. It's been tough with Dean being out sick and all." I tossed that in to see if I'd get another weird reaction.

"I bet," he said, and pulled back the sleeve of his sweater to check the time. "When do you start today? I might come in later."

I glanced at his arm and my heart nearly stopped. Frozen in place, I told my brain to answer. Finally, I blurted out, "At five, so I'd better hustle." I couldn't get out of there fast enough. "Thanks for the drink." I stood up on shaky legs and practically ran out of the apartment and up the stairs to mine. I sprinted in and bolted the door, leaning my back against it. I could feel my pulse pounding in my neck as I tried to catch my breath, my thoughts swirling over each other in a tangled weave I had to undo.

I'd recognized the timepiece on Art's left wrist. It was a Russian Army watch and it looked exactly like the one Jake Hammity had been wearing the night he disappeared.

Chapter Forty-Four

I checked the lock on the front door and thought about what I'd just seen. I tried to tell myself I was being silly—Michael was Art's brother, as Sully had forcefully pointed out. Art was a writer. Writers imagined crimes and murder; they didn't actually *commit* them. How could he have killed Michael and all the other men? Or kidnapped Dean? And had he just threatened me, to boot?

There must be some other explanation for the watch. I'd never seen him wearing it before. Maybe he'd purchased one ages ago like I had and decided to put it on now.

I checked my own watch, an oversized fake Rolex that I'd bought in Chinatown for twenty bucks. I really did have to get ready for work. As I moved toward my bedroom to change clothes, a sudden inertia crept over me. Every ounce of energy seeped out of me and I plopped down on my bed like a woman whose body had betrayed her and left her helpless to move or think.

I must have remained like that for a while when my cell phone rang, pulling me back to the here and now. "Hello," I said. The word came out raspy-sounding, like a foreign language I hadn't yet mastered.

"Hey, it's Kara. Are you coming in soon? We're getting kind of busy, and—"

I cleared my throat and cut her off before she could finish. "Yeah, I'll be down in a few minutes." I got up from the bed and dressed in my bartender black jeans and turtleneck, pulled on my boots, and was out the door in five.

Eric would be home soon. We could discuss my encounter with Art, and I could decide what to do. Garlinger hadn't returned my call from this morning. I know she had her hands full with Simon Portman. Should I call her and discuss my visit with Art Bevins, or was I overreacting?

I sighed as I pushed open the door to The Lounge. The murmur of conversation, the clatter of dishes and silverware, and the soft music on the sound system merged into a comforting and soothing distraction from my jumbled thoughts. It wouldn't last long, I knew, but I'd make the best of it while I could, at least until I stepped behind the bar.

Social hour was almost over when Eric arrived. He took one look at my face and stopped mid-greeting. "What's the matter?" he reached over the bar and took my hand.

"I...I don't know exactly," I replied. "I went to visit Art and—" I was interrupted by a customer at the other end of the bar calling my name. I moved down to speak with her and a few minutes later was back in front of Eric. "She wanted to show me pictures of her new granddaughter." I shrugged.

"Forget about babies. What the hell is going on with you?" Eric was getting frustrated, impatient to hear my story.

I took a deep breath and spit it all out. Visiting Art. Seeing Jim storm out. Art not mentioning Jim's visit, the weird conversation we'd had about the movie, and, of course, the Russian Army watch.

"I don't know what to do," I said and squeezed his hand.

Eric slipped his hand out from under mine and crossed his arms around his middle. "You know, Jude, when a person goes looking for trouble, they usually find it."

It was the same speech I used to get from my mom. I didn't like it then and I didn't like it now. "That's not what—"

He cut me off. "—It is. Art could have had that watch for years. Like the one you said you have. It doesn't prove anything," he added with a shake of his head.

"What about not mentioning Jim's visit?" I wasn't convinced.

"You're not his social director. They're friends. Friends argue. They probably just had a difference of opinion and Jim left in a huff." Now, a wag of his finger. "You've got to stop this over-imagining things." His tone softened and he reached out to take my hand again. "I know I told you to be careful. But Art? After what happened to his brother? I don't think so."

"You're probably right. It just felt so bizarre." I couldn't explain the feeling of unease, of danger just under the surface that I'd felt. I stared up at the ceiling, wondering. "And what about Dean?"

"If it makes you feel better, let Agent Garlinger know. Her team probably found all the souvenirs that Simon Portman stashed in his storage unit, including the Russian Army watch. It won't be long before he confesses and tells them where Dean is."

"What if it's too late?"

"It isn't. I'm sure of it."

How could Eric be so certain? His voice said one thing, his eyes another. He was just as worried about Dean as I was. I came around to his side of the bar, trying to put my emotions in check. I smiled up at his handsome face. It was filled with tension I wanted to wipe away. Even the soft kiss I gave him didn't do the trick. Maybe some food would. I patted his flat stomach. "You look like you're starving. Let's have dinner, then I'll call Elaine."

I picked at my food, moving it around on the plate rather than eating—a rare occurrence for me. Eric tucked in and was finished in record time.

I gestured to his clean plate that he'd wiped down with a piece of bread. "Don't you and Dom have any restaurants or delis you can order from in New Rochelle?"

"Yeah, but none as good as Pete's cooking. I was saving myself for this."

"What? Like a Catholic school girl keeping her virginity safe for her wedding day?" I teased, smiling. Then I remembered how much Dean enjoyed Pete's family dinner, and I could feel my smile melting away. It was always something tasty, not like the hot dogs and meatloaf that some other restaurants served their employees. Just one more thing I'd miss if Pete left The Lounge.

Eric caught the change immediately. "Why don't you try Garlinger now? If she's still unavailable, you can leave another message."

I nodded. "We should have heard something from her by now. She's had Portman all day. How long could it take to get a confession?" I felt frustrated and useless sitting in the restaurant. "Isn't there some adage that people who commit heinous crimes want to confess to them when they're finally caught?"

Eric tried to lighten my mood. "Maybe on *Law and Order*, but I don't know about in the real world." He sat back and took a sip of the wine we'd been drinking with our dinner. "If Portman is the guy, he's been killing people since at least 1999. And he's been keeping it a secret all this time." Eric put down his glass and leaned into the table. "All these years, he made sure that no one found out about his secret life. It might be harder than we think to break him."

This was not what I wanted to hear. It was Dean's life at stake here. If Portman was keeping him somewhere, and no one could find his lair, Dean could die. Or he might already be dead.

I was shaking my head when Sully walked in and marched over to our table. I stood up so fast I almost knocked over the chair. "Did he confess? Did they find Dean? Is he hurt? When can we see him?" My questions came fast and furiously. One look at Sully's stoic expression brought me up short. Something was wrong.

"No. No," I uttered softly. "Don't tell me that Dean is…"

"Sit down, Jude." Sully took my arm and helped me back into my chair. "Elaine just called me, and Portman isn't the guy," he began. "He's a strange duck, but not a serial killer and he didn't take Dean."

"How does she know? How can she be sure?" I wanted Sully to be wrong about this. So wrong that I'd get up, put on a happy face, and waltz him around the restaurant.

"Positive. He had some priors, some violent attacks. His lock up didn't contain anything but old books and household junk. The BAU forensics team went over it inch by inch. Believe me, they were looking hard. There was nothing that ties him to the murders, or to taking Dean."

"I don't understand," Eric piped in. "Why did Garlinger's team pick him up in the first place?"

"They got a tip from someone in the neighborhood who said he'd been acting strange since New Year's. Or stranger than he usually does. Walking around, muttering about knives and blood and getting even. When Elaine went to speak with him, he got antsy—talking wild, shaking, and acting nervous. He started to get physical, tried to push her and another agent out of his apartment, screaming at them to leave him alone." Sully paused and ran his hand through his hair. "They brought him in and searched the apartment. When they found a piece of a blood-stained, plaid shirt hidden under the bed, they thought they had him. It was like the one Michael had been wearing. Elaine said she showed it to him and he started ranting and raving that someone put it there to frame him."

"Did they test the blood for Michael's DNA?" I asked. "That would prove he's connected even though they didn't find the souvenirs from the murders in his storage unit."

"They're on it. The lab is running the test right now, but it will take some time."

I slammed my hand on the table. "Dammit, Sully, we don't have time."

He ignored my outburst and kept talking. "They're not charging him yet, but they're not letting him go. They'll keep questioning him and keep searching for the real killer."

"So, they really don't think it's him, do they?" Eric asked.

"They're covering all the bases," Sully replied, evading a direct answer. "And, I think we should, too."

Sully had my attention. "What do you mean?" I asked, wondering where he was going with this.

He sat back in his chair, took the glass of wine I'd been spinning around out of my hand, and took a large sip. "As soon as I got off the phone with Elaine, I called my friend who does the Bryant Park security. Told him circumstances had changed and I did, in fact, need to see the DVDs from Saturday afternoon." He checked his watch. "I'm going to meet him at his office at ten thirty and take a look.

"If I can figure out who Dean was looking at—and it isn't Portman—we might find the killer."

Sully checking his watch reminded me I hadn't had a chance to relate my story about my visit to Art's apartment. I did it then, filling him in quickly.

"Ummm," was all he said as I spoke.

Frustrated, I asked, "What do you think?"

"I think," he tilted his head toward the bar, "it looks like Jim and Art made up after their little tiff."

Eric and I turned around and took a surreptitious look. The two men were sitting next to each other, heads lowered, sipping their drinks and talking quietly like there was nothing wrong. But something was. I'd seen these men at my bar nearly every day. Today was different. They may have been sitting next to each other, but their posture said it all, each leaning slightly away from the other, keeping their distance. Although it was only inches that separated them, it felt like a giant chasm to me.

Watching them gave me a chill. Maybe they'd shook hands and made up. But my instincts were telling me I was right. Art's reaction when he thought Jim had returned reached a critical mass. Whatever had happened between the two men, it didn't seem could be resolved so easily.

"Stand by until you hear from me," Sully commanded, breaking into my thoughts. "Got it?" What he really was saying was, "Don't do anything stupid, like some jarhead marine."

Eric and I both nodded like good recruits as he walked off toward the bar and the two Irregulars sitting there. Before I could get a word out, Eric stopped me. "Jude, for once, just listen."

"Fine." I stood up from the table. "I need to get back behind the bar."

"Okay," Eric stood, as well. "I'm going upstairs to finish up some work for tomorrow." He came around to my side of the table and kissed my cheek. "I'll be back to walk you home at closing," he added.

"Oh, like a date," I replied, trying to lighten the mood.

"No." He shook his head. "More like Sully's rear guard."

I'd wiped down the bar and gone downstairs to put the receipts in the safe. When I came back up to set the alarm and turn off the lights, I noticed a glass sitting on top of the service area. It hadn't been there when I last looked.

CHAPTER FORTY-FOUR

And it wasn't empty. There was a kitchen knife sticking up inside it.

I swallowed hard and stared at it for a few moments. Angry, I swiped at the glass and sent it crashing to the floor. The killer had left me another message. He'd been in The Lounge tonight and planned this little surprise.

The Irregulars had been here and they'd seemed a little off. Could one of them have snuck back in and done this? And, if so, which one?

I swept up the mess I made, locked up and called Eric to come down. I didn't tell him about this latest episode. I couldn't discuss it. Not right now.

As I walked home holding onto Eric, I couldn't help peering into every shadow. Even when we were inside my apartment, door and windows locked and bolted, I could still feel the hair on the back of my neck standing up.

Chapter Forty-Five

The next day, I called Elaine Garlinger and left another message. She was still unavailable. I'd just about given up reaching her when she came into The Lounge as I was getting ready to close.

The beautiful, well-dressed woman I'd first met on New Year's looked like a shadow of herself. Pale skin, downturned mouth, and bruised eyes replaced her usual determined look. The case was slipping under her skin and pulling her down. She wore her defeat badly, like an old, wrinkled raincoat that had seen better days. Too bad I was going to add to her troubles with my tale from yesterday.

She and I were the only people at the bar. I placed a coaster in front of her and poured her a Maker's Mark straight up without her asking. She lifted the glass toward me in a silent toast and took a long swallow.

I didn't make small talk. I didn't think either of us were in the mood for it, so I got right to the point. "Elaine, I had the oddest experience yesterday with Art Bevins," I began. Then I told her about visiting Art and all that happened, including the Russian Army watch, plus my impression of Art and Jim while they were at the bar.

"How did you find out about Jake Hammity's missing watch?" Her voice was sharp and filled with a displeasure I'd come to recognize. "I believe I told you to stay out of this, Jude."

Right. And leave it all to the experts, I thought, *who were doing so well.* "That's what you want to know, after what I just told you?"

I gave her my "don't be a simpleton" look and proceeded to explain it was right there online. I had just happened to notice two photos of Hammity that were different—one of him from New Year's Eve with the watch on his wrist and then one of his body without it.

The whole time I was speaking, she was shaking her head at me, like Sister Mary Margaret used to do in math class. Well, she was wrong. This time, it added up.

She looked at me with eyes that had regained some of their steel. "Was visiting Art part of your plan to dig for information?" Although her voice was measured, there was anger sliding in under it I didn't appreciate.

"No," I nearly shouted. "I was just concerned about him. Wanted to see how he was doing." I shook my head. "The way he acted…the watch…it scared me. I tried to call you, but…"

"I'm sorry if I was too busy to get back to you." Now she'd switched from anger to sarcasm. "So, Art and Jim? You think they were behaving differently toward each other at the bar?" she asked. "Just acting friendly, for an effect?"

I thought about it before I answered. "Yes. They spoke, but not in the easy way they usually have with each other. You know, a little back slapping, a poke in the ribs, and snarky remarks. There was none of that." The more I thought about it, the more certain I was something was wrong. "They seemed stiff and controlled. It was like they were both playing a part and not doing a very good job of it."

She'd been making notes while I spoke, a strange expression on her face. "Did they say anything that made you think they know something about the murders…or Dean?"

I knew we'd get to Dean sooner or later. I'd postponed asking the one question I wanted to by stalling and relating my experiences from yesterday. Now, with Garlinger in front of me, I'd have to face the facts. I'd been so worried ever since Sully told us Portman most likely wasn't the killer. "Is it true, what Sully said, that Portman didn't do all these murders?"

"I'm sorry, Jude." I nodded silently and let her continue. "We've still got him in custody, but unless we find hard evidence, we'll have to let him go."

"What about the bloody piece of shirt?" I'd pinned my hopes on that belonging to Michael.

She shook her head. "It's not a match." She made a noise deep in her throat that sounded like a sharp bark. "It's not even human blood."

"Not human? Why didn't you know that right away?" My voice sounded angry even to me as I leaned in over the bar and asked, "What next?"

"We keep looking. That's what we do." She leaned back on her stool, moving out of range of my combative stance and taking another long swallow of her bourbon. "I know you're disappointed. So are we. We thought we had him."

"Dean's been gone since Saturday. How long do you think the maniac who has him will keep him alive? Did you stop by just to tell me you have nothing?"

"Jude—"

"No." I held up my hand. "Really, I'd like you to answer that."

My question was met with silence. I left her sitting there and walked to the other end of the bar and picked up my cell. "Hi, I'm about ready to close. Why don't you come down now?" I made my voice loud enough for Garlinger to hear me. She finished her drink, fished out some money from her purse, and left it on the bar. She walked to the door and turned just before she opened it to leave. "We'll find him. We will."

I ignored her and stayed where I was, trying to calm down. Letting the authorities do their job wasn't working. Despite Garlinger's warning, yet again, to stay away, I could see, I'd have do something if I wanted my friend back alive.

Chapter Forty-Six

I woke up early after another fitful night. The sun had barely risen and was beaming weak rays onto the cold January landscape of the Lower East Side adding a shadowy underwater feeling. It usually made me happy to look out my window and see the neighborhood I'd adopted as my own. Not today. Today, it seemed not even the sun could lift my mood.

I didn't want to wake Eric who didn't need to be up for at least another two hours, so I made my way into the kitchen as quietly as possible and put on a pot of coffee. When it was done, I took a mugful into the living room, wrapped myself in a cozy afghan and thought about last night.

My conversation with Elaine Garlinger was still smarting. I hated feeling so helpless and useless. I picked up my cell to call Sully, but I realized even he, an early riser, might still be asleep if he'd arrived home in the wee hours after looking at the Bryant Park holiday market footage. I figured if he'd found anything, he'd have let me know, or maybe he would've slipped a note under my door. Not that seeing another envelope with my name on it would have been reassuring. I probably would have freaked out instead.

I still didn't get what was going on between Art and Jim. And something definitely was. Eric might be right; my imagination was leading me astray and their behavior probably had nothing to do with the murders. I was going to steer clear of Art today, that was for sure. I might have a chat with Jim, maybe walk over to the garage and ask him something about Eric's car. Of course, since I knew practically nothing about cars, anything I asked could make him suspicious. I sipped my coffee and thought about it. I'd figure it out when I got there. I was sure something would come to me.

Asking a car question would be a start, but I still couldn't work out how I could steer the conversation around to what I'd seen at Art's apartment the day before. I doubted he'd mention that he visited Art and left in such a rage.

Naturally, if I told Eric about this, he'd hit the ceiling. Forget telling Garlinger. She would probably make good on her threat to put me in protective custody.

I got up to refill my mug—I hadn't drunk so much coffee since I was in college—and I noticed my notebook spilling out of my handbag, which I'd tossed on the counter.

Organizing my notes on all the crimes was something I could do that wasn't breaking my promise to Garlinger to butt out. It was just reading and writing, two pillars of the three Rs.

I scooped up the notebook and brought it back to the living room where I'd left my laptop. I could feel my mood lifting, like a just-filled helium balloon floating high up into the air. By putting it all down in one place, could I come up with a new approach—or maybe an answer—even though I wasn't supposed to be meddling?

I started typing in the information I'd learned while looking for something among the four victims that tied their murders together.

Besides, each victim being stabbed through the heart, what else had made them so appealing to this maniac? Thoughts about blaming the "victim," as often happened in rape cases, popped into my head. But, of course, these men couldn't help being who they were—a serial killer's preferred type.

What else, Jude? I started listing souvenirs the killer had taken. A Thor's Hammer silver cross, A Fordham University ring, a Russian Army watch, and a silver bracelet. Could they have actually meant something to the killer, or were they just trophies to help him gloat over his kills whenever he wanted?

By the time I finished entering these words, I was frustrated and my head was reeling. I closed the laptop and thought about Dean. Was he still alive? Or was he already dead, his once strong body rotting away?

I thought about another mug of coffee but realized caffeine wouldn't make the pain go away. I could hear Eric stirring in the bedroom. For a minute, I considered showing him the notes I typed up. Thankfully, that crazy idea passed before it took hold. All I'd get was another lecture about staying out of things so the professionals could solve the case. Just the thought made my head hurt more and I got up to get some Advil from the bathroom.

Eric was just on his way in as I was coming out. He mumbled a good morning and a few moments later I heard the shower turn on. I swallowed three Advil and got back to my notes on the computer. What was I missing? What did all these victims have in common?

They were all big men, over six feet and well built. Blond, blue-eyed, and handsome. I had no doubt that all of them could fight off a would-be attacker, or at least try. How had the killer gotten the drop on them? Other than Lukas, they all had ties to the Lower East Side…and maybe to The Irregulars.

It was maddening. I was sure I was onto something—but what, I didn't know. I looked up from the computer and realized the shower had stopped. Eric was standing in the doorway of the living room, wrapped in a towel, watching me with a strange look on his face.

"What are you doing?" he asked, nodding toward the computer.

I put on a bright smile and replied. "Not much. I couldn't sleep, so I was just surfing the net and looking at a bunch of stuff." I closed the computer, stood up, and followed him into the bedroom where he began to dress.

"Hmm," was all he said as he turned to me buttoning his crisp, white shirt. "I hope I can leave you alone today, Jude. I don't want you to get into any more trouble."

I laughed like he was making a joke. "Who me? Never happens."

He tossed a knowing look my way. "Yeah, right. It's a good thing Garlinger is sending Maguire back to watch over you."

His statement surprised me. "She is?" I didn't know about this and I didn't like it one bit. I didn't need a watch dog. I needed to be free to move around without someone following me and reporting in.

He nodded slowly. "She texted me last night after she left The Lounge. Somehow, she didn't believe you'd mind your own business." He paused and finished tying his tie. "She's just being cautious…worried for your safety."

"Of course she is," I said as I helped him tighten his tie. For a second, I wanted to tighten it until he couldn't breathe. But I loved him too much to kill him, even if he was pushing me in that direction.

Chapter Forty-Seven

I waved goodbye to Eric, assuring him I'd be perfectly safe, especially since I'd have big, strong Agent Maguire coming over to mind me. He just gave me another one of his "yeah right" looks and left.

I didn't waste any time in calling Sully. He'd definitely be up by now and probably ready to do a five-mile run. My call went to voice mail and I asked him to call me ASAP. "There's something I need to ask you about. So, call. Okay?" I know I sounded like one of those people who seem like they're expecting an answer even though they know they're talking to a machine.

As soon as I clicked off, I got dressed in a hurry. I wanted to be out of the apartment before Maguire arrived. It would seem ungrateful at best and stupid at worst, but it was crucial to have some time on my own, even just half an hour, to look into one or two things. Nothing dangerous. Just a talk. At least that's what I told myself.

I left my apartment and took the stairs down to the lobby. Peeking out the service door like a would-be robber after a heist, I made sure it was all clear before I slipped out the back door into the alleyway. No Agent Maguire and no press. I breathed a sigh of relief.

Walking to the back of the space, I gave the dumpster a wide berth; it still freaked me out every time I looked at it. My goal was the chain link fence to its left and the passage beyond that led to Jim Deems's garage.

At some point, the fence had been semi-rolled back from its post with just enough give for someone to push it and squeeze through. Sully figured neighborhood kids had done it and he'd been meaning to have it repaired for as long as I lived here. He mentioned it again the other night, but with all that was going on, it slid to the bottom of his to-do list once again.

I knew Jim used the opening every so often as a shortcut from his apartment in Sully's other building to the garage when he didn't feel like walking all the way around the block to Avenue A or when he closed up late.

As I'd tugged at the fence to dislodge the frozen snow that had collected around the bottom, I was happy I'd worn my thick mittens. When the opening was wide enough, I'd bent down and slipped through.

The exit from the fence led to an open space about eight feet wide behind the garage, branching off into a narrower passage about three feet wide that ran along its side with a wooden door to the street at its end. On its other side, there was a five-story tenement building. Deeper than Jim's garage, it had no back yard to speak of and ended close to the property line. That building had two windows on each floor looking out toward the back and two facing the garage. Oscar lived there but I wasn't sure if his apartment was in the front or the back.

I tried to be as silent as possible; I didn't want the tenants in the building opposite to notice me. I crossed the open space of the yard quickly, then crab-walked against the wall, avoiding the litter, leftover snow, and broken tree branches that had collected there. My visit was planned as a surprise. There were no windows on this side of the garage or in the back, so Jim wouldn't see me coming.

The garage itself was tall. A one-story brick building that had been in the neighborhood for a long, long time, it was one of the few remaining vestiges of the old Lower East Side. It had definitely seen better days. There was a rotting, wooden storm door that slanted over what I assumed were steps to a basement with an interior door at the bottom. We'd had one just like it at our house in the Bronx. It was locked with a padlock, but the wood looked so rotten, it wouldn't take much to open it. The brick was crumbling in a few places and the whole building tilted slightly. I figured it would be open by now, ready for any early-morning customers who needed service.

Jim kept his garbage cans in the pathway, just inside the wooden door. I resisted the urge to open the lids and look inside, telling myself I was being crazy. If Jim had something to hide, he surely wouldn't put it here.

The door to the street was on some kind of springy hinges that allowed it to be pushed open in either direction, like the door to the kitchen in The Lounge. I gave a little shove and heard what sounded like a creaky tennis racket. So much for stealth and surprise.

When I poked my head out, I noticed that the lift up metal garage door that led to the interior was still pulled down and the side door for customers had a "closed" sign facing outward. Jim must not have gotten here yet and I didn't know how long he'd be.

I was deciding if I should wait or come back later when I felt a hand touch my shoulder and heard someone call my name. I almost screamed as I spun around and came face to face with Oscar.

"What are you doing here?" he asked with a skeptical look on his face.

"Oh, you startled me," I said, giving myself a moment to think. "I wanted to ask Jim about Eric's car. Eric thinks it might need an oil change." I shrugged in a "what do I know about cars" manner. I couldn't very well tell him I was snooping around about parking after he'd already mentioned Jim didn't provide that service anymore.

Oscar glanced at the garage. "That's strange. Jim is usually open by the time I leave for work." He gestured to the cable company van parked in front of his building.

"In for a busy day?" I asked.

"Always," he replied, starting to stow his equipment in the van. It was cold out and I got the feeling he didn't want to stay and chat. But now that Oscar was in front of me, I couldn't pass up the opportunity to ask him some of the questions that I hadn't gotten to the other night.

"You must know almost everyone in the neighborhood." I reached my arm out in an expansive gesture. He nodded and I could tell he was wondering where this was going. I decided the best way to get a little information was to give some. I didn't know how much more I could pump him for, since we already discussed most of it already. But I'd try.

"I don't know if you heard, but the Feds had to let their prime suspect go. They're still looking for Michael's killer." I hoped I sounded like I knew what I was talking about and let this information sink in before I continued.

"They were discussing the other New Year's Eve murder that happened in the neighborhood from a few years ago.

"I remembered you and I had been talking about it, about Jake Hammity." I paused and lowered my voice to a conspiratorial whisper, as if we were discussing confidential information. "He disappeared after a New Year's Eve party around here, didn't he?"

"Yeah, I knew the guy who threw the party, Jimmy Weslex. It was over on 12th and I stopped by for a little while. I saw Jake there, but I don't know if he was with anyone or when he left." He looked at his watch and I knew I had to speed this up.

"Anyone else you remember seeing there?" I tilted my head to the side and made my eyes big, like I was really curious.

He shrugged. "A bunch of the guys from around here. Art and Jim for sure. Some other people you might not know, Danny Michaels, Vince Cardo, Billy Jacobs. Some of their girlfriends. Maybe a few more. "The Feds probably talked to all of them too, don't you think?

"Yeah, you're probably right," I said with conviction. "Well, I'd better let you get going. Don't want you to be late for your appointments."

"See you around, Jude," he said as he stepped into the van. "Probably be in for a drink later tonight." With that, he pulled out and drove down the avenue.

I'd gotten some of what I came for. Jim and Art had been at the party, along with Oscar, when Jake Hammity disappeared. I was standing on the sidewalk mulling this over when I heard the screech of a metal garage door being lifted. I turned around and there was Jim Deems standing in the opening, wiping his forehead under his red cap with a grease-stained rag and glowering at me for all he was worth. I hadn't heard him approach the garage, and I wondered if he'd been there all along observing my conversation with Oscar.

Chapter Forty-Eight

"Hey, Jim. How you doing this morning?" He'd stepped out from under the metal door, which was three-quarters of the way up, instead of using the door to its right meant for customers.

It took a minute until he answered me, and I could see a bevy of emotions run across his features before he turned his mouth up in a semi-smile. His eyes, that now looked into mine, remained wary. This was his turf and I was obviously, at least to me, the intruder. I decided to ignore all that and began to speak. "You're just the—"

"W-w-hat are you doing out here so bright and early?" he cut me off.

Somehow, I'd made him nervous enough to stutter. I blew into my mitten-covered hands and stamped my boots on the cold pavement. "I'm looking for you." I gestured to the open garage bay, "Maybe we could go inside where it's warmer and talk."

"Uh, sure, w-w-why not." His shoulder went up. "But I gotta warn you, it's not that much warmer in there and it's pretty messy. S-s-so be careful."

I followed him in and took a look around the space. It looked like every commercial garage I'd ever seen, not that I'd been in that many. Given my past, I pretty much steered clear of garages.

Tools were scattered all over a long bench along one side, with a variety of tires, cans, and drums underneath it and posters of cars on top. The left side held one of those hydraulic lifts that would allow a car to be lifted up so a mechanic could work underneath it more easily. On the right was an open space for another car. There were larger tools and machines along that side of the space, some with hoses looped around large pegs set into the brick and I had no idea what they were for. Most of the stuff was covered with dust and looked like it hadn't been used in a while. All except for the door at the back.

The door was metal and gleamed dully in the dim light. It had a padlock that looked newer, sturdier, and more well-kept than the rest of the place. Since there was no second floor, I figured it led to the basement. I wasn't very fond of basements either. Maybe Jim kept the more valuable auto parts down there in case of a break-in. But I doubted it. Nothing I'd seen so far looked like it'd be worth stealing. That lock was big and strong. Maybe it was for keeping more than parts secure.

"Wow," I said. "I had no idea you had all this equipment." I swiveled my head around as though I were taking in the Taj Mahal rather than a lowly auto body dump. "You must be pretty busy."

He'd been standing about a foot behind me to my right. He moved in front of me, turned to face me, and gave me another cold hard stare. "W-w-what can I help you with, Jude?" he asked, getting right to it.

I didn't like him getting so close. I was getting those hair-standing-on-end, back-of-the-neck weird vibes, but I stood my ground and made myself smile. The garage door was still up and I could scuttle out fast if I had to.

"I think Eric's car needs an oil change."

He nodded. "Okay, tell him to bring it in and I'll t-t-take care of it."

"Great." I turned as if to leave, then turned back. "Oh, just one more thing," I said just like that Detective Columbo from the TV show my parents used to watch. "I also heard that you used to park cars here a while ago. "And I was wondering if you might be planning to do it again? Eric is at my place so much and it's been hard for him to find parking when he comes home after work."

"Don't know where you heard that, but it's not something I do." He raised his hand, inviting me to look around. "Where would I put a buncha cars?"

He didn't actually say he never did it. I knew there was an empty lot on the other side of the garage, and I'd bet that's where he used to put them—whether he owned it or not.

"Duh," I rolled my eyes, "that makes sense, unless you had an underground garage tucked away under here."

I could see that I hit a nerve, his hand tightened around the wrench he'd picked up when we entered the garage. "Sorry, I can't help you. Now, if you'll e-e-excuse me, I've got work to do. Tell Eric to drop the car off whenever."

What work? I thought. It didn't look like he'd been busy in a while. Instead of inquiring further, I thanked him and left. Out on the sidewalk, I could hear the shriek of the metal hinges lumbering to bring the door down, closing off the outside world.

I shivered as I walked away, and it wasn't because of the temperature.

Chapter Forty-Nine

I took the long way home, over to Avenue B and around the corner to 10th Street. When I got there, a pissed-off-looking Agent Maguire was outside the building on the phone. Busted. I was in for it now.

"She just got here," he said into the phone. Then there was a long pause. "Yes, ma'am. I understand. Uh huh. I'll do that." His eyes were blazing at me and I could almost feel the heat. "Where have you been?" he demanded.

"Excuse me!" I made the indignation in my voice match his. I must have gotten through, because he cooled down pretty quickly.

"Look, Ms. Dillane…uh, Jude…I'm not your enemy. Agent Garlinger really is concerned for your safety." He paused and took another cleansing breath and I wondered if he practiced yoga. "I'm here to help with that. So, maybe you could cut me some slack and let me do my job."

I nodded. "Okay." He was right, but I hated having someone looking over my shoulder and watching what I was doing. "Why don't we go upstairs and have some breakfast? Sound okay to you?"

"Sure," he said and followed me into the building. So far, he hadn't turned down any meal I'd offered, so that was a safe suggestion.

I was starving. My little early morning jaunt had left me hungry for food as well as more information. I got busy making us some bacon, eggs, and toast, and brewing coffee. I could actually cook if I had to. Not that breakfast was such a challenge. While Maguire was eating at the kitchen table, I took my plate over to the coffee table in front of the couch. I was itching to go over my list and make a few additions. Of course, I didn't want Maguire to see. "I'm going to work on the computer for a while," I told him. "Right here, in the living room, where you can watch my every move." The newspaper had been delivered while I was out, and I'd placed it on the table when we came in. "That's today's paper, if you're interested."

He started leafing through it while he finished his eggs and coffee. And I opened up my computer to my notes.

I'd made a list of possible suspects, starting with the person I now considered my prime one: Jim Deems. Then I suddenly remembered something from New Year's Day. Jim mentioned the knife from The Lounge used to kill Michael. I thought Sully must have told him, even though we were keeping it quiet. I'd have to ask Sully if he had. If he hadn't, well, we'd have to find out who did.

Thinking about this reminded me that I still hadn't heard from Sully. I picked up my cell and speed-dialed him. Still no answer, just his voicemail. "It's me," I said. "I'm waiting for you to call." I turned my back to Agent Maguire as I whispered into the phone. "You won't believe what I have to tell you." Thinking I knew something he didn't should get his attention. It usually worked.

I went back to my notes and added Art Bevins to my list of suspects. He'd really creeped me out when I visited him. It reminded me of Jack Nicholson in *The Shining*. Especially the fact that he's a scriptwriter who mostly writes stories about murder. Like Sully, I still balked at the idea of him being involved in the murder of his own brother. That would really be sick.

I looked up from my laptop and saw Maguire watching me intently. I must have been making odd faces while I was typing.

"Everything okay, Jude?" He finally used my first name without prompting.

I nodded, stood up, and stretched. "Maybe we should go for a walk before we head down to The Lounge."

His face crumpled slightly, but he didn't say no. We both put on our outside gear and left. The sun was shining more brightly now, and the air had warmed up a bit, probably to a whopping 25 degrees. Not exactly strolling-around weather. I snuggled deeper into my parka and pulled up my hood. Maguire turned up the collar of his wool coat and pushed his hands deep into its pockets. I wouldn't keep him out for too long. That would be mean. But I did want to walk back over to Avenue A and pass by Jim's garage.

When we walked past, the metal garage door to the interior was closed tight. Its glass windows at the top were dark and, as far as I could tell, there were no lights on inside. The customer door still held the "closed" sign. The garage looked like it was abandoned. Had I scared Jim with my appearance and my questions?

I really needed to talk to Sully about all of this. I started to pull out my cell but thought better of it. If I reached Sully, Maguire didn't need to overhear my conversation.

"Maybe we should go back," I said, frost forming in the air around my words. "It's too cold."

"Um, okay," he agreed and pushed his hands deeper into his coat. His nose had turned red and he looked miserable. I was sure he hadn't signed on for deep-freeze watchdog duty. We turned the corner and headed for home.

Inside The Lounge, it was toasty warm and the ubiquitous pot of coffee was brewing. We stowed our outerwear in a closet by the kitchen and headed right for the brown gold. Maguire took his mug and settled himself at what had become his regular table and took out his cell phone. He appeared to be busy texting away, probably filling Garlinger in on our walk.

I took my coffee downstairs to my office and tried Sully once more. Still no answer. Where the hell was he? My suspicions were bursting to get out and he was the only one I could tell. *Be patient*, I told myself. *You'll just have to wait until he calls you back.* Since I didn't have a choice, it was the only thing I could do. Well, that and think about my new suspects.

Chapter Fifty

There was always paperwork to do for the restaurant—ordering, scheduling staff, and paying bills—and I made good use of my time taking care of these chores until The Lounge opened for business. That didn't mean I didn't try to reach Sully a few more times and struck out. I hoped he was coming in later. We really needed to talk.

Maguire checked on me every so often. He was going to go out and bring back some Chinese food for lunch and asked if I please wouldn't disappear while he was gone. I said I'd stay put and, for once, I meant it. I told him he better not let Pete see him with Chinese food. He'd be insulted.

Maguire couldn't tell if I was serious or joking and brushed it off with a half-hearted smile. I was just teasing him. Pete would probably commandeer one of those little white cartons and wolf down the contents. He loved Chinese.

I couldn't help thinking about that morning and what might be in the basement of Jim Deems's garage. I had to get a look inside. How I'd manage that, I had yet to determine. First, I'd have to give Maguire the slip, and do it while Eric wasn't around. I'd also have to make sure Jim was not anywhere in, or near, the garage. The only thought I had was to ask Sully for help, that's if I could ever reach him. By the time I mulled this over for the twentieth time, I was no closer to figuring it out than when I started.

I checked my watch and saw that it was time for me to head upstairs and set up the bar. Agent Maguire had moved from his regular table to one where Suzanne, one of our wait staff, was folding napkins for dinner. She was showing him how she turned a plain white napkin into a dove. He seemed to be hanging on her every word.

So, that's why he hadn't bothered me in the last hour, I thought. I coughed to announce my presence and walked behind the bar. I was just finishing up when Sully walked in.

"Finally," I stage-whispered at him as he sat down, looking over my shoulder to make sure Maguire was still occupied. "Where the hell have you been? I've been calling—"

He cut me off with a lift of his hand. He too, looked toward Maguire before he replied, speaking in low tones—an approximation of a quiet, indoor voice. "I've got something to show you." He opened his palm which held a flash drive. "Let's go downstairs and use your computer."

I nodded and started moving toward the stairs to my office. "We'll be right back," I said to Maguire. "I need to discuss something with Sully." He nodded, then turned his attention back to Suzanne.

Downstairs, I turned on my computer. While it was booting up, I started to tell Sully what I'd discovered. "This morning, I went through the fence out back and over to Jim's—"

Once again, he shut me down. "Me first, Jude. You have to see this." His voice was tense and tight as he clicked on a file from the pen drive. It opened on a crowd of people at the holiday market in Bryant Park.

"You got the footage," I exclaimed with excitement. "Did you find anything?"

"It's from the timeframe that Jamila gave us. With all those people, it took a while to go through everything. But you'll see in a minute. Just watch." He was speaking to me, but his eyes were glued to the monitor.

I leaned in closer, as well, and watched the crowd. It felt as if I were snorkeling through a rippling sea with people flowing around and between each other, bodies weaving, arms waving, heads bobbing with the tide. It took a few minutes for the one image Sully wanted me to see to appear. When it did, I jumped out of my chair, nearly knocking it over. "I'd recognize that cap anywhere." Actually, it wasn't hard to—the Deems Automotive logo stood out like a beacon you couldn't miss.

Five minutes later, I'd filled Sully in on my activities that morning and my suspicions about Jim Deems. He was pacing back and forth in my small office, turning every few steps. Finally, he stopped and gave me his version of "the look," eyes squinting, mouth in a grimace, chin tipped up so he could look down his nose at me.

"What?" I asked spreading my hands wide. "Don't you believe me?" I couldn't understand how he could doubt my story.

He shook his head. "It's not that, Jude. Even with all this," he pointed to the now frozen image of Jim's head on the screen, "I just have a hard time thinking of Jim Deems as a serial killer."

"Well, what about the knife?" I asked. "Right after the murder, when Jim was in The Lounge, he mentioned the knife. You got a funny look on your face and I thought you might have let it slip. Did you?"

"I didn't."

"Well, I didn't either. So how did he know about it?"

Sully stopped pacing and sat on the edge of my desk. "It did get me thinking at first. Then I nosed around and figured he probably heard one of the cops talking about it when they were interviewing people."

"Then, the other night, I noticed you got a little weird when he mentioned Dean running all over town with Jamila. What about that?"

"You're right, I was suspicious. But look at Jim. Would someone like Jamila even give him a second glance? I chalked it up to jealousy."

It was so unlike him to be forthcoming with reasonable excuses. I didn't get it.

It suddenly dawned on me that he hadn't mentioned Elaine Garlinger since he arrived. "Did you tell Elaine about the video footage?" I asked.

"Not yet," Sully replied. "I thought I'd talk to Jim first, feel him out—"

It was my turn to cut him off. He was being totally naive. "And what? Ask him if he's a serial killer? C'mon. They don't exactly wear signs around their necks saying, 'Serial killer here.'" I took a deep breath. "Sully, when I walked past the garage again this morning with Maguire, it looked abandoned. It's freaky. I'm not sure you could even find him to have a chat with him."

"He's around. I asked him to meet me for a drink at five thirty. I'll try to figure out if he was the one who snatched Dean. If I even get the slightest hint that he's the guy, I'll make an excuse and call Elaine."

"If he's planning to bolt, Dean could be dead by then." I was shaking with frustration. "We've got to get a look at that basement now. That's the only way to be certain."

"How do you propose to do that?" he asked.

It suddenly came to me. The idea that had been eluding me all afternoon. It would prove which one of us was right. "You're going to help, but first we have to get rid of Maguire."

Chapter Fifty-One

I shut down the computer and Sully and I made our way back upstairs. It was almost five o'clock and the winter sky had turned dark and gloomy, with no moon or stars out to alleviate the blackness.

Agent Maguire was back at his own table, texting again. "Hey," I smiled as I walked over, "Sully's going to keep me company at the bar until Eric gets home, so you can take off anytime you want." I posed it as a casual suggestion, or at least I hoped he took it that way.

He glanced over at Sully, who gave him a thumbs up. *Don't overdo it,* I thought. Maguire looked at me. I could tell he was thinking about Garlinger's command that he not leave me alone even for a minute. "I won't be alone," I said with as much sincerity as I could muster, meaning Garlinger would never know.

"Well, if you're sure…"

"I am. You can go. I bet you have other things to do with your evening. Besides, it's quitting time." I left it at that and walked back behind the bar. I gave Sully a quick wink and went back to my setting up.

Two minutes later, Maguire was saying goodnight. "Jude, please behave and stay here with Sully. I'll see you in the morning."

I resisted the temptation to do a little dance as the door closed behind him. Sully checked his watch. Jim should be here in about twenty minutes. Sully told him he wanted to do something nice for Art, maybe a dinner, and needed his help planning it. I recoiled at the mention of Art's name. I still couldn't figure out why he'd been so weird the other day. I'd mentioned it to Sully—that and the Russian Army watch. But, like Eric, he attributed it to my overactive imagination.

As soon as Jim arrived, I'd leave the bar and go search the garage's basement, taking the same route I took that morning. Half of me was hoping I was wrong and there'd be nothing there. The other part desperately wanted to find Dean before it was too late. If Dean was in the basement, I'd text Sully and he'd get the troops out.

Jim walked in just before five thirty and I made some excuse for having to go downstairs and do some last-minute ordering I'd forgotten. Kara took over for me and I told her to keep Jim's glass full. She just nodded. If she wondered why, she didn't ask. I said I'd be back in half an hour, before we got really busy and before Eric arrived home. If he knew what I was up to, even though I was sure there was no danger involved since no one would be there, he'd try and shut it down.

I grabbed my coat, hat, and mittens and was out the back door in a flash. Of course, my gear was all black, adding to my cover.

This time, I basically sprinted and was at the back of the garage in no time. I'd brought along a small bar knife to use to pick the lock on the stairway storm door. It took a few minutes, but the hasp finally popped open. I'd done all this in the dark, my eyes adjusting to the meager ambient light. Now, after I was down the stairs and had the slanted storm door closed above me, I turned on the flashlight on my cell phone. The interior door seemed pretty solid, with a heftier lock than on the outside. I'd also brought along a small-headed hammer from The Lounge in case I needed to pry the lock off. I did, and slowly pushed open the door.

The cellar was in total blackness. Dank and chilly, a strong smell of ammonia and bleach laid over mold that'd been there for years crept into my nose. The walls were damp with tiny rivulets of moisture running from the ceiling to the floor. It was disgusting, and my body reacted with a heave.

I pushed it back and stepped deeper inside as I called out Dean's name and played the flashlight around the room. It was one big, open space with a set of stairs on the right leading up into the garage and the locked door I'd seen this morning. A stack of cartons was stored behind the stairs, but there was nothing else in the space. I made my way over to them and gingerly peeked inside. Fortunately, there were no surprises; they were all empty. Holding my breath, I rapped on the walls, looking for a hollow space or a tunnel. I stamped on the floor, trying to find a trap door, but came up empty there, as well.

Taking it all in, I realized there was nowhere to hide, and I was certain that the basement was totally bare.

I'd gone over every inch. If Dean had been here, there was no sign of it. No blood or other fluids. Just thinking about that made my stomach lurch again. I checked my watch and realized I'd better get out of there and back to The Lounge.

Outside I shut the storm door and replaced the lock as best I could, trying to make it look like it was closed tight. I was just about to turn back to the passage and the fence, when a hand snaked its way around my neck and over my mouth from behind, stifling the scream that was struggling to come out.

"Don't move. Don't say a word."

The voice was familiar but, in my terror, I couldn't place it. Could it be Jim? No. He was at The Lounge with Sully. I nodded, frozen in place and too frightened to do anything else, my heart hammering in my chest.

"You just couldn't leave it alone, could you? Stupid bitch."

I suddenly recognized the voice. It was Art's. A shudder went through me as my brain registered the danger I was in—alone in a deserted alley with a serial killer.

"I'm going to take my hand away, now. Don't scream, or I'll slit your throat." His knife glinted in the little bit of moonlight that filtered through the clouds as he placed it next to my skin. Was this the knife he'd used to kill those other men? My mind reeled with the certainty I'd be next.

I nodded again, not sure I could scream even if I wanted to. I stood still, trying to swallow the fear welling up inside, waiting for the knife to slice into my skin.

"Turn around. Move!" He shoved me toward the front of the building, checking to make sure no one was watching as he pushed through the wooden door from the alley to the street. Once we were out front, he opened the unlocked customer door to the garage. He must have gotten Jim to leave it unlatched for him.

It was as dark and disgusting as I remembered from that morning. The knife still at my throat, he pushed me inside. Tossing me onto the filthy floor, he stepped back and flicked on a dim light.

I took a deep breath and finally managed to look at him. His eyes were calm. The hand that held the knife, steady. He shook his head slowly from side to side, then laughed so hard he almost doubled over.

"You thought Jim was the killer? What a joke. He's just a wannabe. A sycophant who yearned to be just like his *best friend.*" He gave me a grin. "Look how that turned out.

"He helped me out in the beginning, hunting beside me. It was a partnership, of sorts. He watched and learned as I murdered the men I chose. Sometimes I turned things over to him for the final *coup de grace.* Of course, I was the brains of the operation, and Jim more the muscle."

"But he killed your brother," I blurted out, sorry I'd spoken the moment the words were out of my mouth.

Art shrugged. "Michael was exactly his type. He just couldn't help himself. Then Jim felt remorse, if you could call it that, at killing my sibling. So, he took Dean as a gift for me.

"Where is Dean?" I managed to croak out. "Is he…"

"All in good time, Jude." He glanced at his watch, then smiled again. "There's something you should see before we head to our final destination."

The words "final destination," hit me as hard as if he'd punched me in the stomach. All I could do was stare at him.

Of course, he noticed, and smirked. "Be a good girl, Jude, and scuttle to the back wall. There's a loose tile in the corner. Why don't you lift it up?" he said in a teasing voice.

Trying to swallow my fear, I dug my trembling fingers under the linoleum and lifted the piece away. Inside was a cloth sack tied with string.

"Take it out. Open it." Art taunted from a few feet away.

I did. My stomach recoiling as I looked at the contents. It held the souvenirs from the men I knew they'd murdered. But there was more. Much more. A pair of cufflinks, several wallets, eyeglasses, a wedding band, a driver's license. Too many mementos of death. I couldn't look anymore and twisted the bag shut, trying not to vomit at its contents.

Art's face lit up with amusement at my reaction. "You're such a sensitive soul, Jude. I never knew that about you." He looked at his watch, then gestured to me. "Put it back under the tile. I want the police to find it when they search the garage. They'll be getting a tip in a little while from an anonymous source about Jim and his nasty habits.

"Get up. There's something else I want to show you before I'm finished."

I rose slowly, desperately looking for anything I could use as a weapon. Art saw my eyes darting around. "Don't even try it. We're going for a little walk in the moonlight. You'll like that won't you?"

He opened the door and we slipped outside. "Don't try to run or pull that going slack trick like you did in the elevator." He put one arm around my waist and pulled me close. The other hand held the knife, which he pressed into my side. If anyone noticed us, we'd look like a pair of lovers out for a stroll. He smiled at me. "Behave, or I'll gut you where you stand.

"Where are we going?" I managed to stammer as we made our way east, toward the river through the silent night.

"There's an abandoned warehouse over on 8th Street and Avenue D across from the housing development. I've got a big surprise waiting for you there."

Dean, I was certain, was the surprise. And that Art would kill us both, I had no doubt.

Chapter Fifty-Two

It only took a few minutes to reach our destination. The air had gotten colder, and the night felt even darker, as if it were bearing down on us. There was very little traffic on the street, and it was eerily still. *So, this is it. This is how I'm going to die.*

When we got to the warehouse, Art propelled me around to the back of the building. It was another crumbling brick edifice that the city had let go to ruin. There were old, cracked, and clouded glass windows up high on the first floor, too high for anyone to see into, and a rotted wooden door at the corner of the building.

Art kicked it and the door opened inward. He didn't seem to be worried about making noise. No one was around to hear us. When we entered, it was pitch black. He found a light switch on the side of the door and flicked it up.

Dim light cast a macabre glow. This space was even more disgusting than Jim's garage. An odor of decay hit me immediately. Rats—the ones still alive—scuttled over the bodies of their brethren, and into their bolt holes. Mold covered the walls like abstract artwork. It felt like we'd entered a scene from Hell, and at the far end of the room, in the dimmest part, was a cot with a body lying on top.

"Dean," I screamed as I broke free of Art and ran toward my friend. I hardly recognized him. His face was skeletal and his body had caved in on itself. From his shallow breathing, I could see he was alive, but barely. I sat down on the edge of the cot and picked up his limp hand.

"You monster!" I screamed at Art as I rose from the cot and ran toward him. He held me back with one hand, the knife in the other.

"I thought I'd give you a chance to say goodbye before I killed the both of you." He lifted the knife over his head, ready to plunge it into me.

"Drop the knife, Art." The voice, which had come from behind us, at the other end of the room, startled us both. "Or I'll shoot you where you stand."

Tony Napoli stepped out of the shadows, aiming a gun at Art's head.

"Oh, I don't think so," Art moved quickly and pulled me in front of him, blocking Tony's aim with my body. "I'll be leaving now." He edged me toward the open door and pushed me aside just as he ran out.

"Shit," Tony exclaimed and started to go after him as I ran back to Dean. He was moaning and moving his head from side to side. I needed to get him help.

Just then, Tony came back into the room, a cell phone to his ear. "Elaine," he spoke into the phone, "We found the vic, but the perp got away."

"Tony? Where did you come…why are you…"

He held up a hand. "I'll explain everything later. Let's get Dean some help first. An ambulance is on the way, and so is Agent Garlinger. They'll be here any minute." His voice was calm and measured, but his eyes were telling me something else. He had no idea how bad Dean's condition was.

Agent Garlinger's team arrived right behind the ambulance. They sent the door flying off its hinges and the EMS team rushed inside, followed by the Feds. Garlinger insisted Tony and I stay outside while they cleared the area.

A few minutes later, Garlinger came out. "You're one stubborn woman, aren't you?" I'm sure she saw the pleading in my eyes. I hoped I wasn't going to have to beg for what I wanted to know.

"It looks like Dean Mason will be okay. He's been drugged, just enough to keep him unconscious." She hooked a thumb toward the warehouse. "He's alive and the EMTs are working on him now. They said they got to him just in time." She paused and looked me in the eye. "That's all I know for now." Then she walked away to talk to some of her team.

I slumped against Tony in relief. I still didn't understand what had happened, why Tony was at the warehouse, or any of what was going on.

He read my state of mind perfectly. "I know you have questions, and I promise you'll get answers, but first you need to get back to The Lounge. Sully knows the Feds are on the way and so does Eric.

Chapter Fifty-Three

Back at the bar, Jim and Sully were exactly where I left them. I felt like it was midnight. My body was sore and aching, coming down from the adrenaline rush I'd just experienced. Checking my watch, I saw it was just six thirty. I slipped behind the bar and thanked Kara. I took a deep breath, composed myself, and gave Sully a subtle tilt of my head.

He returned my signal with a quick nod and went back to talking to Jim. He seemed to have already gotten the message, probably from Garlinger, that the souvenirs the New Year's Eve Killer had harvested from all his victims were found in Jim Deems's garage and the Feds were on the way.

Knowing Sully, the smile pasted on his face was only there for show. He'd kick Jim from one end of the bar to the other and back if he had his way. I figured he knew Garlinger would be here soon.

I could see the smile beginning to crack and hoped she'd make it fast. A few minutes later, she and the detectives from the 9th Precinct pulled up outside. They came in and took Jim away so quickly no one at the bar or in the dining room seemed to notice.

Jim was pretty plastered. Sully, with some help from Kara, made sure of that. I only hoped he'd give them a full statement. Because this wasn't over. I felt it in my bones there was more to come.

Eric arrived at The Lounge soon after and somehow knew what had happened. He was stone-faced and angry. I couldn't blame him. I'd gone off on another one of my solo expeditions when I was supposed to be staying put.

"Please, come sit down." I pointed to a table in the back of the dining room.

"Tony Napoli is filling us in on the situation."

He grudgingly followed me to the table and nodded hello to Tony and Sully. "Thanks for calling me before," he said to Tony as he gave me a pointed look.

Tony took the floor. "Jude, Elaine Garlinger asked me to keep tabs on you. She had a feeling you'd try something once we knew Simon Portman wasn't the killer."

"But she had Maguire looking after me. Why you too? I'm confused."

His look told me he could see how well that had worked. Tony leaned forward and his voice became low and intimate, so no one but the three of us would hear. "This is totally confidential. I need you all to swear you won't tell a soul, because I'm trusting you with my life."

His life? What was he talking about? I could see he was serious, and we all nodded. "I'm an undercover detective with a special NYPD narcotics squad. Agent Garlinger recognized me from a few of my cases that involved the BAU and asked me to work with her team."

"A cop?" Sully asked in surprise. "I thought you were—" I kicked him hard under the table and he shut up.

Tony smiled. "I know what you thought." Then he got back to the story. "The last few days, I've been trailing Jude every time she left the building."

I looked at him in surprise. "I never noticed you."

"That was the plan." He continued, "As soon as I saw you sneak over to Jim's garage this morning, I knew you were up to something."

"I wasn't exactly sneaking. I was—"

Tony ignored my protest and continued speaking. "She also asked me to let Eric know that we were watching you so he wouldn't be too worried."

I looked over at Eric. "You were in on this?" I asked. "And you didn't tell me."

"Would it have made a difference?" He asked and raised an eyebrow. He seemed to have thawed a little, but not enough.

"Did Agent Garlinger have Jim down as the prime suspect?" I asked.

"Both him and Art Bevins."

This information came as a shock to Sully and Eric, who both started to shake their heads in disbelief.

"I knew it! When I went to visit Art, he was acting so strange. I just kept thinking something was wrong." I glanced at Sully. "And you didn't believe me.

"Why did Michael have to die?" I asked.

"From what we surmised, Jim couldn't help himself. When he told his 'best friend' about killing his brother, Art went crazy. He didn't want any part of it, or of having Dean as a consolation prize. He was positive Jim had pushed things too far with a murder and an abduction so close to each other. He was sure they were going to get caught."

"That's why Jim was so angry when he left Art's apartment." Now, the words I'd overheard made sense. "I'm surprised Art let me see the Russian Army watch he was wearing."

"He was testing you, trying to get a reaction."

"Well, I failed. I overreacted and couldn't get out of there fast enough." I shivered just thinking about it.

"Neither could he," Tony said.

"What do you mean?" Eric asked.

"Somehow, Art sensed the Feds were closing in, and looking hard at Jim. That's when he moved the souvenirs to Jim's garage where he made sure they'd be easy to find. Of course, Jim didn't know this. Then Art got ready to run. He cleared out his apartment today before Agent Garlinger could get to him. He planned to kill Dean and Jude and pin it on Jim, along with the other murders. The Feds have started a manhunt, and it's only a matter of time before they capture him."

Sully had been silent the whole time Tony was speaking, most likely thinking about the men—the 10th Street Irregulars—he'd befriended and trusted. I knew this would weigh on his conscience for a long while.

I looked at Eric to see if I could figure out what was going through his mind. He still looked hurt and unhappy.

Tony must have been watching. "She was never alone. You know that, right? And not in any danger." Eric couldn't meet my eyes and I wished I knew what he was thinking.

"What about Dean?" I asked softly, afraid of the answer.

"He'll be fine. He was dehydrated and weak. Jim pumped him full of sedatives to keep him quiet and didn't harm him otherwise." He stood up and looked at me. "He was lucky Art wasn't interested, or Dean would be dead."

He slipped on his jacket and started to leave. His voice turned serious. "I'm trusting all of you with my cover. I hope I'm not making a mistake."

"What?" I said. "Who are you really?"

Tony gave me a wicked grin. "If I told you, I'd have to kill you." He looked each of us in the eye then continued, "I've got to get going. Agent Garlinger's waiting for me."

Eric and I were back in my apartment. He was barely speaking, and I wasn't sure if he'd stay or leave. The few weeks since New Year's had taken their toll on our relationship. It was mostly my fault. I'd broken promises and put myself in dangerous situations I could have avoided. Would I lose him for good because of it?

I walked over to the window where he was gazing out into the night. I moved my body close to his and put my arm around his waist. He stiffened at first then, gradually, I could feel his muscles relax. He fit his body against mine and slid his arms around me, his chin resting on top of my head. Would we be alright? I'd just have to wait and see.

A few days later, Agent Garlinger stopped by The Lounge to update Sully and me on Art Bevins.

In the days since they arrested Jim Deems, they'd built quite a file on Art, putting the pieces together from what Jim told them, and reviewing old cases.

I created my own file, as well. I'd searched online for similar murders of young men in and around Cleveland, Ohio, where Art grew up.

It looked like he'd been killing long before he came to the city and he was responsible for at least three other murders in Ohio. The circumstances in the first two deaths had been different, so at first, no one connected them to one killer.

All the victims had been young, blond-haired, blue-eyed handsome men. The first James Reitter had been shot in the temple. The second, Alfonso DeCenso, was strangled. The third man, Larry Akins, was killed by a knife piercing his heart. By then, Art had found his preferred method and brought it with him when he moved to New York.

Had Art known his victims before, or seen an opportunity to strike as he had with Lukas Janssen?

I thought of all the other souvenirs in the sack under the linoleum—I was sure there had been even more murders. Could Art bear to live without his trophies? Would he start killing again and replace them?

I tuned back into what Agent Garlinger was saying. "He'd been perfecting his craft," as she put it. "When he moved here, he most likely saw something in Jim, some need that he exploited, and they began to kill together."

I shivered and wondered what made anyone kill for pleasure. "How did Art get Jim to help him?" I asked.

"Jim is one of those lost souls," Sully replied. "Unhappy, not very popular, or very successful." He paused. "Art appeared to be just the opposite. A well-known writer, with money and friends." He shrugged. "I think Jim would have done anything to be like him."

"He did," I said to Sully and Garlinger. "Didn't he?"

Garlinger nodded. "He won't elude us much longer. I'm confident we'll capture him soon."

Me? I wasn't so sure.

Three Months Later

The sun was shining as I slipped out of bed, the light sliding in through the slats in the blinds making a pattern on the floor. It was finally spring, and I was ready to indulge in the heady feeling of warm breezes, fresh air and new blooms ready to burst into color.

I left my bed and walked to the kitchen with a lightness I'd thought I'd lost forever. Everything seemed brighter today. Even the coffee with its rich, inviting aroma, smelled better. I'd pour a cup after I retrieved my paper from outside my door.

That's when I saw it, tucked halfway under the door—a gleaming white envelope with my name printed on the front. My stomach rolled over and I stopped cold, my body no longer capable of forward motion. My hand trembled as I bent to pick it up. *Please, God, this can't be happening again,* I thought, struggling not to collapse.

Holding it at arm's length like a deadly cobra about to strike, I slowly walked to the kitchen table and wanting to contain the venom I knew it held, placed the envelope on its surface, staring at it for a long time, not moving, not thinking.

Finally, I picked it up and opened it, dreading its contents.

Dearest Jude,

I presume you are well. I can assure you, if I have anything to do with it, you won't be for long. I had the time of my life living and killing on the Lower East Side, until you ruined it. Well, if I'm being totally honest, it wasn't just you, was it? Jim Deems had a lot to do with it as well. I thought I could control him, but...I'm sure the years he'll spend in jail—it's life, I believe—will give him time to reflect on his actions. When I first met you, I saw something in you that led me to believe you might share my inclinations...be a creative soulmate with a longing to match mine. Even though that was not to be, it's important you know you were the inspiration for my best scripts, a muse that made my words soar. As for now, who knows how much time you'll have to think about what might have been and what, I promise you, will be.

Until we meet again.

AB

"No!" I screamed, whipping my head back and forth, and dropped the letter back on the table beside the envelope it had come in. My mind was whirling and my body still in shock. His message disgusted me. How could he possibly imagine that I could be like him. It made me sick and I ran for the bathroom to heave up the bile in my stomach.

Art Bevins was still out there. Every day, I hoped and prayed that they would find him. Instead, he was close enough to be stalking me. I picked up my phone and punched in a number. When it was answered, I said in the calmest voice I could muster, "It's me."

Acknowledgements

Every author says this because it's true: it takes a village to make a book as good as it can be. With that in mind, I'd like to thank my first editor, Joseph Borden, whose knowledge and skill made Last Call infinitely better. I'd like to thank Shawn Reilly Simmons, my editor and publisher, and Verena Rose, publisher of Level Best Books for being so responsive and dedicated to their authors, myself lucky to be included among them. I'd also like to thank my friends who have supported me on my journey, including my sibs at Sisters In Crime NY/Tri-State. I'd be back on page one without you. And, of course, my amazing family, Lauren, Mike and Madison and my wonderful husband, Paul, who has always believed in me.

Recipes From The Corner Lounge

Although the Bourbon Tasting Event at The Corner Lounge was postponed, Jude wanted to share these tempting recipes with you.

Bourbon Cherry Bomb

Ingredients

6 dark red cherries
1 1/2 oz Bourbon
1/2 oz Sweet Vermouth
3/4 oz simple syrup
3/4 oz lemon juice
2 dashes Aromatic Bitters

Instructions

- Add 5 cherries to a cocktail shaker and muddle. Combine all other ingredients into cocktail shaker with muddled cherries. Add ice and shake. Strain into a chilled coupe cocktail glass.
- Top with remaining cherry with stem attached.

Bacon Wrapped Peaches with Balsamic Glaze

Makes 8 servings

Ingredients
4 large peaches
Balsamic glaze*
12 oz bacon
2 tablespoon olive oil
toothpicks

Instructions
Not everyone has a grill and this recipe can be made on the stovetop, as well.

- Set a grill to low and brush the rack with olive oil. Or, to pan-sear, heat a large pan with 2 tablespoons of olive oil on medium.
- Wash and dry peaches. Cut them in half, then cut each half into 4 pieces. Cut bacon slices in half.
- Wrap each peach slice with bacon, using toothpicks to secure.
- Before grilling, brush each slice with olive oil. Grill evenly on all sides until bacon is fully cooked, be careful not to burn it.
- If you're pan-searing, skip the oil-brushing step. Sear until bacon is **thoroughly** cooked. The peach will also brown slightly, which makes it extra sweet and delicious.

*Pete's Balsamic Glaze
You can use store bought glaze or make Pete's recipe below.
2 cups balsamic vinegar
1/2 cup brown sugar

- Mix balsamic vinegar with brown sugar. Place in a saucepan and cook over medium heat, stirring constantly until sugar has dissolved. Bring to a boil, reduce heat to low, and simmer until glaze is reduced by half, about 20 minutes. Glaze should coat the back of a spoon. Let cool and pour into a jar with a lid; store in refrigerator until ready to use.

Sweet Potato Tarts With Pecans And Brown Sugar

Makes 24 tarts

Ingredients

1 medium sweet potato, peeled and chopped
1 tablespoon butter
1 tablespoon maple syrup
1/8 teaspoon ground cinnamon
1/8 teaspoon ground nutmeg
1 package frozen miniature tart shells*
½ cup pecans mixed with ½ cup brown sugar

Instructions

- Place sweet potato in a small saucepan; cover with water. Bring to a boil. Reduce heat; cover and simmer for 10-15 minutes or until tender. Drain.
- In a small bowl, mash sweet potato with butter, syrup, cinnamon and nutmeg. Place 1 tablespoon potato mixture in each tart shell. Place on an ungreased baking sheet. Bake at 350° for 8-12 minutes or until brown sugar has melted over pecans.

Pete's Homemade Mini Tart Shells

If you're feeling ambitions, you can make these easy tart shells from scratch.

Ingredients

1/2 cup butter
3 ounces cream cheese
1 cup flour

Instructions

- In a mixing bowl, cream together the butter and cream cheese.
- Slowly add flour until well mixed.
- Form mixture into a ball and refrigerate for 15 minutes.
- Remove from fridge. Roll into 2-inch balls and place in 24-cup miniature muffin tin.
- Preheat oven to 350 F or 325 F for a dark pan.
- Use fingers to smash balls into tart shell shape.
- Bake unfilled tarts for 5 to 10 minutes.

Grilled Cheese Triangles Made With Saint Andre And Truffle Oil

Makes 8 triangles

Ingredients

4 slices Pullman white bread
6 oz. Saint Andre cheese
1 tbsp. truffle oil

Instructions

- Heat a grill pan over medium heat. It should be hot, but not too hot, or it will burn the bread.
- While it's heating, get your sandwiches ready. On 2 slices of bread, add a big slice of cheese. Top with the top sliced of bread.
- Brush a little truffle oil into the pan, then add your sandwiches. Brush each sandwich top with a little more truffle oil, then place a weight on top. If you have a heavy sauce pan or small dutch oven, heat the bottom and put it on top.
- Cook for about 7 – 8 minutes, or until the cheese is melty and the bread is crisp. Cut each sandwich diagonally into 4 pieces and serve immediately.

About the Author

Cathi Stoler is the author of the three-volume Laurel and Helen New York mystery series, as well as the Nick Donahue Adventures, *Nick of Time* and *Out of Time.* She is a three-time finalist, and winner of the 2015 Derringer Award for Best Short Story. *Bar None* is the first book in her Murder On The Rocks Mystery series. Cathi is a board member of Sisters In Crime New York/Tri-State, Mystery Writers of America, and International Thriller Writers. She lives in New York City with her husband, Paul. You can reach her at www.cathistoler.com.

Also by Cathi Stoler

"Every Picture Tells a Story"
"What If"
"Murder By The Book"
"That's My Story (And I'm Sticking To It)"